Rosie Archer was born in Gosport, Hampshire, where she still lives. She has had a variety of jobs, including waitress, fruit picker, barmaid, shop assistant and market trader selling second-hand books. Rosie is the author of several Second World War sagas set on the south coast of England, as well as a series of gangster sagas under the name June Hampson.

ROSIE ARCHER

The Timber Girls

QUERCUS

First published in Great Britain in 2022 by Quercus
This paperback edition published in 2023 by

QUERCUS

Quercus Editions Ltd
Carmelite House
50 Victoria Embankment
London EC4Y 0DZ

An Hachette UK company

A CIP catalogue record for this book is available
from the British Library

PB ISBN 978 1 52941 930 6

10 9 8 7 6 5 4 3 2 1

Typeset by CC Book Production
Printed and bound in Great Britain by Clays Ltd, Elcograf S.p.A.

Papers used by Quercus are from well-managed forests and other responsible sources.

There is only one dedication possible –
to the Women's Timber Corps of the Second World War.
The commitment and enthusiasm of these
young women seeded my idea for this novel.

Chapter One

'On your lonesome, pretty li'l gal?'

'I was until you barged in on me!' Trixie flicked back her bleached-blonde hair, which fell across one eye in what she perceived as a fair imitation of film star Veronica Lake's peekaboo style, and stared at the American sailor standing before her. Even in the cabin's dim light of the ferry boat that would shortly set sail to Portsmouth from Gosport, she could see his smile and it made her feel like all her birthdays and Christmases had come at once.

More men were trundling noisily down the metal stairs, filling the once empty cabin. They were high-spirited sailors with accents that previously she'd only heard at the pictures. Wearing pea jackets over navy blue outfits with wide-legged trousers and perky white upturned-brim hats, they brought American brightness and glamour into the murky cabin.

'Hobo, make with the blues harp!' sang out the tall sailor, as he sat himself down on the narrow bench beside her, causing Trixie's suitcase to topple at her feet.

'Jeez, I'm sorry, honey,' he said, bending quickly and nimbly to set the battered object upright again before making himself comfortable. Trixie tried to wriggle along to make room for him but found herself now wedged tightly between him and another sailor. He laughed, showing even white teeth, and his breath smelt of chewing gum. 'Cosy this, huh?'

The muskiness of sandalwood cologne swept over her. She liked it. It made a change from the stink of sweat that usually emanated from the bodies of early-morning workers pressed together in small spaces.

'The name's Cy Davis. What's yours, pretty gal?'

'Trixie, Trixie Smith.'

A few minutes earlier, alone, she had been apprehensive, worried that the momentous decision she'd made to change her life was the right one. But, now, the appearance of this young man had inexplicably caused her thoughts to melt like snowflakes in the sun.

Trixie had to glance away from his dark brown eyes

flecked with gold because looking into them made her feel she had known him for ever and that he could see deep into her soul.

'And where's Trixie Smith sailing off to on the first ferry of the day?'

She took a deep breath. Not only was he gorgeous, but he was incredibly forward. The war made a lot of people realize there might not be a tomorrow. The Allies, especially the Americans, were very sure of themselves. Most English men still spent ages deciding whether it was the correct thing to do to approach a girl, never mind ask her name and where she was going.

'Scotland, to join the Women's Timber Corps, the lumberjills.' Her words tumbled out and the moment they left her mouth she knew the decision she'd made to leave the relative safety of home, and work to help save her country during this awful war, was an exciting step forward into the unknown.

Trixie smiled at his bewilderment, then added, 'I'm going to learn how to chop down tall trees.'

'Jeez! A lady logger?' He was staring at her with renewed interest, as if she was the most revered person in the world.

Trixie guessed it was more than probable he knew where Scotland was in the British Isles. But meeting a woman lumberjack obviously wasn't an everyday occurrence for him. Not that she was a fully fledged lumberjill yet!

She nodded. The man Cy had called Hobo had pulled a mouth-organ from his pocket and was playing 'You Are My Sunshine' skilfully, the men's voices harmoniously joining in.

Cy spoke close against her ear but the noise inside the cabin now made it almost impossible for her to hear him clearly. 'You travelling on by train at the harbour station?'

The ferry's engine surged as it began its short journey across the Solent waters between her birthplace and Portsmouth. 'Yes,' she said.

'Okay if I walk with you? Maybe we can grab a coffee before you board.' He rolled back his coat cuff and looked at his watch. 'I got time before we're recalled from liberty to the USS *Ready* at the Dockyard.'

Trixie remembered seeing the anchored gunboat across at the naval base as she'd walked down Gosport's jetty to board the ferry. 'You're not backwards in coming forwards, are you?'

'I know that cute English saying,' he said, winking at her. 'And this one, "If you don't ask, you don't get!"'

She laughed, thinking there was nothing she'd like more than to remain in his company until her train left. It would be a fine send-off from Gosport to her new life. She moved her shoulders happily to the music.

'You know this tune?' His mouth, breath warm, close to her ear made her heart flutter.

She nodded. She wanted to tell him she frequently played the popular song on the piano and it was one of her favourites, but he was now jiggling his body and tapping his feet to the harmonica's jaunty notes. In any case, the noise in the cabin had heightened even further so instead of trying to talk she began to sing with the men.

He stared at her, admiration in his eyes. Then in a clear tenor voice he too joined in with the singing and she saw Hobo wink good-naturedly at him. Eventually the tune changed to 'Chattanooga Choo Choo'. Trixie sang lustily.

When she'd left home that morning, she'd been apprehensive of venturing into the unfamiliar, leaving the town where she'd been born, which wrapped itself round her like a comfy old overcoat. In Scotland she knew nothing of the people or the work expected of her but now she felt reassured. If these brave boys could come across the seas to England from America to help fight the war against Hitler, she certainly had no need to be afraid of travelling a few hundred miles away.

Again, the song changed. Hobo began playing 'Don't Sit Under The Apple Tree'.

Cy covered her hand with his own, squeezing her fingers

gently. She didn't recoil. His touch, the singing, the music made her feel warm inside.

Then the craft's engine changed volume and the boat juddered to a stop as it nudged against the safety of the fenders hanging from Portsmouth's wooden jetty.

The music stopped abruptly as Hobo shouted, 'We're here!' The singing petered out. Trixie knew the boatmen would be tying ropes around bollards making the ferry safe for passengers to disembark.

Cigarette smoke swirled in the cabin and escaped with the American sailors as they clambered the stairs to the outside world. Cy waited until most of the men had departed before picking up her case and helping her to her feet.

Emerging from the cabin Trixie found a weak sun had broken through the previously dull skies. Automatically she stared towards the dockyard where *Victory*, Admiral Lord Nelson's flagship was, as usual, moored. The old and the new, she thought, looking more closely at the clean lines of the convoy escort gunboat docked nearby, showing the American flag.

As Trixie stepped down from the ferry she was aware of the queue of passengers waiting to board it back to Gosport. She walked carefully, mindful that her high heels could slip between the planks of the wooden pontoon. Cy, still carrying her suitcase, said, 'There she is, Trixie, honey, USS *Ready*. She's one of your ships, built in Belfast, borrowed by us on the lend-lease programme. You provide the boats we fill 'em with men to help win this war. We're all in this together now after Pearl Harbor.' He slipped his free hand into hers. 'We docked early yesterday for remedial repairs. Because of liberty I was sure destined to meet you. I call that Fate.'

'Do you believe in it?' she asked. Trixie firmly believed that 'What goes around comes around.' She tried to be fair in all her dealings and never willingly to hurt anyone.

Cy stopped walking and faced her. 'I come from New Orleans, honey, where everybody believes in Fate.' His eyes twinkled knowingly.

The light August breeze was ruffling Trixie's blue dress. She smoothed the cotton material with one hand, then adjusted her gas mask and bag slung across one shoulder. With Cy still clasping her other hand, she followed the crowd up the pontoon towards Portsmouth Harbour railway station nestling on iron pilings in the mud between the Hard, the bus station and the entrance to the Dockyard.

So many people were jostling up the steps to the trains that Cy let go of her but he caught her up as she showed her travel warrant to the ticket officer and bought a platform ticket for himself.

'Platform two, Waterloo train's late. Change there for Dundee,' said the uniformed attendant at the barrier.

'How late?' Trixie was worried she'd not make the connection for the Dundee train.

The attendant shrugged. 'There's a war on, love, or hadn't you noticed?' He suddenly smiled. 'It's on its way. Listen for information.'

Trixie consoled herself with the thought that at least the train wasn't cancelled.

'What did I tell ya?' Cy murmured in her ear, 'It's Fate! We've been given more time together.'

He pulled her through the early-morning crowd of servicemen and workers towards the tea room. Inside, the air was thick with cigarette smoke from the customers sitting at small tables, or standing huddled in cliques drinking from thick cups. Unappetizing sandwiches curled beneath a glass dome on the counter.

'Two coffees,' said Cy, to the frizzy-haired young waitress when she looked at him for his order.

She immediately raised her eyes heavenwards, turned and spoke loudly to an older waitress with fierce metal curlers in her grey hair: 'Another Yank wanting coffee!'

The older woman tutted and shook her head. 'No coffee,' she mouthed through brown teeth. 'Tea or cocoa?'

'Two teas, please,' cut in Trixie, and watched as the younger woman set a cup beneath the spout of a large steaming metal urn, flipped up a tap, and liquid the colour of tar filled it. She slid the overflowing cups onto thick saucers. 'Milk? Sugar?'

'No,' said Cy.

'Yes,' said Trixie.

'Make your minds up!' snapped the young woman. 'That'll be fourpence.' She glared at the ten-shilling note Cy held out. 'Nothing smaller?'

Trixie was already fumbling in her bag and slipped the coppers onto the counter. The waitress picked them up and transferred the money to the drawer of the till, dismissing them both.

'Coffee's difficult to get,' said Trixie, sliding onto a chair vacated by a British soldier lugging away a kitbag. Cy sat on the empty seat across the table from her. He piled food-encrusted plates on top of each other to make room for their cups and saucers. A wireless was playing and Trixie could hear Frank Sinatra crooning 'Be Careful It's My Heart'.

'I'm sorry, I didn't mean for you to pay, honey. But don't let's talk about coffee. Tell me about you.'

She was aware of the firmness of his jaw, the dimple in his cheek caused by his broad smile as he watched her, with those long-lashed gold-flecked brown eyes. She wanted to put her hand across the table, lift it and touch the tight dark curls peeking below his jaunty sailor hat, but it seemed an improper gesture to make to someone she'd only just met. He picked up his cup in both hands, took an exploratory sip and grimaced, putting it down on the saucer. Trixie laughed. 'That good, eh?' She saw his hands were large, calloused, capable.

He noticed her staring and said, 'Okay, let's start with me. I'm twenty-two, unmarried. I worked in Jackson Square for the New Orleans Steamboat Company. A paddle-steamer, the *Natchez*, sailing the Mississippi river . . .' She must have looked amazed for he hastened to add, 'Below deck, shovelling coal. Money was good but I wanted to see the world so I joined the Navy.' He pushed back his cuff, looked at his watch, then said, 'Now you, honey.'

'I was born across the water in Gosport nineteen years ago and I've never been anywhere else. I live with my mum. I'm not involved with anyone. My dad's dead. He served in France during the Great War, and Mum's met this lovely man who wants to marry her. I think they deserve a life without me hanging about, getting in the way. I gave up my job in a greengrocer's to join the Land Girls only I got persuaded to go to Scotland instead and chop down trees.'

He was listening carefully and his eyes hadn't left her face all the time she was talking, but now he foraged in the pocket of his pea jacket. He drew out a stub of pencil and a scrubby piece of paper and began writing, careful not to let the paper soak up the spilt tea on the table. When he finished, he sat looking at her again. 'What d'ya mean, you got persuaded to go to Scotland?'

Trixie laughed. 'I thought the Land Army would be a cut above working in a shop, and I'd be doing more to help England win this war. The assistant at the Labour Exchange suggested the Women's Timber Corps, a newly formed branch of the Land Army. She said they needed strong young women to work in forests to provide lumber for pit props, telegraph poles and such. I liked the idea that I'd be useful and I'd travel. I didn't know then that I might be sent to Scotland but I didn't need much persuading.'

Trixie liked it that he'd given her his full attention. She gave him a small smile and lifted her cup to her lips, noticed the smear of bright lipstick that wasn't hers and replaced it on the saucer, which was swimming in tea.

He shook his head. 'It was stupid of me to bring you in here to say goodbye. Trixie, you're worth more than this.'

She was aware of the overfilled ashtray, the loud chatter, the myriad body smells, the dog ends trodden into the wooden floor. 'There's a war on.' She shrugged, remembering the ticket attendant's words.

Billie Holiday was singing 'Trav'lin' Light'.

'That's us,' he said, 'both travelling to places we've never been, to do things we've never done . . .' His hand snaked across the table and covered hers. The piece of paper crumpled against her fingers. 'Will you write to me, honey?'

Trixie nodded, slipping the paper inside her bag.

'Eventually I'll get your letters,' he said.

'I don't have an address . . .' she began.

'Fate'll take care of it,' he said.

'It probably will,' she replied but her words were cut short as he leant across and she felt the warmth of his breath before he kissed her, gently and with mindful desire. Then he put his hand on the back of her neck and pulled her towards him until the one innocent kiss became as hot as the fire burning inside her. She wanted to hold him closer, wrap her arms about him.

Behind the counter, the elderly waitress coughed dramatically. Trixie opened her eyes to see customers about them, staring. She dragged herself away from him. Instant attraction, she thought. Like a sudden thunderclap. The kind only ever experienced once or twice in a lifetime.

'What's it like in New Orleans?' she asked, trying to speak

more calmly than she felt and all the while thinking she'd rather be kissing him than talking to him. 'I've seen the place on newsreels and read about it in books.'

'Nothin' like on film or in books!' he responded. 'You got to feel the place. You got to experience New Orleans. It's special. It's magical, especially the music coming from the bars in the heart of the French Quarter . . . Me and Hobo play jazz in the Blue Moon—'

Trixie couldn't help interrupting, 'You play an instrument?'

'I play bass saxophone.'

She knew it! They both loved music! Oh, how she'd love to hear him play. Trixie wondered if the notes bubbled around inside him, as they did with her, longing for freedom. 'Can you read music?' The words tumbled from her mouth.

He shook his head. 'Did you see Hobo playing to sheet music?' He didn't wait for her answer but carried on, 'Music comes from the depths of a person.' He paused. 'Listen to Billie Holiday. She's one of the best singers ever! She never learnt to read music but she manipulates the tempo and phrasing, and what comes out is pure magic. Your Vera Lynn's spellbinding, too. Another terrific singer who doesn't need to read notes . . .' The excitement in his voice tapered off. 'I'm sorry,' he said, 'running off at the mouth when I want to know all about you.'

Trixie was smiling. She wanted to tell him she loved listening to him, discovering things she never knew, hearing him praise the singers she admired. She said, 'I have nothing very interesting to tell you. I have such a little life. But I do love playing the piano by ear,' she added.

Another smile creased his face. 'Trixie Smith, karma has pushed us together because it can't bear for us to be apart any longer. Fate won't care about time or distance. When this war ends, whether it's in America or England we'll be together. And that's a promise.'

He picked up her hand. It looked small nestling in his strong-looking brown fingers. She could feel the heat of him transferring itself to her, making her conscious of her already heightened emotions.

'You don't have a little life, not to me, Trixie,' he said. 'We'll write to each other. Tell each other everything that goes on in our hearts and minds.' He was leaning across the table and she felt again the warmth of his breath. The musky smell of his heated maleness filled all her senses. His face was close, so close that she couldn't help herself because it seemed the most natural thing in the world to do. Her hand left his and she rested it on the back of his neck, feeling the silkiness of his crinkled hair before she pulled him towards her. His lips, full and supple rested on hers for a moment, and then he kissed her, at first, gently, then with mounting passion.

His tongue met hers, played inside her mouth until Trixie felt she wanted to devour him but, coward that she was and mindful of the sudden silence that had once more filled the tea room, she pulled away, just as the obscure voice announced, 'The train on Platform Two will shortly be leaving for Waterloo . . .'

'I have to go . . .' Her words were muffled as the proclamation was repeated over the loudspeaker system.

Cy had already picked up her suitcase. Hastily they made for the tea room's door. Once they were outside, he grabbed her hand and they began running along the platform, her gas-mask case bumping against her hip.

The smell of steam and oil filled the station. Passengers scattered to and fro searching for the right platforms. The London train was already packed with civilians and men in uniform as Trixie hoisted herself aboard.

She stood in the corridor by the open carriage door, her suitcase at her feet. Cy gazed up at her, every so often stepping aside as people climbed onto the train.

'I wish we'd met . . .' The last of her words were lost in the blast of a whistle. Just along the platform the uniformed guard was waving a flag and then he was walking towards them, slamming doors shut.

Cy grinned, too late to mask his sadness. She blinked because tears prickled the backs of her eyes.

Something seemed to click into place and Trixie knew they were no longer two strangers going in opposite directions. Somehow, sometime, they would meet again.

She'd fallen in love with Cy as soon as she'd met him. A rush of unhappiness flooded her. It was easy to be cynical about love at first sight. But sometimes, if someone was lucky, they met somebody. All she could think of was that the timing wasn't right and she didn't want to leave this man, who was still clutching her fingers, making her feel warm and wanted.

'Shut the window,' the guard demanded.

Cy's fingers abandoned her hand and now she felt bereft. Tears stung her cheeks.

The train was moving out of the station. She strained to peer through the glass as the engine gained momentum but its smoke made it difficult to see.

A huge sigh left her as she leant her head against the cold glass She felt as though part of her had been torn away.

Chapter Two

Trixie, her heart in torment at being dragged apart from Cy, bent down and stood her case upright. Travellers stumbling against it had left it overturned. She looked about her and saw servicemen and other passengers sprawled on the littered floor, some chatting, some snoozing and most using kitbags and luggage as seats or pillows. Already stale air and cigarette smoke filled the corridor.

Opposite her was a carriage, door open, its seats crammed with people, parcels and bags tucked into their laps, wielding newspapers. Fingers waved lit cigarettes denoting claims to passengers' spaces. Trixie sighed. The journey to London could perhaps take a couple of hours. Any dreams she'd had of sitting on a seat with her head next to a window and thinking about Cy had already disappeared. She had resigned herself to joining the others sitting on the floor, when a voice called, 'Room for a little 'un here, ducks.'

A well-upholstered woman, wedged between a sullen-looking, thin-faced young girl sitting by the window and a little boy kneeling on the upholstery of the seat next to her, was waving a small kitchen knife at Trixie. She was grasping a bright red apple, its peel dangling, in the other hand. On the floor, jammed between her knees, was a wicker basket. Apples bulged from a brown-paper bag. The child squirmed, waiting impatiently for his next slice of fruit.

'Shove up, Norman, and let the young lady sit down.'

The child stared rudely at Trixie, then crawled awkwardly from the seat, exposing socks around his ankles and sandals with mud-caked soles. He leant now against his mother's plump knees.

'Um . . .' began Trixie, but got no further for her suitcase was hauled through the carriage's doorway and shoved across spent matchsticks and dog ends to the sliver of seat between the thin girl and the stout woman, who had now moved along the seat.

'All the way to London, is it? We're a bit late starting off but we'll get there.'

The woman shoved her knife in front of Trixie almost

before she had managed to squeeze onto the seat. Startled, she realized she was supposed to take the speared apple slice, and answer the question. Trixie nodded. 'Thank you,' she said, sliding the apple from the blade into her mouth. The fruit was sharp and crisp. The child glared at her. Perhaps he begrudged her the piece of apple, thinking it should have been his. Trixie tried a smile at him – he was perhaps three or four years old. Beneath his overlong fringe, pure mischief gleamed from his eyes.

Trixie wondered if his mother cut his hair by putting a basin on his head, then using the knife to hack around it.

Wrestling with her shoulder bag and gas mask, Trixie saw the knife now held another slice of apple. She screwed her eyes closed in anticipation of a wail from the child, accompanied by a gout of blood spouting into the air as he made a grab for the fruit. When nothing happened, Trixie cautiously allowed herself to raise her eyelids to find the little boy's face inches from her own.

'Leave the lady alone, Norman,' said the woman. The apple was still on the knife.

Relief flowed through Trixie when he slid to the other side of his mother.

'Sorry, love, do you want a piece?'

Now the large woman was addressing the girl, who was

tightly pressed next to the window. Shaking her head, she shrank from the knife.

Newspapers rattled as the train clattered along the track.

Trixie gazed at the unkempt back gardens of Portsmouth's bombed and bedraggled houses, hung about with washing lines pegged with grey clothing. Tin baths were nailed to outhouses or propped against the brick walls of sculleries. Discarded broken furniture bloomed like strange flowers.

Last night there'd been no wail from Moaning Minnie so householders had had the luxury of sleeping in their own beds instead of crowding into public shelters. Trixie disliked camping in the damp Anderson at the bottom of their garden next to the lavatory but it was a lot better than being blown to kingdom come.

The south of England was still taking a right battering from Hitler's planes. Portsmouth's dockyard, Priddy's munitions factory, Daedalus' airfield and St George's barracks were only some of the local bases the Germans wanted wiped off the map but most of the time their aim wasn't true so the smell of cordite hung in Gosport's devastated streets, like a shroud.

She wondered what the landscape looked like near Shandford Lodge in Angus. She'd borrowed a book from the library and had been amazed at the pictures of Scotland's wide-open gorse-covered spaces without a dwelling in sight. Majestic mountains had taken her breath away. The great expanses of water called lochs had filled her head with wonder, and she'd stared in awe at the photographs of pine trees, whole forests of timber, that she would be expected to cut down to help win the war.

The woman opposite, her knees touching Trixie's, had conjured a flask and was pouring what looked like tea into the cup. Trixie held her breath, envisaging the liquid spilling everywhere, but most likely on herself. She breathed a sigh of relief when, tea drunk without mishap, the flask disappeared back into the holdall at the woman's feet.

'I bet you didn't dream this journey would be so nerve-racking,' whispered the girl at her side.

Trixie turned her head and smiled.

The girl's pale, thin face was framed by long dark hair that hung below her ears. Despite the August warmth she was dwarfed by a dark blue gaberdine mackintosh. Trixie was about to answer her when a doorstep of bread topped with dark red jam was shoved in front of her. 'Would you like it, love?' the fleshy woman offered. The child was already messily eating a slice.

'No, thanks,' said Trixie.

'Yes, please,' said the girl.

'Good! I like to see people eat,' gushed the woman, dropping the now empty and crumpled bag that had contained the sandwiches into the basket at her feet. 'The preserve is home-made. Brambles I picked meself. Had to use saccharine to eke out the sugar now there's a war on . . .' Trixie heard no more because she was transfixed by the heavy bruising about the girl's thin wrist and arm. It had previously been hidden by the long sleeves of her raincoat.

Now the girl was pushing the sandwich into her mouth and swallowing quickly. Trixie saw discolouration covering her other wrist. She wanted to say something, ask questions about the marks, but knew the girl wouldn't relish her nosiness because she had tried to hide the bruising. Why else would she be wearing a coat on a warm day in August? She was also very hungry.

Trixie thought about the corned-beef-and-onion sandwiches, nestling in greaseproof paper, in the corner of her suitcase. The girl was now wiping the corners of her mouth on her sleeve. If she was ravenous, and clearly she was, thought Trixie, one slice of bread wasn't going to satisfy her.

Trixie wondered if she dared try to extricate her suitcase, which was jammed next to the woman's basket, and take out her own food. She'd planned to eat on the Dundee train, having had toast for breakfast before leaving home, but she felt she ought to offer the girl something. Her sandwiches, carefully made and wrapped by her mother, had been placed inside her case, along with a flask of tea, the top screwed on firmly so Trixie wouldn't have to carry too many items while changing trains.

'Your shoulder bag, gas mask and the suitcase are more than enough to have to worry about,' were her mother's words.

However, even supposing she could withdraw her case there wasn't the slightest possibility, in the tight space, that she could lift it up to her knees and open it without the contents spilling everywhere, not something she relished.

She stole a glance at the girl next to her. She had now closed her eyes, apparently dozing. Trixie took a deep breath and, despite the thick smell of cigarette smoke, the noise from the servicemen in the corridor, and the rustling of papers in the carriage, tried to relax. She looked at her watch. Des, the man living with her mother, would now have arrived home from working the nightshift as a porter at the War Memorial Hospital.

She smiled remembering the five-pound note, an enormous amount, he'd slipped into her handbag. 'Don't you try to give it back to me. You'll hurt my feelings,' he'd said.

'Go on, love, take it,' her mum had added.

Des cared about her, and worshipped her mum. He was always giving Rose little tokens of his love. A bunch of flowers, usually wild ones, now that gardens and allotments contained vegetables. Sometimes he brought home biscuits he'd saved for Rose from his tea break.

Trixie didn't remember her own father. He was still in hospital long after the Great War had ended, her mother had told her. He'd left Rose as a young man full of hope to fight and win a war but had been brought back from France a quivering wreck. When the hospital had finally allowed her to care for him, he was fearful of leaving, first the hospital, then the house. Bitter, disillusioned, not even reading the books he loved, he preferred to sit alone in the front room, or his shed where before the war he had enjoyed carving. Now he touched neither wood, nor tools, nor books. His nightmares were horrendous. He couldn't, or wouldn't, bring himself to tell her mother of the horrors that had changed his personality. Trixie was four when her father had hanged himself from the wooden beam in the shed.

Three years ago, Rose, a cleaner at the hospital, had met Des, a widower, and Trixie was happy that the skinny, red-haired but balding man, who reminded her of a Swan Vestas match, had that special gift of making her mother laugh again. A year after meeting Des, incendiary bombs had burnt his house down. Rose asked Trixie how she'd feel if Des moved in 'as a lodger'. It was no secret that he wanted to marry Rose, and no secret that the neighbours would gossip when they set up home together.

'When the war ends, we'll tie the knot,' Rose promised.

Trixie believed her mother was scared of allowing herself the happiness she deserved. She was frightened that, as with her first marriage and the Great War, this war would change things, possibly for the worse.

Trixie was growing discontented at the greengrocer's, weighing vegetables and chopping off the greenery from bunches of carrots.

At weekends the Alma pub's piano became her salvation. It was time for Trixie to move on with her own life, she'd decided, and to force Des and Rose to get on with theirs. In the town, the shop-window advertisement for the Land Girls caught her eye. Upon visiting Gosport's Labour Exchange to ask about joining up, she'd been persuaded by an official that the new branch of the women's services, the Timber Corps, were looking for recruits, so here she was, travelling towards the great unknown.

'We're getting off at Woking. It's the next stop,' said the large woman. She began gathering her bags and admonishing her child, who was crash-landing a wooden toy Spitfire plane on every surface within his reach.

'It's been nice meeting you,' said Trixie. The woman had been kind.

'You too, love,' the woman said. 'Say, goodbye, Norman.'

Behind his mother's back Norman stuck out his tongue.

Quite a few passengers disembarked, including several from the crowded carriage, so Trixie moved across to the opposite window seat, relishing her new-found freedom of space.

She watched the girl with the bruises, who had fallen asleep, wondering how old she was. Possibly a similar age to herself, she thought. But sleep seemed to have softened her face, making her appear younger. Apart from the remark about the overcrowding in the carriage, the girl had offered no conversation. Trixie decided she was probably one of those people who kept themselves very much to themselves, sometimes with good reason, and only became sociable when she had to be.

The carriage, now quieter, gave Trixie the inner calm to think about Cy. Her body still tingled at his touch. She couldn't resist smiling as she remembered the feel of his hand pulling her towards him. She'd enjoyed his talk. She liked his looks. She thought of their kisses and smiled again to herself. That they both shared a love of music was a common denominator. That he was self-taught, like her, proved to Trixie that his determination to express himself, through playing the bass saxophone, knew no bounds. She couldn't believe how alike they were.

Her thoughts went back to a wet, miserable lunchtime at school, when she'd wandered into the empty hall where Mrs Edwards thumped out the hymns for morning prayers. The piano lid was up and Trixie had sat on the stool, randomly touching the keys. After a little while, she found she was playing the chords to 'Good-night Sweetheart', a popular song. Not expertly, of course not, but after experimenting, she found that as long as she knew a tune, her fingers went to the correct keys. She wasn't supposed to touch school equipment or wander about unsupervised so she left the hall before she was discovered.

She kept her secret to herself.

And then came the day a neighbour wanted to get rid of a redundant upright piano to create more space. Trixie begged her mum to take it. At first Rose demurred, but eventually she gave in. 'It'll be a while before I can afford to pay for piano lessons,' her mother said.

'I can borrow music books from the library and practise, Mum,' wheedled Trixie.

The piano was brought round and pushed into the front room, and Trixie borrowed books from Gosport library. She found she couldn't tell a quaver from a crotchet. Her memory wouldn't retain the meanings of the notes or their corresponding sounds. Her playing improved when she gave up trying to read music.

Her fingers knew the notes.

Rose told everyone she had 'perfect pitch' and was proud as Punch when Trixie began playing the piano on Friday and Saturday nights in the Alma pub, at the end of their road. When she left school at fourteen to weigh potatoes and vegetables in Watt's greengrocer's her job was only bearable because she had the weekends to look forward to when she could play the piano for her own and others' enjoyment.

Trixie yawned. The rumble of the wheels along the track was hypnotic. She was aware the whole journey to Scotland by train would be practically endless. She hoped the delay at the start of her journey wouldn't mean she'd miss her connection to Dundee.

She thought of Cy asking Hobo to play his harmonica. He hadn't needed a music book to get the cabin full of people singing, had he? Cy had said he could also play by ear.

Later tonight when, hopefully, she finally arrived at Shandford Lodge she would write to Cy. Trixie thought of the new Parker fountain pen, in her suitcase, which her mother had bought for her to write home. She'd thank Cy for making the start of her new life so enjoyable. Those kisses had been heavenly, even if the assistants in the café were affronted by them! Not that Trixie had ever been kissed in public before. And certainly never like that. He'd made her feel alive! Cy wasn't a bit like any of the lads in Gosport she'd been on dates with. Not that there'd been very many. Dates were usually composed of walks, visits to the pictures and pubs, but the excitement appeared to wear off quickly and apathy soon followed.

Would that happen with her and Cy? Perhaps, perhaps not. Letters flowing between them would ease the tension of being away from home, for him and for her. Fate would take care of the rest, she thought. Hadn't Cy said so?

When she arrived in London, she would need to change trains. She'd have to find the correct platform. The next part of her journey would be even longer if the delay at Portsmouth meant the Scotland train had gone. She'd hope for the best. On the Dundee train she would eat her sandwiches and drink her tea. Her mother had told her she shouldn't rely on there being a buffet car as the war had changed so many things.

Trixie slept.

Chapter Three

'Wake up! Wake up! It's the end of the line!'

Trixie opened her eyes to feel and see the girl in the mackintosh shaking her. For a moment she wondered where she was and what was happening.

'The train's stopped! We're at Waterloo!'

'Oh,' Trixie said. They were the only two people left in the compartment and the train was at a standstill. 'Thank you,' was all she could manage as she scrambled unsteadily to her feet, then groped about the carriage floor for her suitcase. 'Thank you,' she repeated, then saw she was alone. The girl had gone.

Trixie yawned as she walked unsteadily along the busy platform, the suitcase at her side, her shoulder bag and gas mask bumping against her hip. The smell of steam and oil accompanied her as she battled through people coming and going towards the main concourse.

Servicemen and -women were everywhere. People were walking quickly or grouped together talking, queuing at barriers, and children were fretting. She made her way to one of the enquiry booths to find out which of the many platforms she needed to board the Scotland train and was delighted to discover the delay to the Portsmouth train had not caused her to miss her connection to Dundee.

So many people, so much going on. Newspaper sellers calling out headlines, porters pushing trolleys piled high with suitcases. A disembodied voice from a loudspeaker was making no sense at all. She shuddered to think what might have happened if the girl in the mackintosh hadn't woken her when the train had arrived at Waterloo station.

At long last Trixie was waiting behind the barrier for the guard to pull back the metal gates to allow passengers to board the train.

She breathed a sigh of relief: she was in the correct place for the second part of her journey and looking forward to relaxing once she found a seat. She was thirsty – she should have bought a cup of tea on the platform, perhaps a sandwich as well, but she hadn't wanted to dawdle in case she forgot the instructions she'd received from the guard at the enquiry desk. As soon as she was on the train she'd get out her flask and sandwiches. She patted her shoulder bag, containing her travel information, ticket, ration book and identity card, and waited.

At Dundee she was to stand outside the station's main entrance where she would be collected and taken by road to Brechin, Angus. There she would have four weeks' training at felling trees and learning all she would need to know, before she was transferred to where her employment would begin.

It was all very exciting. She wondered whereabouts she would eventually be detailed to work or if she would be moved about the country or, and here her heart began to beat fast, whether the Timber Corps might decide she was totally unsuitable for the job. Trixie cast the negative thoughts from her mind. She could do anything she put her mind to. It had been her decision to stop playing gooseberry to her mum and Des, which she hadn't made lightly, so it would be up to her as to whether or not she made a success of becoming a lumberjill.

Twenty minutes later Trixie was sitting next to a window in a third-class carriage with her suitcase above her in the rack, waiting for the train to leave the smoky station. Beside her were her shoulder-bag, gas mask, and a brown carrier bag containing her sandwiches, flask and an Agatha Christie novel she'd brought to pass the time.

The carriage was filling quickly now. No bowler-hatted

businessmen, as there had been on the London train and, so far, no children. It wasn't that she disliked children, on the contrary she loved them. She smiled grimly, remembering Norman from the previous train.

Trixie caught a whiff of flowery perfume. Two young women were now making themselves comfortable on the vacant seats opposite her. Their excited chatter further raised her spirits as they began putting cases and bags in the overhead rack.

Carriage doors were slamming and whistles were blowing. As the train began to move, she caught snatches of conversation between the two girls. It seemed they too, like herself, were eager to get to the end of their journey. Trixie moved her carrier bag to her lap and began unscrewing the flask, already anticipating the taste of the tea.

'That's a good idea,' said the girl wearing a tailored silk costume. Trixie could tell by the cut it was expensive. She stood up, took off her jacket and put it high on the overhead rack. Her long-sleeved white blouse with a pussy-cat bow was immaculate. She then brought down a cloth drawstring bag, which appeared quite heavy. 'Do you want your sandwiches, Jo?' She looked down at the other girl, who seemed to be deep in thought. 'Jo!' Her voice was louder now. 'Do you want your sandwiches?'

Jo seemed to shake herself from her reverie and answered, 'What? Oh! Yes, please. That sounds like a good idea, Hen.'

Trixie was immediately aware the girl called Hen had an upper-class voice. She pronounced her words as though she had all the time in the world to do so.

Most people from Gosport, including Trixie, and the girl called Jo, sounded more like London Cockneys and gabbled, putting their own interpretations on words they weren't completely at ease with. Trixie thought the two girls in the carriage seemed an unlikely pair.

Hen moved an expensive leather suitcase along the rack to take down a brown string-handled carrier bag similar to Trixie's, which she handed to Jo, then sat down again.

Trixie took a sip from her flask cup: the last home-made tea she would experience for a while. She told herself not to start getting homesick or feeling down before she'd even reached her destination.

Hen took out from her bag a smaller, lumpier drawstring bag. Pulling the top loose, she asked, 'Would anyone in the carriage like an apple? These ripen early in our Alverstoke orchard and we usually have so many to spare . . .'

Mutterings of thanks and acceptance came from the other passengers in the carriage.

Trixie noticed Hen had small hands with well-shaped nails that were painted a delicate coral. When the bag was handed to her, she smiled her thanks and tried to hide her own bitten nails as she took out one of the apples. The fruit was hard and smelt delicious. Today seemed to be one where everybody offered her apples, she thought. She'd picked up on the name Alverstoke.

'This tastes lovely,' she said, after biting into the crisp flesh 'I know an Alverstoke.'

'Do you?' replied Hen, a smile breaking across her face. 'It's part of Gosport, on the south coast.'

'I come from Gosport,' said Trixie.

'So do I,' said Jo, staring at Trixie with interest.

'I say, you're not making for Shandford Lodge, are you?' Hen asked. Her blue eyes glittered. Her hair, unlike Trixie's, was naturally blonde, the white-gold that not many girls were lucky enough to possess. It was also very long and she wore it plaited and wound about her head, making a frame for her striking looks.

Trixie nodded enthusiastically, 'Yes! Are you?'

'And I wouldn't mind betting there are others like us on this train,' Jo said. 'Did the Labour Exchange call you back, ask loads of questions and make you take a medical?'

Trixie nodded.

'I had my medical a few days ago. Jolly quick off the mark, aren't they? Must want us girls pretty bad,' chimed in Hen.

Trixie thought Jo was probably the eldest of the three of them. She looked tired and her red hair was scraped back into a ponytail, which didn't do her any favours. There were remnants of red lipstick still clinging to her lips and she wasn't as expensively dressed as Hen. There was an air of sadness about her. Her blue-flowered, button-through, puffed-sleeve dress with a sweetheart neckline was obviously well-washed. But it was wartime and most women were making do with cherished clothes they already had in their wardrobes. Rationing and shortages had taken their toll on fashion.

'Where do you live in Gosport?' asked Trixie.

'Bedford Street, near Ann's Hill. Do you know it?'

'Yes, you're not far from me. My mum lives in Alma Street.'

'How extraordinary,' said Jo. 'I'm Jo. My real name is Joan but it's always been shortened to Jo.'

'Mine's Henrietta but that's such a bind to say, so Hen will do fine.'

'I'm Trixie.' Trixie replaced the cup on the flask. She took another bite of the apple. She could feel her spirits rising. It wasn't that she was worried about arriving at Shandford

Lodge on her own but how much nicer it would be to turn up with friends she had already made on the journey to Scotland.

'Have you two known each other for long?' Trixie asked. 'Gosh, this apple is delicious,' she added.

Hen laughed. 'Have another.' She pushed the bag at Trixie, who shook her head. She didn't want to appear greedy.

'We don't know each other at all, not really. We met on the train from Portsmouth. Thought we were going to miss this one because of the delay to Waterloo. We palled up after finding out we were both bound for Dundee,' Hen said. 'Wouldn't it be jolly if all three of us ended up sharing living accommodation?'

'Might be nice,' replied Jo. 'Three Gosport girls together.'

Trixie glanced out of the window at the bombed brick buildings surrounded by piles of rubble. She saw dust-covered hedges and trees, rosebay willowherb flowering in the burnt earth. London's battered and smoky city was slowly disappearing as the train rumbled along the track towards Scotland. Trixie wondered what her new life had in store for her.

She answered, 'Yes, it might be fun.'

Chapter Four

'It's awfully cold and dark.' Hen pulled her thin costume jacket tighter across her breasts. 'And I never expected it to be as breezy as this.'

'Do you have anything warmer in your suitcase to put on?' Trixie asked. After reading the books she'd borrowed from the library, she'd anticipated Scotland's climate to be less welcoming than she was used to in the south of England. She'd folded a short jigger coat as small as she could in her luggage and now felt the benefit of wearing it.

'No,' said Hen. 'I knew we'd be given serviceable uniforms.' She sighed. 'But I did pack a couple of very nice party frocks to wear somewhere special in the evenings.'

Trixie smiled to herself. From what she'd read about Shandford Lodge and the sort of work they'd be learning to do, they'd be too tired for glamorous evenings out, if indeed there was anywhere to go.

Jo, now on the pavement crouching over her opened suitcase, held up a thick hand-knitted woollen cardigan. It looked as though it might have been made from unpicked jumpers. 'Put this on,' she said. She clicked her case closed and stood up, her fitted gaberdine raincoat falling snugly over her. 'A friend of mine comes from Aberdeen and he says it rains a lot in Scotland and it's windy. This'll keep you warm. At least it's not raining,' she added.

Trixie was surprised Jo had even noticed the conversation going on between her and Hen. She had been standing with her back to the wall, a faraway expression on her face as if she was somewhere else entirely. Trixie's mum, noticing someone seemed to be out of touch with reality, called it being 'away with the fairies'. It was obvious to Trixie Jo's thoughts weren't always on the present subject and that something was worrying her. Perhaps, in time, she would confide in her new friends.

Hen took the cardigan from her. 'Thanks, Jo. You're an angel. I wish our transport would hurry up and arrive.'

Trixie had only known Jo for a short time but it was clear that the young woman was sensitive to other people's feelings. She didn't smile and laugh as easily as Hen did.

Trixie knew nothing about Jo's background other than that she came from the same town as herself. They hadn't poured out life stories on the train journey but from short conversations she'd guessed they'd come from similar households.

Hen, Trixie quickly deduced, came from a far more privileged background. Her parents lived in Western Way in Alverstoke, the monied part of Gosport, and she'd mentioned she'd been boarded out at a school near Winchester.

Trixie's one claim to fame was that she'd been milk monitor at St John's School in Forton Road. It would be interesting, she thought, to find out more about both of her new friends and why they'd decided to apply for a job so far from home.

Trixie shivered. Standing in the inky blackness outside the creepy Gothic building of Dundee railway station was only bearable because she wasn't alone.

It was too late for any shops to be open and there was no traffic on the silent road. The blackout was a deterrent against aiding enemy planes to discharge their loads. About twenty other girls were standing on the pavement, chatting in small groups. She had overheard some talking about the Lodge so was thankful to know she'd arrived at the right waiting place.

'Here's a couple of lorries!' someone called.

Trixie could make out two bulky shapes trundling along the road. Their headlights were mere slits in the darkness. The lorries shuddered to a halt and a man jumped down from the first. He was small and grizzled, well wrapped up in shapeless clothing. As he walked up and down, observing the girls, the smell of cigarette smoke wafted from him. He reminded Trixie of an ashtray that needed to be emptied.

'Shandford Lodge?'

When he'd received his answer, he waved a hand towards a metal foothold at the back of one of the lorries and told them to climb inside the vehicles, taking their luggage with them, and in an orderly manner. He began ticking off names on a sheet of paper. Trixie had to listen carefully to his instructions because his accent was so alien to her. She stayed close to Hen and Jo, fearful they might be separated. Once she had climbed up into the wagon, which smelt strongly of petrol, she discovered a wooden bench positioned around three sides of the vehicle. She sat down next to Hen, who had bagged a seat behind the driver's cab.

Part of the hood, which was stretched over an iron framework, had worked itself loose. She tucked the offending canvas behind her while praying that it wouldn't rain before they reached their destination. If it did, she'd get wet. The lorry, she decided, had definitely seen better days.

'Doesn't look like it would keep bad weather off us,' whispered Hen.

'Let's hope the journey's not too long then,' answered Trixie, marvelling that after travelling all day Hen's flowery perfume still managed to help mask some of the more unsavoury smells in the vehicle.

Jo was trying to prop her suitcase in front of her knees. The once empty space in the middle of the lorry was now full of the girls' luggage.

Trixie overheard someone moaning about how tired she was. Although she'd spent all day travelling and mostly sitting, she could hardly keep her eyes open. It seemed ages ago that she had been singing at the top of her voice in the ferry's cabin with Cy and the other American sailors. Thinking of Cy sent a warm feeling through her and a smile touched her lips.

'I wonder how far it is to the Lodge?'

The driver had obviously overheard Hen.

'Och, dinna fash yersel'. We'll arrive when we arrive,' he growled, with just the slightest turn of his head.

Hen looked at Trixie, grinned and shrugged, still no wiser.

It was dark in the back of the lorry and only the odd word here and there came from the girls. Trixie, leaning forward, watching over the driver's shoulder, wondered how on earth he could see where he was going with only the merest flicker from his headlamps showing the way. The road, if indeed it was a road, seemed full of potholes, making the vehicle judder and twist. She wished she hadn't drunk all the tea in her flask – she was so thirsty now that she could have sold her soul to the devil for a cuppa.

A few snores and snuffles came from the girls who were lucky enough to have fallen asleep. The smell of petrol was mixed now with stale perfumes and the muskiness of unwashed bodies. It was draughty and cold. Hen's head was resting on Trixie's shoulder and her even breathing suggested she, too, was now sleeping.

Trixie had no idea whether they were still somewhere in Dundee or had left the city behind. Looking through to the back of the vehicle she could just make out the front of the other lorry with its dull lighting. She decided this wasn't the first crowd of girls the two drivers had collected from the station. They probably knew the road backwards, forwards and sideways.

Next to her, Jo snuffled in her sleep. Trixie liked her tremendously and hoped they'd become really good friends. She closed her eyes.

'Wake up. We're here!'

Jo was shaking Trixie's shoulder. Trixie realized she must

have dropped off. Some of the girls had already jumped down from the wagon and were waiting in a group, suitcases at their feet, outside what appeared to be a very grand ivy-covered stone lodge.

'This looks lovely,' she managed.

'Aye, and you'll be lucky to see much of it,' said the gravel-voiced driver, heaving himself over to the huge oak door and tugging the old-fashioned bell pull.

Trixie looked at Hen, who was now standing at her side and unnecessarily patting her plaited hair, which hadn't fallen out of place.

Hen shrugged. She, too, thought Trixie, wondered what his cryptic remark meant. The door creaked open and a well-built woman in a green woollen jumper and riding breeches stood in the doorway. Trixie thought she looked like a horse, with her long face and protruding teeth. Loudly the woman announced, 'Welcome, everyone.' Trixie was surprised for she had expected a Scottish accent, not an upper-class English voice. 'My name is Maud Styles. I'm your representative for the Women's Timber Corps. A hot meal will be served without delay, and then you will be shown your sleeping quarters. Leave your luggage *tidily* in the vestibule and follow me.'

Within moments the outer door had closed, burying them

all inside the high-ceilinged baronial hallway, and then they were following the woman down a long, wide corridor. Stags' antlers were mounted high on wooden plaques. Trixie was horrified to see stuffed animal heads between the antlers. Stone and wooden carvings of ugly heraldic beasts also adorned the walls. She shivered. Everything smelt highly of polish.

As Maud Styles walked past closed wooden doors, with clearly marked plaques, she called out their names. Trixie wondered if she was doing so in case some of the girls were unable to read. Later, she was to wonder why Maud Styles had bothered, considering none of the girls were allowed to set foot in the other rooms. She remembered the lorry driver saying they'd be lucky to see much of the Lodge.

Finally, they arrived at a large stone-flagged dining room, its door propped open by a cast-iron Scottie dog. Two long tables, with benches, were laid with jugs of water and thick glasses, cutlery and condiments. Trixie noted thankfully there were also cups and saucers set at all places. It looked extremely clean and business-like. More tables and benches were stored at the back of the room so Trixie decided it was used regularly. Again, the medieval theme prevailed. There were no curtains at the enormous, leaded-glass windows. Trixie was reminded of the hall at St John's School in Gosport, but, of course, the school version was much less elegant.

'If you'd like to line up by the hatch and serve yourselves,' Maud Styles announced. 'Remember, there's a war on. Take as much as you can eat but eat as much as you take. It's probably better if you decide where you're going to sit first, then help yourselves to food. It will save wandering around with filled plates.'

A metal blind was raised to show a selection of steaming vegetables in square metal dishes and a huge pot of something meaty in gravy. It smelt delicious, Trixie thought. Closed doors behind the serving counter probably led into the kitchen, she decided. A pile of white plates was stacked at one end: the starting point for them to line up and help themselves.

The warmth inside the large room after the chill of the lorry journey made Trixie feel tired again and she stifled a yawn. Hen had bagged a space for three at a table, setting down her handbag and gas mask to mark the territory.

'I don't know that I want a meal,' said Jo. 'I'm too tired.'

'Have a look. You might be pleasantly surprised,' said Trixie. 'And you ought to eat something nourishing after all the travelling.'

Other girls had already shed their coats on the benches to reserve places and were queuing for food.

'You ought to try a little, Jo,' Hen said, 'It'll help you sleep better.'

'I'm so weary I could sleep on a clothes line,' Jo replied.

Hen said, 'Since we haven't been shown our rooms, you may have to!'

They trooped over to where girls were shuffling along, using serving spoons and filling plates.

'If we're fed like this at every meal, I'll be very happy,' said Jo. Trixie looked at Jo's plate. Despite her saying she didn't feel as though she could eat, her food was piling up nicely. Trixie counted four roast potatoes nestling among peas.

'The food won't come free. It'll be deducted from our wages,' said Hen. 'As will our board.'

'I suppose so,' said Trixie. She was now standing opposite the huge pan of thick brown gravy. She couldn't remember the last time she'd been offered such an enticing dish. Rationing meant frugal cuts of meat that women queued outside butchers' shops to buy to feed their families, hoping against hope that when their turn came to be served the man wouldn't say, 'Sorry, sold out.'

After helping herself to a portion that couldn't have been described as over-generous she returned to her seat and began eating. No one stood on ceremony. Here, it was collect your food and get on with it.

'I really thought I was too tired to eat,' said Jo, looking at her clean plate, 'But that was the cat's pyjamas.' She patted her stomach. 'Now I could do with a cup of tea.'

'And it looks like we're being served one,' said Hen.

Trixie saw two aproned women, wielding large brown enamelled teapots as they worked their way through the tables, pouring tea. Many of the girls were sitting back on the benches, with a satisfied air. Some were lighting cigarettes.

'I think I've fallen asleep and gone to Heaven,' said Jo, patting her stomach again. She had a big smile on her face.

'Oh, here comes Maud Styles,' said Hen.

'I hope you're all feeling better now.' Maud, standing in front of the closed shutters, didn't wait for an answer but carried on: 'Before you're shown to your sleeping quarters, I need to explain that this palatial home, this shooting lodge, has been commandeered for the duration of the war. You will eat here,' she waved an arm encompassing the dining room, 'but the rest of the building is totally out of bounds.' Trixie could see the girls looking at each other, clearly confused. 'Tomorrow, after breakfast, here at six o'clock,' she added, 'you will be issued with a standard uniform. Training is for four weeks. Please bring your ration books to hand in. You will be given more information tomorrow. Goodnight, everyone.' Without another word she left the room.

People began chatting, finishing their tea, moving from their benches.

In the doorway two young women were dressed in green pullovers, beige shirts, green ties, riding breeches and jaunty green berets with badges depicting trees.

'They look very smart,' said Hen. 'I suppose they're here to show us to our quarters.'

Hen had guessed correctly. First everyone was marched back to the front door to collect their luggage and the impressive oak door was opened. Trixie made sure she wasn't separated from Hen and Jo as, divided into two columns, the girls were led away into the night.

Summer it might have been but Trixie felt the keenness of the cold air. She shivered, looked up into the heavens and gasped aloud. Never before had she noticed the brightness of the stars. They shone like diamonds in the inky blackness.

Her eyes became accustomed to the darkness. She could feel small stones beneath her feet that gave way to grass and the air she was breathing tasted different. There was an earthy freshness, untainted by the stink of cordite that floated everywhere in Gosport. She'd become inured to the smell of the exploded bombs, the brick dust, the stench of burning wood after the nightly visits of Hitler's bombers.

An owl hooted and Trixie almost froze with fear before

she chided herself. What did she expect out here in the countryside?

Trixie breathed deeply. Ahead of her she could make out the shapes of tall trees and of smaller, oval-roofed buildings. 'Doesn't it smell lovely and fresh?' she said.

One of the young women guides opened the door of a wooden hut and announced to her party, 'This will be your home for the time you're with us. Please choose your beds. The ablutions shed is there.' She gestured at a door at the far end. 'And the lavatory is through the door next to it. It's up to you to keep everything clean.' She paused. 'A single paraffin lamp has just been lit to welcome you. You'll note more lamps, unlit, dotted about the room. By all means use them but please be aware of the blackout regulations and the necessity to economize on paraffin. Some girls buy candles locally, when the shops have them. There are a few precious unused stubs on saucers there.' She motioned to a windowsill where, along with the candle ends, Trixie saw several boxes of matches. The blackout curtains had been drawn tightly about the windows.

The girls wandered inside the hut, looking about them in awe.

A pot-bellied unlit stove stood in the middle of the wooden floor. Logs were piled next to it. The young woman motioned towards it. 'You will be responsible for maintaining this and supplying its fuel.'

Gasps could be heard. Hen looked at Trixie and pulled a face.

'I suppose she means we're to lug home logs for it from the forest.' Hen's whisper was loud.

Metal beds lined the large room. Each had a metal cupboard at its head, and a pile of scratchy-looking blankets, coarse sheets, and a pillow at its foot.

Hen giggled. 'I thought at least the beds would have been made up.'

She received a glare from the guide.

The long room looked functional, Trixie thought. Scrupulously clean but without any sign that it had been and would be inhabited by young women. If they were to be living here for four weeks, that would soon change.

Trixie was consumed with staying close to Hen and Jo and listening to the young woman's instructions. She was about to share a hut with approximately half the girls who had been waiting outside the railway station. How would she sleep with so many others in the same room?

The guide made another announcement: 'Be in the dining room by six tomorrow morning. Sleep tight, everyone.' And then she was gone.

Trixie hoisted her suitcase onto her bed. She opened it, found the pen and writing paper and set them on top of her locker. Hen and Jo had bagged beds at either side of hers. She said a little prayer of thanks that the three of them were still together. Tiredness overtook her and she sat down on the lumpy mattress.

'Don't stop now, Trixie. Make up your bed and put out your stuff for tomorrow before weariness stops you,' Hen said. 'I've a feeling we daren't be late for breakfast.'

'I suppose you're right,' said Trixie, pulling herself to her feet. After making up her bed she put her Agatha Christie novel on top of her locker, then stuffed inside everything from her suitcase, except her nightgown, towel, soap and toothbrush. She realized she could no more walk down to the washroom, than fly to the moon so she sat down on her bed and looked about her. The general chatter in the hut had dulled to a faint murmur and she could hardly keep her eyes open but she had promised herself she would write a letter to Cy. A smile lifted her lips just thinking about him.

She glanced along the line of beds occupied by young women who probably felt as she did, tired and a little scared of what tomorrow might bring.

The washroom door opened and a young woman came out. She was clutching about her a gaberdine raincoat over a flannelette nightgown that hung almost to her bare feet. She climbed into her bed wearing the coat. Then, when she was hidden beneath the covers, she glanced about furtively, presumably to make sure no one nearby was watching, wriggled out of the coat and placed it at the foot of the bed.

Trixie looked away, feeling guilty for staring, but curiosity pulled her eyes back. Her first thought was that the girl was shy.

It was then Trixie recognized her. The dark hair, the long face. It was the girl she had shared a carriage with on the Portsmouth to Waterloo train. The one with the livid bruises who had kindly woken her.

A thought ran through Trixie's mind. The first few days here would be extremely important for making friendships. The girl seemed determined not to be noticed, which might be construed as standoffishness and she certainly wasn't like that: hadn't she reminded Trixie that the train had stopped? It might be prudent to talk to her, Trixie thought, possibly thank her again. Of course, she'd not mention the bruising. Another thought entered Trixie's mind: had the girl passed her medical to join the lumberjills with those bruises? If so, how had she explained them?

If she had received them since, who would have been so violent to her?

Trixie went over to the window-ledge and took back to her locker a nub-end of white candle, a saucer and a box of matches, the paraffin lamp having already been extinguished. She lit the candle and heated its base so that the melted wax would enable it to stand upright on the saucer. Sitting in bed, listening to the sounds of tired girls mumbling as they fell asleep, she began to write:

Dear Cy

If you only knew how many times you've entered my thoughts today you would be amazed. I'm just a girl leaving home for the very first time and I never expected to meet anyone as wonderful as you on the ferry to Portsmouth. I would like to write you a long letter but I hope you won't mind it being brief as we've been travelling all day and I can hardly keep my eyes open. By 'we' I mean the rest of the girls but especially Henrietta, who is blonde, and Jo, who is a redhead. I met them on the train and I do hope we become firm friends. I missed you as soon as my train left the station. I love your smile, I love your looks, I love the way your eyes crease at the corners when you laugh. I love the way you think, and that you adore music as much as I do. I really love your kisses and the way you make my skin tingle when you touch me. I've never met anyone like you in my whole life and I wish we'd had more time to talk in that café. I felt we were the only ones in there, surrounded by a sort of cocoon. I couldn't help wanting to show you how alive you made me feel, and that's why I pulled you close for our second kiss. That's never happened before, with anyone, so please don't think I make a habit of kissing men I've just met in public places.

I'm proud of you and the sacrifices you're making in fighting against Hitler. Please look after yourself.

I hope I hear back from you soon. The above address is where I'll be for some weeks.

Yours Trixiexx

PS I do believe in love at first sight.

Hardly able to keep her eyes open, Trixie kissed her line of written kisses, then set the pad on top of her locker. Tomorrow she'd address the envelope and post her letter. She blew out the stub of candle and caught the smell of its burning wick as she snuggled down in the darkness.

Chapter Five

'Did you sleep well last night? And finish your letter?' asked Hen. She was tucking a hairpin into one of her long white-gold plaits, anchoring it next to the other. Her hair had come adrift while she was dressing in the cotton shirt that was part of the uniform she and the other girls had been issued with after breakfast. Without waiting for an answer, she added, 'We've had such a lot of information thrown at us today – we've hardly had time to breathe.'

'I think so,' answered Trixie, to the sleep question. She didn't want to say she'd been woken by someone crying softly in the darkness. From all around inside the hut she had heard snuffles and snores but it wasn't the predictable sounds that had woken her. She'd listened carefully: if she could comfort someone who was homesick, she would have intervened but, hearing no more, Trixie had drifted back to sleep.

Now she thought of the girl who had woken her in the train. It might be a friendly gesture to go along and say hello to her, but the girl's bed was neatly made, her effects put away, and there was no sign of her. Well, greetings would keep, Trixie decided. After all, it was highly unlikely that women sleeping and possibly working together wouldn't soon get to know each other.

After breakfast, Trixie had been awed by the sight of so many others purposefully going about their business in the Lodge grounds. The camp was home to a multitude of girls, in various stages of their training and all residing in huts, like her.

Last night she had arrived in darkness at Shandford Lodge and today Trixie was eager to explore the grounds and post her letter to Cy.

Trixie smiled at Hen, who looked smart in her khaki dungarees and work-boots. The hut buzzed with laughter and conversation, while a portable gramophone was playing 'Frenesi' by Artie Shaw and his orchestra, making her feet tap. Trixie wondered who had managed to carry a gramophone and records as well as all her belongings to Shandford Lodge. The music added to Trixie's feeling of wellbeing.

She folded her corduroy breeches and green woollen pullover, then gazed at her wellingtons and oilskin raincoat with its matching sou'wester. Where on earth was she to put all these clothes? Yesterday she'd placed her own clothes in the locker and now she had to repack them in her suitcase and tuck it out of sight beneath her bed. It didn't look like she'd be wearing summer dresses and high heels anytime soon.

'Talk about passion-killers!' said Jo. She struck a pose in front of Trixie and Hen, dressed only in elasticated knee-length bloomers and a long-sleeved vest. 'Come and get me, Clark Gable! I'm all yours!'

Hen, laughing, threw her bottle-green beret at her, but it tumbled onto Trixie's bed. Trixie grabbed it. As she returned it to Hen, she said, 'Don't chuck your lovely hat about. It's practically the only item of clothing that distinguishes us from the Land Army girls. Their hats are trilby-shaped and brown. And we've got this super little badge of two crossed axes to pin on ours.' She held it up.

'Land Army girls work in the fields doing the work of men who are away fighting for our country. Lumberjills chop down trees needed as pit props to keep the coal mines open, railway sleepers, and in shipbuilding. The country needs lumber, and us girls will provide it,' Hen said. 'That means working in forests and sawmills and making sure the timber is deposited at the railway stations.'

Jo grimaced. Hen was repeating the mantra drummed into them this morning in the dining room by Maud Styles.

'That's quite a difference between the two groups of women, Hen,' Trixie said. 'The Land Girls are well provided for. I hope we'll—'

'Who could want more than this beautiful underwear?' Jo interrupted, and attempted a pirouette, which was anything but graceful.

Trixie laughed. She was happy to see Jo so light-hearted for she was sure it had been her she'd heard crying softly last night. Trixie didn't want to pry. She was discovering Jo was a very private person.

'Actually we're already looked after more than adequately, given board, lodging, uniforms, these comfy knickers, and later today we'll be issued with our tools of the trade after the meeting to explain what's expected of us at work.'

'Well, I don't enjoy being treated like a child,' said Trixie. 'At home I didn't have to go to bed after cocoa at nine o'clock and be locked inside this camp at ten.' That probably accounted for the lack of people they'd encountered when they'd arrived last night, she decided.

'I presume that's only while we're in training,' said Hen. 'Anyway, there probably isn't anywhere to go around here, and once we're actually chopping down trees and being out in the open air all day, we'll be too tired to go dancing.'

'Go dancing!' Trixie squeaked. 'We're in the middle of nowhere! Who are we going to dance with? There aren't any other camps around us and that makes a mockery of another of their silly rules that no men should hang around this camp.'

'I thought you told us you'd already met the man of your dreams,' chipped in Jo. Trixie had already been plagued with questions about the letter she'd written. Of course she had told Jo and Hen about everything that had happened on the ferry and in the station café.

'That's quietened you down and made you think, hasn't it?' laughed Hen. 'I do hope I meet someone like that.'

Then Jo surprised Trixie: 'This war can destroy life in a flash. Grab love and hold on to it tightly.'

Trixie coloured. Visions of the young American floated into her mind. 'I so needed to write to Cy last night . . .' So much was happening in such a short time that it now seemed ages ago that she had met him.

'I hope later I won't be writing to tell him I didn't pass the test we all have to take at the end of the four weeks,' Trixie said, brushing aside her glossy fall of hair. She was thoughtful. 'And I hope we three can stay together when we're moved on to wherever we'll be posted.'

'That will depend on whatever the authorities decide we're best working at,' said Hen. She stared at Jo, who was still prancing about in her vest and bloomers. 'I suppose you're aware your underwear has War Office stamped all over it?'

Jo twisted, trying to see where her knickers and vest were labelled.

Trixie smiled at her. It was like she had a double personality, she mused. One moment she was thoughtful and sad, the next like a puppy let off the lead, excited and scatty.

Hen sat down on Trixie's bed, suddenly serious. 'This is the first time I've ever worn trousers,' she said. She stroked the rough material of her dungarees. 'Mummy and Daddy didn't agree with me wearing so-called men's clothing. They said they hadn't spent a fortune on my education to have me looking like a hobbledehoy.'

'What on earth is that?' Trixie exclaimed.

'An awkward boy,' supplied Jo, clearly pleased with herself. 'Are they very strict, your parents?'

'Very. I saw a picture in a shop window advertising lumberjills working in the woods. It was requesting volunteers. The girls looked happy. It was so inviting.' She paused. 'I decided the only way I could have a life of my own would be to sign up. Surely, I thought, Mummy and Daddy wouldn't berate me for wanting to do my bit in helping to win this war . . . Of course they did. Only by then it was too late. I'd already enlisted and there was nothing either of them could do to stop me. I left home to break free from the traditions they've been making me stick to all my life.'

In her mind's eye Trixie could see Alverstoke's Western Way. Huge houses in tree-lined plots, cars in the drives and probably no worries about petrol coupons, or the lack of. Inside bathrooms instead of a lavvy at the bottom of the garden and real lavatory rolls, not cut-up squares of newspaper hanging from a nail. So very different from the terraced houses with front doors opening onto grubby pavements that she was used to. Cars were unaffordable down her street. Bicycles were the normal mode of transport, and buses, of course.

It didn't seem to Trixie that money and tradition were so awful. But what did she know of such things? Rose, her mother, had no money, but had never stopped Trixie wearing slacks.

Humping hundredweight sacks of potatoes and string bags full of vegetables at the greengrocer's since the age of fourteen, when she had left school, meant comfortable, serviceable clothes were the norm. She was aware, though, that slacks on women were frowned upon by certain more traditional people and even some men. 'So, Amelia Bloomer wouldn't be invited to a dinner party at your mum and dad's house, then?' she said.

'God, no!' Hen giggled.

Jo frowned.

'Amelia Bloomer helped to make trousers popular with women when bicycles came into fashion, Jo,' supplied Trixie. '"Clothes for women should be suitable to their wants and needs,"' she said, in an affected voice 'That's what Amelia thought. And I reckon dungarees and trousers for women while they're working in factories and out in the fields are practical. We're not going to help win the war dressed up like porcelain dollies, are we?'

'Definitely not,' said Hen. 'And you can keep Clark Gable!' Jo threw up her hands and gasped in mock-horror. 'I've already fallen in love with my dungarees!'

Chapter Six

'When I woke up this morning, I never thought all this would happen today,' said Trixie. 'I feel like I've been run over by Alf's horse and the cart!'

The firelight danced above the ash and smoke rising from the dead branches of the brash fire. Trixie and the other girls had been warned to stop feeding the smouldering mass of fragrant pine. They'd been told that soon it would be time to stamp out the ashes and dig over the charred earth in readiness for planting young trees. The saplings would replace the pines now being brashed, then felled.

Day one of training almost over, Trixie looked about her at the other exhausted girls relaxing around the embers while sitting on logs or lying on the undergrowth. All wore dungarees or slacks, shirts and heavy boots.

Tomorrow Trixie determined she would wear the gloves

her mother had slipped into her suitcase. The pine resin from the branches had caused a sticky substance to build up on her fingers.

She and Jo were waiting for Alf, who was of indeterminate age. He had a limp, and an unshaven though kindly face, and would take them back to the Lodge on his cart. Alf didn't seem to have another name. He was, he had informed them, the timber foreman and their boss for the next few weeks.

The forest air and a healthy breeze, which Trixie had first decided was exhilarating, had helped to wear her out. She thought Jo looked as if she could drop with weariness, but she wasn't going to comment because she guessed she looked exactly the same.

The trees, so tall, so beautiful, which she'd been learning to chop down and also to brash, now seemed to be closing in on her. She thought longingly of her bed in the hut.

She was still smarting from the remarks Alf had made earlier. All the girls around her had laughed but Trixie knew it would take her a long time to live down her mistake.

'Use your right hand!' said Jo, as though reading her thoughts and elbowed Trixie.

'Don't you start!' said Trixie, but with good grace.

'Are you going to tell Hen?'

'Probably won't need to because everyone else will,' said Trixie.

She thought back to when Alf had explained about brashing. 'Use the brashing saw and cut the lower dead branches from the conifers. Usually you'll need to clear at least to a height of six feet. Not only does this get rid of the dead wood but it allows access to the forest.' The command had seemed clear enough to Trixie.

She was working next to a girl named Maisie who had started straight away. Trixie, armed with a saw, followed her every move. After a while, getting sweaty was all Trixie was achieving, while Maisie seemed to have the knack of quickly and cleanly hacking off the lower twigs. She pulled on them, holding them fan-shaped, then cut as near to the trunk as she could. Trixie copied her but to little avail. Maisie was soon removing the brash so speedily that Trixie couldn't keep up with her. She was appalled that she couldn't cope with such a seemingly simple task.

She was near to tears when Alf appeared. He watched them both at work, then removed his red neckerchief, wiped his forehead with it, and retied it around his neck.

'Left-handed, are you, Trixie gal?'

Trixie shook her head.

'Well, I can see that young Maisie is. Copying her is

no good. Why don't you use your right hand to saw the branches?'

Trixie stared at Alf, then at Maisie, who had dropped her saw into the undergrowth so she could search her sleeve for a handkerchief with her left hand. She blew her nose loudly. 'Sawdust dun 'alf get up yer nose, don't it?' she said, replacing the hankie.

Next to Maisie, her friend Dolly, oblivious, was hacking away with a saw at the lower branches. She was right-handed and doing the job reasonably well. Certainly better than Trixie.

'You use your right hand, Trixie gal,' Alf repeated. A smile creased his face. 'No good copying someone else. You got to do it yer own way!' Maisie, meanwhile, had realized what was going on and was cackling like an old hen. Pretty soon other girls were giggling.

Trixie was wishing the earth would open and swallow her. Tears of shame stung her eyes.

Alf touched Trixie's shoulder. 'I bin watching you, Trixie,' he said. 'If I had as many gals who put their backs into a job, like you, I'd be a happy man.' The laughter stopped, as if a tap had been turned off.

Trixie took a deep breath and, with the brashing saw now in her right hand, the left steadying the old growth, didn't speak but instead found a steady rhythm as she sawed.

'Good gal,' said Alf, fumbling in his pocket for his pipe. 'You use your right hand.'

Trixie knew the girls would tease her about her mistake, possibly for the rest of the day, probably for all of the time she was to spend at the Lodge.

'I ache in places I never knew existed,' Jo said, bringing Trixie back to reality. 'And I'm starving. It seems years ago we ate our packed lunch.'

'That doorstep sandwich of grated cheese and mashed carrot was good,' said Trixie, remembering, 'but now I'm so ravenous I could eat a horse!'

It wasn't only the gnawing ache of hunger and the promise of their evening meal that was making the trip back to Shandford Lodge enticing but the simple act of washing off the sweat and lying down to rest her painful arms and shoulders. Sleeping, without having to wield a heavy saw to cut branches, seemed absolutely heavenly.

'You'd better not let Alf hear you say you could eat a horse,' Jo said. 'He's very fond of his Lulubelle!'

Trixie thought about the solid grey Shire horse, with soft brown eyes, that the grizzled man spoke to quietly and treated as gently as one would a child. Yes, Alf was a kind man, she thought.

She took another swig of the thick brown tea brewed over

the fire. A clear, gurgling stream ran through the woodland so Alf had provided a billy-can and tea leaves and introduced them to the delights of using amenities that were at hand. There was no sugar or milk but Trixie thought she'd soon learn to drink it without, and like it. She was sure the afternoon tea breaks had added energy she hadn't known she possessed.

Trixie's head was spinning with the information she had been forced to take in. It seemed impossible that there was still more to learn.

'How on earth am I going to be able to work a full day when just half a day leaves me like a dishrag?' she asked Jo.

Was it really only this morning, after being presented with her uniform, that she'd thought she might stroll around the Lodge and find her bearings? Or even walk outside to discover the village, which she had been told was close by? But there'd been no time for that because they'd been ordered to work in the forest. She was thankful she'd been able to post her letter to Cy after discovering the red letterbox just outside the Lodge gates.

On the journey in, and throughout the afternoon, their timber foreman had added nuggets of information. 'Can you remember what Alf told us about the sawmill?' she asked.

'Not much,' answered Jo. 'But he promised we'd have a look round one. I dare say we'll get used to it all and everything will fall into place, eventually.'

'The wanderer returns!' A smile lit Trixie's face as Hen walked towards them with a grin. Without speaking she eased herself down onto the undergrowth in her usual unhurried way.

'You're back then! Where did you go and what happened? I suppose you'll be working in different places from us now.' Jo's mocking words fell over themselves. She moved along to give more room for her friend to stretch out. 'I hope you won't think you're too posh to talk to us.'

Hen gave her a wry look, then winked at Trixie to show she wasn't worried by what Jo had said.

Now she'd got to know Jo a little more, Trixie knew there was no malice in it. Her moods could be mercurial but her heart was kind.

'Yes, a bit of a surprise that was,' Hen said. Trixie thought she looked quite pleased with herself. 'To be singled out like that. Any tea left in that billy?' She waved at the can resting in the warmth of the ashes.

Trixie picked up the tin mug she'd been using and threw away the grouts, refilled it with tea and passed it to Hen, who smiled gratefully at her. She set the metal can on the earth away from the fire's embers.

'I expect it was that posh school you went to,' said Jo. 'Sets you apart from us Gosport riff-raff.' She grinned at Hen. 'I was never any good at maths.'

'Nor me,' added Trixie. 'I once managed two out of ten for arithmetic. Bottom of the class I was.' She giggled. 'However, after working in the greengrocer's I defy anyone to say they're quicker than me in adding up pounds, shillings and pence correctly.'

Hen laughed and put down the empty mug. 'I needed that,' she said. 'I was parched.'

Trixie added, 'The government knows all about us from the Labour Exchange. Our strengths and weaknesses. Including what we're likely to be good at. I suppose the people here have all our details on file.'

'I don't mind that,' Hen admitted. 'I've nothing to hide. Anyway, I do like working out problems in my head and a measurer has to do just that. The first thing Alf showed me and the others was how to measure the height of a tree.'

'Blimey!' gasped Jo. 'Did you have to climb up it with a tape measure?'

On their arrival in the forest Alf had taken a scrap of paper from his pocket and called some of the girls' names,

Hen's included. Jo had been worried that Hen had done something she shouldn't, until they'd discovered that she had been chosen to become a measurer. Later, she'd be expected to visit privately owned forests and give a price that the government would be willing to pay the farmer for the timber, if it was considered good enough. The job involved a good head for figures and penmanship. Measurers received a wage increase of ten shillings a week, Alf had said.

'Well done, Hen,' Jo said. 'Tell us how to do it.' She turned to Trixie. 'Is that billy empty now?'

Trixie nodded. She'd rinse the can out in the stream, maybe bring back some water to drench the fire before Alf came to collect them.

'It's a really clever system,' continued Hen. 'You hold a straight stick by its base at arm's length, walk away, stop when the stick in your hand is the same length as the tree. Then you measure how far you've moved from the tree and the measurement, in feet, is the tree's height.' Hen frowned. 'At least, I think that's the right way to do it,' she added. 'I think I can remember how to measure the circumference as well.' She paused. 'Using a regular tape, measuring around the tree trunk at a height of four and a half feet should give the actual circumference of the tree . . . Or have I got everything mixed up? I think I need to get away from all these trees. It's difficult trying to remember everything.' She handed back the mug to Trixie. 'Thank you.'

'It wasn't only you learning about measuring, was it?' Jo asked. She'd stood up and was now rubbing her aching back. 'Did you get on all right with the other girls?'

Hen nodded. 'There wasn't time to chat, not properly. They seem fine. I was told there's a pretty lively pub up the road – well, lively when they've got beer, that is.' Jo and Trixie looked at each other and smiled broadly as she continued. 'I didn't see the pub but we walked miles looking at different species of trees and being told what their wood was used for. There were four of us women being shown aspects of the work, then being made to work out sums in our heads,' carried on Hen. 'Alf left us in the charge of a stern woman from the Lodge. She had a loud voice and was a bit how I imagined a sergeant major in the army would be, very bossy. Eleanor Yates, her name was. But she seemed to know her stuff.' Hen paused again, then said confidentially, 'Apparently, there are Canadians felling trees here in the forest, needed because our men are away fighting. We heard them calling to each other but we never saw them. We might get to work with them later, so I was told. None of us dared to go and find them. We didn't want to incur the wrath of Eleanor Yates. She's terrifying. There's an airfield not too far away, more Canadians, and sometimes dances at that pub.' She laughed. 'But tell me what you've been doing.'

Trixie saw her glance at the dry branches lying about on the earth. 'We heard about the pub too,' she said. 'It's called the Yellow Duck. We've been brashing. Alf came back to us after he'd disappeared with you. We were told how to prune those dead branches from the trees. I'm not going to tell you what happened to me because you'll hear about it soon enough and I feel such a chump . . . Anyway, I'm not the only dunce here. One girl was actually climbing a ladder to reach the topmost tree branches. She must have misheard Alf's instruction to cut to about six feet from the ground. Alf really shouted at her. She's in our hut – Dolly's her name.' Trixie pointed out the girl sitting on a log some distance away. 'She was sawing off green branches near me, but then she disappeared. "What the hell are you doin' up there? And didn't I say dry, dead branches only?" Alf yelled at her. She fell straight off the ladder! Luckily the branches broke her fall on the way down, so she wasn't as badly hurt as she might have been, just a few scratches.' Trixie sighed. 'It's difficult, if you've never used a heavy saw before and aren't sure what you're supposed to be doing.'

'I agree,' said Hen. 'But I wouldn't waste too much time feeling sorry for Dolly. Apparently, so I heard, she's one of those girls who never listens when she's told something. Always thinks she knows best. She sounds as if she might be a bit of a liability. It's so important to listen carefully and do as we're told. But why do that to the trees? Brashing, you said?'

Trixie answered her: 'Apparently it encourages them to grow straight and tall, which means a better price for the owners, when the trees are cut down and sold for pit props, telegraph poles and suchlike.' She added, 'Alf said it makes it easier to walk through the trees to have a good look around. Anyway, the dry branches that fall are gathered up and burnt.' She indicated the remains of the fire they were sitting next to, and another ashen patch, further off, surrounded by chatting girls. 'All the embers must be completely dug over before we leave,' she added. 'During the hot weather, fires spread easily, so we have to be careful.'

'I hope we won't be split up,' said Jo, in a small voice.

Trixie realized she had probably become bored by their conversation, and had slipped into a world of her own.

Hen put her hand on Jo's arm. 'Even if measurers are taken to different locations during working hours, I'll still be sleeping in the hut with you.' She squeezed her arm. 'At least for the next four weeks while we're learning to be lumberjills.'

'Good,' said Jo, with a smile. 'But I'm not sure I like learning on the job. I thought we'd be taught stuff in classrooms.'

'Perhaps we will, later,' said Hen. 'I think it's easier to get on and do it, than sit and listen to someone telling us what we should be doing.' She was quiet for a moment. 'There's quite a few women in these woods learning different forestry stuff and there's more men.'

'More men!' exclaimed Trixie. 'Where?'

'The other side of the forest,' Hen said. 'They're guarded while they're working, so they're probably prisoners of war,' she added.

'What nationality? Did you speak to any of them?' Trixie asked.

'We weren't allowed anywhere near them. Anyway, why are you so interested? You've got Cy, haven't you? Are you going to write him another letter, tonight?'

Trixie pulled a face. 'The way I feel I don't think I could hold a pen. I'm so tired. All I want to do is sleep and eat,' she added.

More women and girls were returning to the clearing now. It seemed obvious to Trixie that Hen was right about them being at different stages of learning about forestry. Some of the tools looked so heavy she wondered how anyone managed to carry them, let alone use them.

Further down the stream a horse and cart had pulled up and some of the women and girls were clambering aboard.

'I wish that was us,' said Jo.

Trixie said, 'So do I, but our lift back is with Alf and Lulubelle. Surely they won't be long now.'

It was then her attention was caught by one of the girls walking towards the cart. Most of the young women were grouped in twos or threes, laughing and talking. She, however, was hunched over and shuffling through the undergrowth rather like a small solitary creature that wanted to disguise itself.

It was the girl from the train. The girl in their hut who'd got into bed wearing her mackintosh. Trixie's heart reached out to her – she looked unbearably lonely, and she had been plucky enough to speak to her in the crowded carriage. 'I bet you didn't dream this journey would be so nerve-racking' had been her words when Trixie was worried that the woman opposite was about to spill her flask of hot tea over Trixie's knees. Later, as well, the girl had woken her at Waterloo station . . .

This time she was not wearing the long blue raincoat.

Her dungarees were practically hidden by a baggy brown jumper, high in the neck and with sleeves to her wrists.

But even from the distance between them, Trixie could see she had been crying. She felt ashamed that she hadn't yet spoken to her.

Chapter Seven

'You're not really going to bed?' Dolly Farrows stared at Trixie, whom she'd caught in the act of climbing into her bed. 'It's not even seven o'clock and the best part of the evening is yet to come!' Dolly, bright red lips, eyelashes clumped together with heavy mascara and her dark hair victory-rolled, shook her head in disgust.

Behind her, her friend Maisie, also heavily made-up and wearing a box-pleated skirt with a fluffy red jumper, frowned as she asked in her Birmingham accent, 'Aren't you coming down to the Yellow Duck?'

Trixie sat on her bed. 'I'm worn out with all the work we've done today.'

The two girls had come from the end of the hut where their beds were. This afternoon, briefly, Dolly, Maisie, Jo and she had been together, brashing trees. The pub in the village had been mentioned.

'You're a lightweight! That's what you are!' Maisie laughed.

Trixie noted that Hen, already in bed, wrinkled her nose and pulled up her covers. The smell of lily-of-the-valley scent, in which Maisie and Dolly had soaked themselves, was overpowering.

'If you're like this after one afternoon, what'll you feel like after a full day tomorrow?' Dolly idly kicked the leg of Trixie's iron bed. 'Downing a couple of pints of shandy and having a bit of a sing-song will do you much more good than lying there.' Evidently Dolly's tree fall hadn't unnerved her one bit.

'Aren't you two tired?' Hen stared at them. Her face had a healthy glow from working outside in the warm breeze and fresh air.

'Of course. But we're not going to mope around in bed, like you two, imagining that every ache and pain is worse than it really is, are we, Maisie?' Dolly dug Maisie in the ribs so she shook her head in agreement. 'We're going out to have a laugh. Work hard, play hard,' she said. 'Otherwise our training is all work and no fun.' She raised her eyebrows and grinned. 'Besides, we heard it's where the Canadians drink.'

'Why didn't you say so earlier?' Hen, her flaxen hair loose, threw back her bedclothes, exposing a flannelette nightie, and stepped down onto the wooden boards. In moments she was on her knees pulling her suitcase from beneath the bed.

'What are you doing?' Trixie could see her riffling through her folded clothes.

'What you should both be doing.' Hen looked up at Trixie, then across at Jo, who had just come back from the ablutions room. A towel was wound turban-style around Jo's head because she'd washed her hair. Wet tendrils hung about her forehead and she was wreathed in the fresh, homely smell of talcum powder. 'I don't want my memories of training to be work and sleep. I'm looking for something to wear and then I'm off to the village,' Hen said.

'You just like the idea of being with the blokes,' mumbled Jo. Dolly and Maisie laughed.

'And why shouldn't I?' Hen asked. Trixie heard a hint of sharpness in her reply. Hen was holding up a long blue chiffon dress. 'What do you think of this?'

'Don't be daft!' broke in Dolly. 'It's a pub, not a ball we're going to. Keep it simple. Blouses and skirts. And wear your wellingtons or boots. Take shoes to change into, if you must. That last lot of rain might be lingering in potholes, and twice a day cows are driven up that lane. You don't want to be stinking of—'

Maisie broke in: 'It's still quite light outside now but later it'll be dark and there's no lighting because of the blackout.'

'I get the idea,' Hen said. Then, 'Why don't you two carry on up to the Yellow Duck and we'll come when we've got changed? No sense in you losing drinking and flirting time because of us.'

Maisie nodded.

'All right,' agreed Dolly. 'We'll see you there. You can't miss it, the pub's about a mile up the lane.'

'Bye, then.' Hen was busy wriggling into a blue gored skirt beneath her nightie, grumbling quietly because her unplaited hair was getting in her way. Trixie watched Dolly and Maisie leave the hut, shouting goodbyes and closing the door behind them.

'You really are going out, then?' asked Jo.

Hen stopped what she was doing now that she'd pulled on a silk blouse atop her skirt. She dropped her nightdress onto her bed and stared at Jo. 'Of course! And, believe it or not, I feel better already now I have something besides cocoa, breakfast and work to look forward to. You are both coming, aren't you?' She picked up her make-up bag from the top of her locker.

'I suppose so,' said Trixie. She looked at Jo.

Jo was pulling back her blankets. 'I don't want to,' she said.

'It's not because I ache all over, which I do, but I don't feel like being jolly when I'm not in the mood.'

'Don't be a misery,' said Hen. 'You'll like it when we get there.'

'If she wants to go to bed, let her,' said Trixie. She had realized that Jo was temperamental and if she needed to be quiet it was best to let her get on with it.

Jo gave Trixie a grateful smile and sat on the edge of her bed. Pulling the towel off her head, she used it to begin drying her hair.

'You sure you'll be all right on your own?' Trixie frowned at her.

'I'm not exactly on my own with a hut full of girls around me, am I?' For a moment Trixie thought she could see the brightness of tears sparkle in her friend's eyes. Jo blinked and sighed. 'Go! Have a nice time. Don't wake me if I'm asleep when you come in but tell me all about it in the morning.' She gave Trixie a smile that told her she'd made up her mind and didn't want to be persuaded otherwise. Then she turned away and continued rubbing her hair with the towel.

Trixie wondered if Jo was homesick. Today she'd thought a great deal about her own mum. Earlier, she'd decided that tonight she would write again to Cy, and send a letter to Rose telling her all her news. Several of the girls were already complaining about being away from home and missing familiar faces. It might explain Jo's moodiness or at least some of it, she thought. After she'd delved into her case and grabbed a pair of grey slacks and a short-sleeved mauve jumper, she gathered up her toothbrush and toiletry bag.

Walking down the middle of the hut towards the washroom, she noticed that the bed where the girl from the train slept was still perfectly made up. Her first thought was that she had gone out for a walk. It was still reasonably light outside. Trixie had noticed that the summer darkness didn't fall in Scotland as early as it did in Gosport. But when at last it was dark, the night was blacker than anything she had ever encountered at home.

The girl was kneeling on a chair looking out of a nearby window. Trixie thought she was in a world of her own rather than staring at something going on outside. She walked up to her. The girl had freshly washed hair and had changed out of her work clothes into a loose cotton dress that buttoned firmly at cuffs and neck. The faded pattern of the material and its worn appearance told Trixie it wasn't new.

She took a deep breath. 'I don't expect you remember me but thank you for waking me when I fell asleep on the London—'

'I do remember,' the girl broke in. 'Forget it. It was nothing.' Her dark brown eyes held Trixie's.

'It wasn't nothing,' Trixie insisted. 'I could have missed my connection if it hadn't been for you.' The next words that came out of her mouth were totally unplanned. 'Look, me and my friend Hen are going down the village pub. Why don't you come along with us? As a thank-you?' Trixie's eyes swept over the girl's angular face. The dejection she had seen before was now replaced by apprehension. And fear.

'I . . . I . . .' She frowned. 'I can't,' she said.

Something seemed to have happened to Trixie. She knew she had to make the girl come with them. She didn't want to take no for an answer. But the girl was one step ahead of her. 'I don't have any money,' she said. Her voice was no more than a whisper.

Trixie smiled. 'I'm inviting you because you did me a good turn. I'm paying, so you can't refuse.'

Without giving her time to utter another word Trixie walked towards the ablutions room. Before she had time to let herself in, the door opened and out swept Hen, dressed and wearing make-up but with her long hair still hanging down her back. 'I forgot the pins for my hair,' she said. 'I'd lose my head if it wasn't screwed onto my neck! Are you going to be long getting dressed?'

'I'll be ready before you,' Trixie told her, as the door closed behind her.

It took her very little time to dress, and as she scrubbed her teeth, she stared at herself in the mirror. Trixie was aware she was no beauty, and certainly not glamorous like Hen. Her heart-shaped face was all right, she thought, and she quite liked her blonde hair, which reached to her shoulders. She'd combed part of it forward in the way Veronica Lake wore hers. It wasn't exactly the same style but she'd copied it as best she could, and Trixie decided it would have to do. She wished it was naturally blonde so she didn't have to use peroxide and ammonia when her mousy roots grew through. Her green eyes were her best feature, large and luminous. She gave one last spit onto the tiny blue brush, ran it across the solid lump of mascara and gave a final coat to her eyelashes. Then she gathered up her things, opened the door and made her way towards the girl, who surprised her by standing up and smiling at her.

'Ready?' Trixie asked.

'Ready,' answered the girl, and followed Trixie down the hut to where Trixie threw her make-up bag and nightdress onto her bed.

Hen had just finished pinning her hair into two perfect coils around her head as Trixie said, 'My new friend's coming with us, Hen.'

Hen smiled at the girl and Trixie was relieved she didn't ask Trixie for her friend's name because she didn't know it. The girl smiled apprehensively at Hen and said softly, 'It's very kind of you to let me come with you. You know what it's like if a woman goes into a pub on her own, she gets herself a bad name. My name's Vi, short for Violet.'

'You're welcome, Vi,' came Hen's answer. Trixie breathed a small sigh of relief that Hen's impeccable manners allowed her simply to accept Vi's reason for joining them.

Hen grabbed her handbag and gas mask and started towards the hut door. 'Come on, then, you two,' she called. Trixie saw her glance at Jo's bed. Jo had stopped drying her hair and was now under the covers. 'Canadians, here we come!' Hen laughed.

Stepping out into the night, Trixie wondered at Vi's seemingly easy acceptance of being practically bullied into going to the pub. And Hen's obvious delight to be meeting the Canadians made Trixie wonder if she had ever been out with a man before.

Chapter Eight

Trixie blessed the moon for brightening the way along the dirt lane. It was spoilt by deep potholes and dark patches that all three girls tried to steer clear of. The air was scented with wild fruits, and summery blossoms reaching maturity. The more pungent smell of animal waste couldn't be ignored because it was the most powerful of all. Trixie was glad she'd heeded the advice of Dolly and Maisie and worn her sturdy black lace-ups. They didn't exactly complement her outfit but they kept her feet clean and dry.

High ragged hedges lined one side of the track, and opposite, it yawned into fenced fields of heather and gorse. Fields that yielded lumpen shapes with huge horns and shaggy coats, either lying down or wandering about with steam billowing from their nostrils. Trixie could see they were cattle and to her they looked like something out of a cowboy film. Totally unlike the black and white cows she had seen on Hampshire farmland. These, she decided, were Highland cattle, recognizable from pictures in books borrowed from Gosport library.

'I'm glad those huge beasts aren't wandering along the lane towards us.' Her voice had broken the silence that had fallen after the initial chattering between them had withered.

Trixie had grown tired of propping up a dying conversation. Hen was obviously preoccupied, either with her proposed new job or something she wasn't willing to discuss while Vi was present. Hen wasn't being overtly rude – it wasn't in her nature to be so, Trixie thought. She was just being Hen.

Vi was monosyllabic whenever Trixie tried to include her in a conversation. This afternoon when she had seen Vi, she'd been alone, obviously upset enough to cry. She could understand Vi's reticence. Why should she spill out her feelings to virtual strangers? And while the shapeless button-through dress concealed the bruises on her skin, she must have been aware that Trixie had seen them. Trixie had never mentioned meeting her on the train, or her bruises, to either Hen or Jo. All she wanted to do was befriend the girl. Neither Vi nor Hen responded to her observations on the cattle.

It was the noise that reached Trixie first. Her heart immediately lifted at the hearty, though out-of-tune, strains of 'Roll Out The Barrel' coming from the dark shape of the pub silhouetted in the moonlight, and now not far away.

'We're here, at last,' said Hen excitedly. With renewed enthusiasm the girls practically ran towards the Yellow Duck.

Hen turned the door handle and fought her way through the blackout curtain covering the door. A fug of cigarette smoke and beer enveloped Trixie as she followed her friend into the brightness of the crowded bar. Hen didn't wait for either Trixie or Vi and was immediately swallowed into the throng.

Vi grabbed her hand and Trixie halted.

'Trixie, I'm not sure why you made me come here. If it's because you think I'm going to tell you how I came by the bruising, you're mistaken. I know you've seen the marks – you first noticed them on the train, didn't you?'

Trixie looked at her apprehensively, fearful even of what Vi might say next. This was the first time the bruising had been mentioned.

'Somehow, though, I don't think it was just curiosity that's made you bring me here. If that's so, thank you for trying to be a friend . . .' Her voice tailed off.

Trixie was at a loss as to how to answer. Vi, standing

close, bowed her head. They needed to move from the doorway, so Trixie said lightly, 'You're not so green as you're cabbage-looking, are you?' Vi was certainly nobody's fool, she thought.

Vi laughed and immediately Trixie knew they understood each other perfectly. They would talk, but it would be in Vi's own good time.

Together, they stepped into the warbling mass of customers. 'Oh, by the way,' said Vi, grabbing at her arm, 'I don't drink alcohol, so if you're buying, I'd like a lemonade or orangeade.'

Pushing through the bodies with Vi at her heels, Trixie looked about for Hen, but she had disappeared.

Eventually Trixie elbowed her way past men drinking pints and couples singing or chatting, and stood waiting to be served by the harassed barmaid. Horse brasses hung from wooden beams and the ceiling was brown from cigarette smoke. But the pub had a homely feel. Many of the customers were now singing soulfully and tunelessly to the Ink Spots' current popular song, 'I Don't Want To Set The World On Fire'.

Way down at the other end of the long bar, she could see a man who looked like the publican, large-bellied in a striped apron and with a drooping moustache. He glanced her way, but didn't move from the beer pumps, which he pulled on constantly, filling pint pots. The pints seemed to disappear from the barmaid's hands like magic as soon as they landed on the bar.

A voice came from the serviceman now standing next to Trixie. 'You'll never get served, darlin'. It's always men first. Want me to add your order to mine?'

It was on the tip of Trixie's tongue to tell him he was a fast one to try to pick her up. She managed to stop herself just in time as he added, 'They've been without ale here but had a delivery this morning. That's why the place is packed.'

Trixie mentally chided herself for her unkind thoughts and treated him to a wide smile. The soldier's blue eyes twinkled and he gave her a warm smile in return.

'Thanks,' she said. 'I'd like that. It's half a shandy and a lemonade.' Since she had no idea where Hen was, she couldn't ask her if she wanted a drink.

Vi had said something earlier to Hen about lone women in bars being unjustly classed as tarts, but equality between the sexes was slowly being won, especially now women were forced into doing the jobs of men who were away fighting. Trixie had noticed it in the Alma, when she played the piano, that men were always served before women. So, it was no surprise when at last the tired-looking barmaid sauntered up to the soldier, ignoring Trixie, and asked, in a Scottish burr, 'What can I get you?'

To Trixie he said his name was Tom. He was billeted in the village. Trixie had to insist he take payment for their drinks. She and Vi followed in Tom's wake as he carried the tray to the area in the corner where the singing was loudest.

Hen, with a glass in her hand, was sitting high on what seemed to be a piece of furniture covered with a sheet. Her long, slim legs, crossed at the knees, were being much admired by the men standing about her.

'I've been looking for you,' said Trixie.

Hen was crooning 'We'll Meet Again' in a throaty voice, but stopped long enough to say, 'I'm so glad we came. I'm having a lovely time. I'm sure Jo would have liked all this.' She swept an arm theatrically around the room, then sipped her drink, put it down, and continued singing.

Trixie was about to apologize for not buying her a drink when Hen spotted the glasses on the tray, stopped singing again for long enough to give Tom a wide smile, and said, 'Thank you, handsome, for the drink.' Tom was blushing.

'That's what you call a fast worker,' said Trixie.

'Our Hen's a very popular girl,' said Dolly, draped over a chair and raising her glass to Hen. Trixie caught the sarcasm in her voice.

Maisie giggled. 'Tom's smitten with her already. We haven't bought a drink since she got here!'

Vi was frowning at Dolly and Maisie. Trixie realized she didn't like the way the two of them were exploiting Hen. 'What this place needs is a piano player,' she said. She gulped some of her lemonade.

'I can play,' said Trixie, 'but I need a piano.'

'What d'you think she's sitting on?' An airman, in air-force blue, with blond curls almost as pale as Hen's hair, said, 'It's only covered up because Donnie McKay has no one to play it and he thinks that with a sheet over it nobody will spill drinks on it.' Before Trixie could utter another word, the airman had shouted above the tumult, 'Donnie, d'you mind if this girl tickles the ivories?'

Almost immediately, the landlord shouted back from behind the bar, 'Sure, Ken. Help yoursel', lassie. It's no locked. It's no been used for a wee while, and some of the keys are stuck.'

'Come on down, girly,' said the blond airman to Hen, who grinned at him.

'Catch me, handsome,' she said, falling from the piano top into Ken's arms.

He held on to her, thought Trixie, just a little longer than was necessary.

'Oops!' he said. 'You could have done yourself a nasty injury if I hadn't grabbed you.'

Hen gazed into his eyes. 'But you did, didn't you, darling boy!' Then she turned to Trixie. 'Let's get you a piano stool . . .'

Hen didn't move to look anywhere but her words caused the men around her to scatter in the hunt for a stool. Vi shook her head and smiled a knowing smile.

Trixie thought Hen released all her inhibitions when men were around. And they loved it. She pushed away her incomprehension at why Hen, a truly beautiful girl, needed so much approval.

From behind the Bentley upright piano, a stool with a green velvet seat was produced, hoisted over and set down. Trixie lifted the lid of the piano and looked at the keys. 'C'mon, Trixie, play, so we can all sing in tune!' Hen begged.

Trixie made herself comfortable, said a little prayer to herself that there were no professional pianists about to find fault with her playing by ear. And with Vi standing at her shoulder, she began with one of the favourites, 'Yours', which she'd played many times in the Alma.

Cheering started as Trixie's fingers touched the notes. Cheers that halted, as the crowd about the piano began listening in earnest. Hen, standing next to Trixie, began to hum the tune, then to sing along in her husky voice.

Clunk, then another, clunk.

Two notes in the middle of the keyboard were reluctant to be played. Trixie's fingertips touched the keys but instead of a sweet sound, only dull thuds emerged. Trixie told herself not to let it worry her. It was possible the piano had reacted to changes in the humidity of the bar. Other customers had immediately joined in singing, seemingly ignorant that the tune wasn't as it should be.

Hen's voice was dreamy and the airman, Ken, hovered alongside her, like a bee ready to collect pollen.

But Trixie couldn't bear the awful sounds that interrupted the flow of music. 'Time to refresh your drinks, everyone, while I look at the piano to find out why the keys are sticking.'

Taking her at her word, the customers pushed towards the bar. She looked in the direction of Donnie, and saw him put two thumbs up as he smiled a thank-you, glad of yet more trade.

Trixie peered at the black and white keys then tested each note. As she had already thought, it was a couple of the central white keys that couldn't be depressed. Carefully she felt along and around the notes.

It didn't seem that dampness was to blame, after all, she thought. Surely more keys would be malfunctioning if that was the problem As she peered all around the faulty keys her keen eyesight detected a sliver of silver.

'Well, look at that, Vi. Can you see? Is it metal?'

Vi leant over. 'I don't see anything.'

'Well, I do,' Trixie insisted. 'Hen, can I borrow one of your hairpins?' Hen obliged, after breaking her gaze into Ken's eyes.

Poking, lifting and more than a few swear words later, Trixie finally held between her fingers the tiny culprit of the jammed keys.

'Well, look at that,' said Hen, pushing back the hairpin back into her plait. 'Who would have thought a threepenny joey would have caused so much bother?'

Trixie stared at the tiny silver coin with its flattened and worn edges.

'Who's that on the face of the coin?' Vi asked, peering at Trixie's hand as she turned it over.

'It's Queen Victoria,' Hen said. 'I wonder how long it's been jammed between the keys.'

'Ever since someone playing the piano emptied a pocket to pay for a drink, I expect,' said Trixie. She handed the tiny coin to Vi. 'Hold on to that,' she said.

Her fingers touched the notes and the true sounds they made caused her heart to lift and her lips to curve into a smile.

'I'll be back in a moment,' Trixie said, rising from the stool and taking the coin from Vi. As she squeezed past her in the crush around them, she heard the girl's sharp intake of breath. It was obvious Vi had other bruises that Trixie had accidentally touched. The look that passed between them said more than words.

'Here you are, Donnie.' Trixie pushed the coin into his hand. 'This is the cause of the piano's sickness.'

'You're a bonny lass!' He looked at the silver threepenny piece, then leant across the counter and enfolded her in his brawny arms. Letting her go, he said, 'I'm that pleased I'm going to put it in a frame and stand it on the shelf. You'll nae pay for another drink in this place as long as I'm the boss here,' he said. 'No one's touched that piano since young Stuart O'Gilvey said it needed tuning. He used to have the customers singing and dancing . . .'

'Where is he, now?' Trixie asked.

'He joined the Navy and didnae come home.' A glazed look came into his eyes. He was remembering happier, then sad days, Trixie thought.

'Maybe the coin belonged to him and accidentally slipped between the keys,' she said.

'Aye, maybe,' Donnie answered. He seemed to pull himself out of his reverie and shouted down the bar, 'Fiona!

This young lassie drinks free in here from now on! Och! Wasn't it a lemonade for your pal and a shandy for you?'

His middle-aged barmaid waved to show she'd understood and gave a frosty smile at Trixie. Trixie, overwhelmed, could hardly breathe her thanks to Donnie. She ignored the rogue thought that Fiona might always be too busy serving the men to take her order.

'What did he say?' Vi asked, when she returned to the piano, drinks in hand.

'I'll tell you later,' Trixie answered, after she'd handed Vi a fresh lemonade. 'Where's Hen?'

Vi frowned. 'She said she was going outside for some air. With that air-force bloke, Ken.'

'What happened to soldier Tom who bought the drinks?' Trixie asked.

Vi shrugged.

Trixie smiled knowingly at her, then sat down and began to play 'Sleepy Lagoon'.

The singing started again. Trixie felt as if she was part of the music now the notes flowed freely. Happiness filled her whole being.

Despite there being little room to move, couples melted into each other's arms, dancing together as if, for a little while at least, the war and all it represented could be blotted out. To come along to the Yellow Duck in the evenings for the next few weeks and play the piano, with free drinks thrown in, was a bonus, she thought. 'At Last', followed by 'Over The Rainbow', tumbled from the keys and Trixie felt as if she could go on playing for ever.

Chapter Nine

'Not much stops you playing, does it?'

Trixie looked up from the writing pad on which she was pouring her heart out to Cy. It took her a moment or two to realize someone was talking to her.

Vi stood beside Trixie's bed, the blue mackintosh covering her nightdress, its belt tied tightly around her middle. The hut was practically in darkness but the girl in the bed opposite was reading by a candle in a saucer, which enabled Trixie to see to write.

Trixie pondered Vi's words. She remembered it had taken a wave of enemy bombers arriving to force her to lower the piano lid in the pub and crawl beneath a heavy table for safety, until Donnie extracted her, while the German planes droned above. As soon as the all-clear came, she continued the sing-song. Just as happy as the customers who cheered her on. She'd finally stopped playing when Vi had shouted at her above the music that all the girls from Shandford Lodge had disappeared.

'Thanks for reminding me we should get back here before we got locked out,' Trixie said. Like Vi, she kept her voice low as most of the girls, including Jo, were asleep. She looked at the empty bed next to hers. 'I wonder where Hen is.'

'Last seen disappearing into the darkness with some feller, Ken, I think,' Vi said, with a grin, picking up the envelope with a Gosport address. 'To your mum?' she asked, replacing the letter on the bedside locker.

Trixie nodded. 'She'll worry if she doesn't hear from me.' Then, 'Have you let your family know how you are?'

She saw a shadow pass across Vi's face. 'My mum'll be more worried if she does get a letter from me,' she said.

It was on the tip of Trixie's tongue to ask what the girl meant by that cryptic remark, but she decided not to pry. Hadn't she already made up her mind that if Vi wanted her to know about her home life she would tell her?

'Anyway,' said Vi, 'I don't want to wake these sleeping beauties.' She waved an arm encompassing the other slumbering girls. Her voice had become so soft that Trixie had to listen carefully in case she missed anything. 'I just wanted to say thank you for one of the best nights I've had in ages and . . . and . . .' she seemed to be searching for the right words to say before everything came out in a rush '. . . I really would like to be your friend, if you'd let me?'

Trixie smiled at her. She thought Vi looked like a naughty three-year-old standing there in her shapeless coat, worried enough to cry.

'We're already friends,' Trixie said, putting out her hand and closing it over Vi's fingers. She saw the tension leave Vi's face, and tried to lighten the mood even more. 'And that means if you get to the dining room before any of us for breakfast in the morning, you're to save all our seats.'

'Even Hen's?' Vi gave a small smile.

Trixie looked across to Hen's empty bed and said, 'Of course. But I do hope she comes back soon. I'm getting worried.'

'Don't be,' Vi said. 'I heard some of the girls saying earlier that there's a break in the fencing surrounding the Lodge.'

'Hen won't know that.'

'Maybe not, but I bet that blond airman does!'

Trixie immediately felt better. She grinned at Vi, who said, 'Nighty-night,' cheerily and went to her bed. She decided to stop worrying about Hen: she was a grown woman, wasn't she? And Hen, like all of the girls, was aware of the rules concerning their training and men friends at Shandford Lodge.

She finished her letter to Cy and, after sealing the envelope, she wrote BOLTOP and SWALK on the back of it. Although he was an American, she guessed he'd be familiar with 'Better On Lips Than On Paper' and 'Sealed With A Loving Kiss'.

She picked up her Agatha Christie book but there was so much going on in her mind that Trixie found she was reading the same lines over and over and not taking any of them in. The novel was relegated to the top of her locker. She glanced over towards the girl who was reading. She looked up from the page at Trixie's movements and mouthed, 'Goodnight,' smiled, then continued reading.

Trixie slid down in the bed and pulled the blankets up to her chin.

She felt quite warm and safe in the hut with the other girls. She had spoken to only a few but no doubt by the end of their training they'd all be pals, she thought.

Her mind returned to tonight's air-raid. Hitler sent his planes over Gosport on the south coast so frequently that whole families had reserved spots in public shelters. Most local people had Andersons in their backyards or Morrisons in their homes. Trixie was aware Hitler's aim was to raze

Portsmouth Dockyard, the airfields, Priddy's armament yard and St George's barracks out of existence, so why was she surprised that an air-raid had occurred here in Scotland? Was it because in all the books about Scotland she'd borrowed from the library, pictures showed mostly miles and miles of heather-covered hills and sparkling lochs? Houses were like sheep, lone white dots on the landscape. She knew about its forests, lonely sandy beaches, and had read of the wild animals that roamed free. But she had actually learnt nothing of Scotland's people or its heritage.

When she was hiding beneath the table, Donnie had battled his way from the bar, through his customers, most of whom hadn't bothered to take cover, to stand in front of her saying, 'Don't worry. If it gets bad, we'll camp in my cellar.'

Trixie said, 'As soon as the siren goes at home, my mum and I run out to the Anderson shelter. We don't come out until the all-clear sounds. I've never actually witnessed a night raid – too scared,' she added.

He had stared at her, smoothing his moustache. 'Come along and see this one then, Trixie, lass.' He put out a hand and helped her up. 'You an' all, Vi,' he added. Trixie looked around for Hen, couldn't see her and decided she must be sheltering somewhere else, probably with her man. She and

Vi had followed Donnie outside into the night. He stood where the shadows were darkest.

The sounds were unlike anything she'd heard before, not even while watching the daylight dogfights between the Spitfires and the Messerschmitts in the skies over Portsdown Hill from the relative safety of Gosport's town centre.

The noise was horrific.

Scores of little shapes, like silverfish, darted around larger aircraft. The smaller planes, she knew, were German fighters. But never before had she seen aircraft shaped like those Donnie was pointing out to her. They were long, thin, deadly machines, too many to count. Trixie shivered. 'What on earth are they?'

'They're nicknamed, Flying Pencils because of their shape and they fly low down so it makes it harder for our night fighters to get at them. Cleverly designed,' he added. 'They've self-sealing fuel tanks.' He looked down at her before he pointed upwards again, 'And see their twin tails?'

Trixie shuddered. She knew the pilots couldn't see them as they watched but the planes were frightening to look at. Even so, they intrigued her. She realized she hadn't heard the *whump, whump* of bombs falling and exploding, which was almost a nightly occurrence back home in Gosport. It made her think these planes' objectives were further away.

'What are they really called and where are they going?' she asked. There seemed to be no end to them.

Donnie said, 'They're called Dorniers and they're hoping to hit RAF Leuchars air base, the coastal command station.'

'I thought we were in the middle of nowhere,' Vi said.

Donnie gave a low laugh. 'It might seem like that here, lassie, but Scotland has huge shipyards, submarine bases that are made possible by our deep lochs, then defence systems and coastal batteries to stop the enemy landing. And, of course, we've got the Loch Ness monster – Nessie'll look after us!'

Vi laughed, then stopped suddenly. 'Should you be telling us this? How do you know we're not German spies?'

'Oh, yes!' Trixie said. 'What about the slogans on posters? "Loose lips sink ships" and "Be like Dad and keep Mum"?'

Donnie chuckled, a rumble that came from deep inside him and left his mouth in a great loud burst of laughter that made his moustache jiggle. When it ended, he said, wiping his eyes, 'You two lassies are English girls who've been vetted by the government to help win this war. Dinna be so daft!' He put his beefy hand on Trixie's shoulder. 'You still frightened of the planes?'

'Not with you around,' Trixie said.

'Get back in the warm and start playing the piano again,

lass,' he said. 'In no time at all, you've become a fine asset to the Yellow Duck. You've brought memories, music and life back to this place and that's made me happy. And if you come in regular and it rains – it rains a lot here – I'll make sure you get back to the Lodge dry and safe.'

Trixie decided Donnie McKay was a good man to know, and that she liked him a lot. They watched the planes until they disappeared and the night was quiet again, punctuated only by the bellowing of the Highland cattle. She hoped and prayed that every single one of the Dorniers wouldn't find a target.

Now the darkness inside the hut enfolded her as the girl in the bed opposite extinguished the candle.

Trixie slept.

Chapter Ten

A cold breeze was blowing through the open window of the dining room, which had been set up for the lecture. Trixie pulled up her shirt collar and wished she'd put on a warm jumper. Maud Styles, impeccably dressed in her green Timber Corps uniform, entered the room and took up her stance at the table. Her voice was clear as she faced her audience.

'Good morning, all. Some of you might like to understand a little of the background that brings you to Shandford Lodge, also to know what is expected of you during your training here.' She looked around the room before she began again.

'Lady Gertrude Denham, president of the Women's Voluntary Service and director of the Women's Land Army, approached the minister of agriculture to form the Timber

Corps. In 1939 Britain was the largest wood-importing nation in the world but in 1940 wood stocks were predicted to last just seven months.' A few gasps were heard from the audience but she carried on: 'The German occupation of Norway is causing a shortage of imported timber. The enemy is blocking sea routes in the Battle of the Atlantic. Our own timber production *must* be increased. Approximately two thousand lumberjacks have been recruited from Canada and Newfoundland to teach and work alongside you and other volunteers in different parts of the British Isles. This year in April, in England, in May, here in Scotland, twelve hundred women were recruited from the Land Army to found the Women's Timber Corps. Approximately a hundred and twenty girls volunteer each month and are trained. The Timber Corps is now a separate organization.

'You have enlisted to help your country win this war, and for this you have my and our country's heartfelt thanks.'

Here she took a sip of water from the tumbler on the table in front of her. Vi looked at Trixie. 'She's good, isn't she?'

Trixie smiled back but glanced away as Maud Styles began speaking again.

'I promised myself I wouldn't keep you long. Most of you have already started instruction in some of the work you'll be expected to do when you leave here. Please pay attention to your instructors. They will show you the correct techniques. Injuries may result from inattention to detail.

'As lumberjills you will fell hundred-foot trees with axes and six-foot cross-cut saws. You'll lift heavy timber with bare hands and haul it from forests to roads. Some of you will make complex mathematical calculations based on the cost of cubic volumes of wood. Those of you who are over twenty-one will drive tractors and lorries. You'll learn char-coal burning, saw-milling, and how to identify and protect young trees. This and much more you will be taught. In return you will be well fed. You'll receive a wage from which bed and board will be deducted. You'll be looked after here at Shandford Lodge. You've probably heard . . .' here she smiled conspiratorially, '. . . that once upon a time women couldn't work on the land or in factories. Men's work, it was said . . .' There came jeers and catcalls from the audience but she went on, silencing the girls, 'That proved to be a fallacy. Women work during wartime at men's jobs because they can, because it's necessary to win this war.

'Being a lumberjill isn't an easy job. It's jolly hard work! You'll see your bodies change, become fitter as you acquire muscle. But more than that you'll gain confidence and make friends. When your training is over you will move on to where your talents are needed. I hope you'll benefit from your stay here. Enjoy the camaraderie. Thank you, and God bless you all.'

Maud Styles raised a hand to quell the noise that had started and, as if remembering something she had forgotten to say, gave a slight cough and added, 'Those of you who would like to apply for a travel warrant for a long weekend home leave after training and before taking up Forestry Commission placements please apply to me as soon as possible.'

The clapping started. Maud Styles nodded at her audience and quietly left the room.

There were murmurings and the sound of benches being moved across the floor as the young women crowded towards the door that led to the corridor exit.

'Straight and to the point,' said Jo. 'At least we know what's in store for us.' She added, 'I'm not going back to Gosport. I'd rather stay here.'

Hen looked at Trixie and frowned. Trixie thought it best just to accept Jo's decision and not ask questions. She thought Jo looked tired, even though she was the only one of the four to go to bed early last night.

Expending energy at the Yellow Duck playing the piano, Trixie decided had done her the world of good. She felt full of beans and although there were aches in places in her body she had never known existed, she was glad she'd taken Dolly and Maisie's excellent advice and visited the pub.

'Will you go home?' she asked Vi.

Vi was thoughtful. 'I'd like to check up on my mum.' She sighed. 'Can I talk to you later about it?'

It seemed a peculiar answer.

Trixie said, 'Of course. It's just that those of us who want to travel back down to Gosport, well . . . I thought it'd be nice if we travelled together.'

'Count me in, then,' Hen said. 'I'd be banished from my family home if they ever discovered I had a chance to see dear Mama and Papa and didn't take it!' Jo and Vi laughed. Hen was remarkably happy this morning.

Trixie had had no idea what time Hen had got back to the hut last night. It might even have been in the early hours of today, but when Trixie opened her eyes this morning, Hen was lying in her bed snoring quietly.

Trixie had seen that only she was awake in the hut. After dressing, she had left the sleeping women and walked out into the grounds. It had rained during the night: the grass was damp and the air smelt fresh and clean. Oak, ash, hazel and birch abounded. Trixie was fast remembering things she'd been told and leaflets she'd been handed to read. She could practically taste the pine scent of the fir trees, which reminded her of Christmas.

She was eager to take a stroll around the area before the place became a hive of activity as the girls congregated for breakfast.

Birds were singing lustily, their wings making sudden thrashing noises as she disturbed their early chorus. Pigeons, sparrows and sea-gulls were birds she knew well for they scavenged the streets and beaches of Gosport. But here among the greenery, fluttering and singing, were feathered species she'd never set eyes on before. Walking on the pine needles, she was trying so hard not to crush the numerous tiny plants, their colourful leaves and petals fading, turning brown as summer wound to an end. The trees seemed to swallow her.

She stopped. Her heart was beating fast. A scrabbling movement in the tree in front of her had caught her attention. Raising her eyes to a branch she saw a pair of eyes staring down at her. Little paws, like tiny hands, held something she couldn't quite make out to its mouth, and it was gnawing furiously, as though its life depended on it. Trixie knew what the creature was but she'd never been so close to a red squirrel, or indeed any squirrel, in her life before.

'Oh, you beauty,' she whispered, marvelling at the rich

chestnut colour of the animal's coat and the proud plume of its bushy tail.

For a few seconds she stood perfectly still. The squirrel had lost interest in eating and was still staring back at her. Then the nut dropped from its grasp, and with a huge bound the creature leapt into the next tree and was obscured by leaves, gone from her sight.

Her mother would be almost as excited as Trixie was to hear she had been so close to a red squirrel. But she knew she probably wouldn't tell the girls of her encounter. It was a treasured intimate moment between herself and the wild creature, in the glorious natural surroundings she was lucky to find herself living in.

She thought of all that had happened since she'd left Gosport.

There was a smile on her face as she remembered Cy and the way he'd encouraged her to sing on the ferry. She would never forget his kisses, which had awakened something new inside her.

She thought of the friends she'd made, and the hard work yesterday that had tired her but not so much that she hadn't walked down to the Yellow Duck. She remembered playing the piano and the joy it had given her, the pleasure on the faces of Donnie's customers as they'd sung along to the music.

She was glad she'd made the decision to leave home and become a lumberjill.

Trixie returned to the hut just as Hen and Jo were leaving for breakfast.

'Enjoy your walk in the woods?' asked Hen.

'We guessed that was where you'd disappeared to,' added Jo.

Trixie had nodded, then smiled.

And now, after porridge, toast and tea, mulling over Maud Styles's lecture, she was looking forward to today's work.

Her thoughts were interrupted by Dolly's voice: 'Going to the Yellow Duck later, Trixie?'

'Of course,' she shouted back.

'See you there, then.'

Yes, Trixie decided, she liked being a lumberjill very much indeed.

Chapter Eleven

'Still writing that letter?'

Cy, lying on his berth in the cabin, was about to say something to Bruno, when Hobo answered for him. 'Jeez, man! That ain't the same letter. What's another to add to his collection to send.'

Cy saw Bruno's amazement at the letters stacked in a pile on his locker.

'You sure that dame can read?' Bruno laughed uproariously and slapped his thigh. He stopped when Cy glared at him.

'Don't you give no mind to what Bruno d'Angelo says,' Hobo interrupted. 'Everybody knows that Italians cain't read or write!' He winked at Cy. 'Bruno reckons everyone's dumb as him.' Hobo ducked before the pillow thrown by Bruno reached him.

Cy leant down from his bottom bunk and picked up the pillow that had been meant for his buddy. 'She's gonna write to me. An' when I gets mail from my Trixie, I gotta make sure she gets enough mail back telling her how much I love her.'

And he did love her. He'd never really believed in love at first sight but the moment he'd spotted Trixie sitting alone in that ferryboat cabin his heart had done a double somersault. He wasn't some stupid kid: he'd had more than his fair share of girls back in New Orleans and since he'd joined the Navy. English girls too. They flocked around the American guys like bees around honey, said they loved their accents. Cy sometimes found it difficult to understand the way those girls spoke because they used different words for everyday stuff, like sidewalks and elevators. But he'd hung on to every word Trixie had uttered because she had somehow cast a magic spell on him and he knew he couldn't let her disappear from his life.

Yet wasn't everything against him ever meeting her again? Trixie in Scotland and him moving further away from her with every nautical mile?

His mother wouldn't say so for she believed in the African religion that was connected to spirits, ancestors and nature. In his head he could hear her beloved voice telling him, 'My son, God don't interfere in daily lives but the spirits do. An' if spirits mean to change your life, then life is sure gonna be changed.' And if a son couldn't believe his mother's words, he wasn't worthy to be called her son, was he?

All he could do now was believe, write Trixie letters and pray she hadn't lost the bit of paper he'd written his mail details on. He thought once more of what his ma would say: 'If it's meant to be, so it will be.'

Cy threw Bruno's pillow back at him. It was caught by the Italian who said, 'Trixie sure is a pretty gal. It was lucky how you two met.' Those words exactly compounded what he was thinking.

The pillow was returned safely to Bruno's bunk. Bruno picked up a pack of cards from the top of his locker. 'Fancy a game, you two?'

Both men answered at once, 'Yeah!'

'Give us a moment to finish this,' added Cy, his head bowed once more over his pen and paper.

'You know where we're headed?' Bruno asked.

The colour of his glossy dark hair exactly matched his long eyelashes. No wonder the girls gravitated towards him, thought Cy. He had film-star looks and was the first at any saloon's bar with money in his hands to buy a round of drinks, but the big sap never bothered to read the bulletins on the notice-board.

Cy folded the paper, tucked the pages inside the envelope and put it on the growing stack all waiting for Trixie's address to be added. When she wrote her first letter with her return address, he'd hand all his letters to the mailman.

Cy heard Hobo say, 'Caribbean, you dope.' A blissful look crossed his face. 'Maybe girls in grass skirts handin' out coconuts,' he said. 'An' I'll take whatever else they're handin' out!'

Cy laughed. 'That's after we've done a stint supporting the fleet and tankers, and looking out for submarines.'

Hobo grinned back, 'I don't believe there's U-boats there, but yep! That's what this British tub is for, guarding supply ships. Small and fast, she might only have twenty guns on her top deck but she'll look after us—'

'It's a hell of a long way to go,' interrupted Bruno, 'the Caribbean.' He was shuffling the cards now, and sitting at the table, waiting. 'Just because we're going there don't mean we'll get there! Japs and Germans, they sure don't like us.'

Hobo ran his fingers through his short crinkly hair, then pulled up his chair opposite Bruno. 'You can be a right crazy bird of ill omen, when you wants!' he said.

'Well, I thought that operation was all taken care of,' Bruno said. 'Operation Neu . . . Neul . . .'

'Operation Neuland,' put in Cy. 'But you know how it is in war, win some, lose some. Sweep up the mess others have left. We don't ask dumb questions, just go where we're needed.' His chair scraped across the cabin's floor as he joined them.

'American, ain't we?' he continued. 'The USA was well positioned to defend the Florida Strait but not enemy access from the Caribbean. The Venezuelan oil fields still gotta be protected. Britain needs the oil as much as we do. The USA also depends on minerals brought over for road-building and bauxite for aluminum for our aircraft. With enemy U-boats hanging about and sinking whatever they can, real or not, we gotta go where we're told.'

But Bruno's attention had already wandered from the war.

He asked, with a grin, 'What we playin', guys? Pinochle or poker?'

Trixie had no idea why she'd agreed to go to the dance in the tin hut tonight at the back of the Yellow Duck.

She'd planned to write another letter to Cy. It was amazing, she thought, how one thing led to another when she was spilling her heart out to him on paper. She knew she had to be careful what she wrote about in case her letters were read by someone else, like the enemy. She certainly hadn't told him there were aircraft bases in the area and neither did she mention anything pertaining to the war that she read in the newspapers or heard on the wireless. But she filled pages and pages telling him about herself, her hopes and dreams, and with every sentence her love for him was growing stronger. He'd promised to write and she knew he'd keep that promise. In the meantime, she would show him she cared by constantly writing to him.

Then she remembered the anguished look on Vi's face when Trixie said she'd really prefer an early night to going out. 'Go with Hen – she's going,' she'd implored.

Every bone in Trixie's body ached. Wielding an axe and a saw all day today, and the past few days, in the depths of the forest, where tiny flying objects called midges had tried to eat her alive, had caught up with her and all she wanted to do was curl up in her bed, read, then sleep.

'But Hen will disappear with a Canadian or some other bloke as soon as we get there and I'll be left on my own. Besides,' a blush stole over her face, 'I want to go with you because I feel safe with you . . . and I've never been to a proper dance before.'

Trixie thought of all the dances she'd been to at the Connaught Hall, the Sloane Stanley Hall, and the Lee Tower Ballroom in Gosport and was amazed that Vi had missed out on so much fun. 'You're having me on,' she said.

Vi shook her head. 'I wouldn't lie to you, Trixie.' She looked like a kiddie who'd lost her sweets and Trixie's heart melted.

'All right, then, I'll come,' she said resignedly. Then she remembered it would be Vi's first outing to a dance, so she gave her a grin and determined to make it a night Vi would never forget. 'You're right about Hen, though. It doesn't matter where we go. If there are fellers around she gravitates to them, like nails to a magnet,' she said. 'Then she's gone all evening!' They smiled knowingly at each other. 'How could I trust her to look after you?'

In the time Vi and she had become friends, Vi's bruises had faded sufficiently to allow her to wear shirts with the sleeves rolled up and to stop wearing the blue raincoat. She still didn't attempt to mix with the other girls in their hut, though, preferring instead to stay close to Trixie, Hen and Jo, but she was slowly thawing towards people and, unlike Jo, becoming less reclusive.

Jo had already said she'd give the dance a miss. Trixie knew Jo wasn't one to mix and laugh and joke with the other girls. She wasn't standoffish, not at all, but she preferred being on her own, often taking herself for walks alone in the forest. It was no surprise to Trixie that Jo didn't want to go to the dance: she was the 'loner' of their group.

Then Trixie was kneeling on the floor scrabbling in her suitcase beneath her bed for something to wear. A pale blue dress was the answer, she thought, buttons down from its V-neck to its knee-length hem. The last time she'd worn it was at the Criterion picture house in Gosport to see *Sun Valley Serenade* with Sonja Henie starring in it. She wondered if Hen had copied Sonja Henie's hairstyle of long blonde plaits twisted around her head just as Trixie had copied Veronica Lake's peekaboo hairstyle. She was suddenly aware of Vi still hovering over her. 'Go and get dressed then! We don't have a dispensation to stay out late because of a dance.'

Vi lowered her eyes and a pink blush stole up from her neck. 'Actually, I don't have anything nice to wear . . .' Her words came out in a rush. 'Could I borrow . . .'

Vi was being honest with her, Trixie thought, and it had taken the girl a great deal of courage to admit she had few clothes. Vi often accompanied her to the pub in the evenings but, like many of the girls, after working all day, she simply washed, combed her hair, brushed her teeth and put on some make-up, then changed into a clean shirt and dungarees that she would put on again in the morning.

There were always makeshift lines of washed and wet clothing hanging about the hut and in the trees outside. The woodstove was lit and burning now the evenings had become cooler and its heat was marvellous for drying wet socks. Some of the girl's mums had even started sending clean clothes by post!

Trixie remembered seeing Vi only once in a dress and that was the very first time she'd persuaded her to accompany them to the Yellow Duck. She was about to mention it but decided against it. If that was Vi's one and only frock and it was torn or needed washing, the girl would feel even more humiliated. After all, it must have taken Vi a great deal of courage to ask to borrow clothing.

Trixie grabbed Vi's hand and pulled her down beside her. 'Of course you can. Have a dig in here and see what you fancy. We're about the same size. My stuff's not posh but you're very welcome.'

Vi had already seized a dark green dress with shoulder pads and was holding it against herself.

Trixie thought the colour suited her admirably. But she saw the brightness of tears forming in Vi's eyes. She didn't want to embarrass her so she looked away, but not before the girl had said, very softly, 'Trixie, thank you so much.'

Chapter Twelve

'Look at all these girls,' said Vi.

Trixie and she had reached the tin hut at the rear of the Yellow Duck to find a line of women, chattering and laughing, the queue snaking almost round to the front of the pub.

The smell of cheap perfume in the air vied with the scent of roses and night scented stocks in Donnie's walled garden. Unlike many Scottish householders whose gardens were left to thistles Donnie was very proud of his well-tended plot at the rear of the pub. He favoured flowers and didn't have much time for vegetables despite the Dig for Victory initiative.

Joining the queue, Trixie stamped from foot to foot to get her blood circulating. Her feet had become damp tramping down the mud-slicked lane in the wet work boots she'd worn all day in the forest. Her favourite black high heels were clutched in a brown-paper bag. She prayed she'd be able to squeeze her feet into them when she took off her boots. Wearing them each day had done her feet no favours at all. Like most of the other girls she suffered from blisters that wouldn't heal, even though she'd rubbed the insides of her leather boots with Vaseline to soften them. Vi had worn her boots but brought her lace-up shoes to dance in.

'Why are we waiting?' moaned Vi. 'Girls always get in for nothing. Loads of girls entice the men to come along. The men pay for entry and buy Donnie's ale, so why isn't this queue moving faster?'

'As usual it's the blokes who are to blame,' said a Scots girl in front. 'The Canadian airmen got paid this week and none of them have any small change.' Then she added, 'Donnie's tearing his hair out because it's taking all his copper from the bar's till and Fiona's hopping mad because she has to keep asking people if they've got the right money.'

'Canadians?' asked another girl. 'No Yanks?' She sounded disappointed.

Trixie wondered if the girl had ever met an American lad. Perhaps not. That might account for her dismay. Her words reminded Trixie of Cy and that as yet she'd not heard from him. Each day she eagerly awaited the post for a reply to her letter. A sudden wave of sadness overtook her that she quickly dispelled by remembering his kiss. She felt happier still as the queue started moving.

She could smell the cigarette smoke and hear the music long before they reached the hut. Music? She stared at Vi, who was looking as mystified as herself. Trixie's heart dropped. Where was the saxophone? Drums? The sound filling the air was nothing like the band music played on the wireless. In fact, it reminded her of the Scottish dancing she'd learnt at school, except that the slow music now coming from the hut was more like a soulful waltz! She could definitely hear an accordion and a violin. Did that mean the evening would be filled with Scottish music she'd never heard before, and dances like 'Strip the Willow', which she had definitely done at school?

Trixie had so wanted Vi to hear big-band music playing fast tunes, like 'In The Mood', and to learn how to jitterbug.

The long queue was edging forward. Trixie decided all these people must be expecting to enjoy themselves or they wouldn't have come. If nothing else, the dance at the Yellow Duck would be an experience.

Donnie greeted the pair at the door. 'So, Trixie, you'll no be playing the piano in the bar tonight.' He stated the obvious. 'Well, this dancing is thirsty work, so come for a drink anytime you're ready.'

'I shall,' Trixie answered. He was here to collect entrance money and afterwards would disappear back inside the pub.

'I'll no be sayin' enjoy yourselves because I ken you will,' he added, showing them inside.

Because of the music she wasn't so sure of Donnie's promise, but she managed to grab a couple of spaces at the end of a long bench set against the side of the hut near a small table.

'Well, we're in now,' she said, bundling Vi onto the seat. She began pulling off her boots. As she took her high heels from the brown-carrier bag, her heart constricted. Would she be able to stuff her poor swollen, blistered feet into her beloved favourite shoes? And, if so, would she be able to stand upright in them? Or dance?

She realized these dances could be quite profitable for Donnie MacKay. Not only did the men have to pay to enter but it was only a few steps into the Yellow Duck's bar to buy a pint. She looked around the hall, which was already heaving with Brylcreemed men and perfumed girls either dancing or waiting to be asked.

She looked at her legs, which were beginning to colour nicely in the last warmth of the summer's rays. Like the other girls she'd begun rolling up her dungarees to look like shorts; catching a bit of sun helped disguise the fact that there were no stockings to be had in the shops because of war shortages. The last pair of nylons she'd seen had been on Hen's shapely legs and she'd wondered how she'd got hold of them. They'd been in a hurry tonight so Trixie hadn't bothered drawing a line up the backs of her legs with eyebrow pencil to resemble the seams of nylons.

Trixie stood up. Her shoes were very tight. Oh, well, she thought, she could always dance barefoot! Her mum had announced, 'Pride's painful,' whenever Trixie had allowed her hot tongs, which had been heated on the gas flames, to burn her skin when she was curling her hair. Her mum was quite right, thought Trixie, but in wartime, with so many sacrifices to be made, what was a little pain if it brought the desired effect?

Thinking about her mum and home made her realize that one benefit of not living on the south coast was getting a decent night's sleep, even though it might not be for many hours. Back in Gosport, Moaning Minnie was relentless in her warnings of enemy aircraft coming to destroy the many naval, army and air bases, and the armament factories.

Of course, there were air raids here. They'd had one the other night, hadn't they? But it wasn't like Gosport where you never knew from day to day if, when you went to the air-raid shelter, your home would still be standing when you returned.

She was getting maudlin again and this wasn't the time to pander to her emotions. She gazed around the large hut where all the occupants seemed to have left their worries at the door.

The four men playing instruments were on a small raised stage at the end. No piano, she noted, but the accordion player, in a red tartan jacket, was smiling widely. A flute, recorder and a fiddle, all played by quite elderly men, began harmonizing beautifully as the St Bernard's Waltz started.

'Oh, I know this one! We did it at school!' Vi had finished struggling with her boots, kicked them beneath the bench and was standing ready to move into action, a grin running from ear to ear.

'C'mon, we don't need a man to dance this one.' Vi was like a whippet after a rabbit, pulling Trixie onto the floor.

Trixie loved dancing – she'd missed it so much. Vi was right. This was a sequence waltz and she was executing the steps perfectly. She turned back to Trixie, still grinning. 'I'm so glad we came. It's like being at school, only with grown-ups!'

Across the crowded floor Trixie caught sight of Dolly dancing with a Canadian airman. The place seemed full of Canadians. Dolly spotted her and waved. Of Hen there was no sign but Maisie was there, sitting the dance out, talking to a sailor so Trixie waved to her as well. Trixie began to relax and enjoy herself, especially when the next dance was the Dashing White Sergeant, a Scottish country dance, where people moved on to new partners.

Trixie told herself her feet didn't hurt, even though they did, because she wanted Vi to enjoy herself.

The four musicians, whose hand-painted board propped at the side of the dais proclaimed them to be the MacAndrews Brothers, had progressed to playing a selection of Glenn Miller favourites and Trixie was thankful of a chance to sit down.

She laughed at Vi. 'I'm just not cuddling up to you during these waltzes. You need a feller for that.' She made her way to the bench, Vi following.

She'd been worried Vi might not want to stay on the floor if she stopped partnering her. The girl had been eager enough to attend the dance but Trixie had noticed on the few occasions she'd paused for a quick rest because her feet hurt, Vi had automatically and determinedly looked away whenever a man approached her. It was almost as if she was daring them to ask her to dance. Trixie resolved to push the girl to her feet the next time a man came looking for a partner. After all, that was what a dance was, wasn't it? Couples dancing together?

Trixie never got as far as a sit-down.

'Fancy a dance?'

Trixie looked at the man in front of her. Blond Brylcreemed hair and blue eyes, he filled his air-force uniform as though it had been sprayed onto his athletic, broad-shouldered body.

'Go on, you daft thing! Dance with him, Trixie. You're eager enough that I should accept dances! I'll still be here when you come back,' Vi said.

Trixie had just kicked off her shoes and they'd skittered beneath the bench. She didn't want to refuse the tall stranger and she'd caught him looking her way during the dancing, but it was out of the question that she could push her swollen feet into her tight shoes again, if she could find them. 'Thank you for asking but I need to sit down now.' She saw his face crumple so she quickly added, 'Can I take a rain-check?'

Immediately his face brightened and he said, 'Would you like a drink, then?'

Trixie didn't like to refuse him twice so she nodded, 'That would be nice. An orange or lemonade would be lovely.'

A smile lit up his white, even teeth. He looked briefly at Vi, then back to Trixie. 'I'll get one for your friend as well,' he said. He didn't wait for a reply before moving towards the door and becoming swallowed in the crowd.

'Rain-check?' Vi couldn't conceal her mirth. 'What are you? An American now?'

'Well, I think he's Canadian but he'll know what I mean,' said Trixie, sitting down. 'I heard an American use it when I was working in the greengrocer's and I was asked for potato chips and put some spuds in the bowl to weigh them. I thought he was going to get someone to fry him chips. He said he'd take a rain-check! How was I to know he meant crisps?'

'You dopey thing!' said Vi, a smile across her face.

'Anyway, I asked him what rain-check meant, and he said when people pay for a baseball ticket and it rains, the teams can't play. The spectators are given a ticket so they don't have to pay again when play restarts.'

Trixie leaned forward and lifted Vi's chin to close her mouth – Vi was staring open-mouthed at her. 'He seems nice,' she said to Vi, changing the subject.

'I thought you had a feller,' said Vi, sharply. 'What about your Cy?'

'This one's buying me a drink, not asking me to marry him,' said Trixie, quickly. 'Anyway, you seem to have changed your mind. Just now you were urging me to dance with him.' She bent down and began massaging her swollen feet.

Trixie felt bad for snapping at Vi like that. She tried to

make it better by asking, in a calmer tone, 'Enjoying yourself, Vi?'

Vi's sullen face softened. 'Very much,' she said, then grinned at her.

Trixie hadn't realized just how stifling it was in the hut. The blackout meant the door had to be kept closed with a heavy curtain shielding it, and although some of the windows were open, they were covered with thick curtains. She could feel perspiration running down her back as they sat and watched the dancers. Trixie sighed. Something cool was just what she needed, she thought. And, as if by magic, the man came back with a tray of drinks.

'Thanks,' said Vi, 'but there's only three of us.'

Four glasses and two bottles stood on the tray. The man placed it on the small table and selected a glass of orangeade. 'I had to wait in the queue and when I got served the woman behind the bar suggested I take extra now, as later the bar gets crowded.'

Trixie was looking longingly at the glass of orangeade in his hand.

'Excuse me,' he said, leaning across Vi, his fingers holding Trixie's drink mere inches from her face.

Trixie saw Vi wrinkle her nose in distaste almost as if the drink in his hand offended her.

He said to Vi, 'God this place is crowded.'

'I suppose so,' Vi answered.

Trixie took the drink and gulped it down, leaving very little in the bottom of the glass.

'Oh dear!' she said. 'But I needed that!'

'Good thing I bought extra,' The airman grinned. 'My name's Ben, Ben Tate. What's yours?'

'Trixie,' she said, ignoring the narrow-eyed look Vi was giving her.

She heard Vi say to Ben, 'I'm Vi. Which drink is mine?'

Trixie looked at the tray with three remaining tumblers of orange next to the two bottles of Scotch Ale. Ben selected and pushed one of the tumblers towards Vi. 'Take this one,' he said.

Trixie saw Vi give him a funny look before she raised the glass to her lips. She took a tiny ladylike sip. 'Thanks, Ben. Much appreciated.'

Trixie noticed Ben watching Vi as she made short work of the rest of her drink.

'I'm ready to dance when you are,' Trixie said, finding her shoes, pushing her feet into them and waiting until Ben had set his empty bottle back on the tray.

He was a lot taller than her and she fitted into him quite well. He certainly knew how to dance and how to hold a woman.

Many men didn't and they shuffled around the floor, not leading but expecting their partners to dance like Ginger Rogers. Trixie felt herself relax. She wondered what it would be like dancing with Cy. Then she told herself to stop making comparisons between Cy and every other man she met. She knew why she did it, because even though she'd fallen in love with him, she actually knew little about him, except that he came from New Orleans, loved music and, like her, believed in Fate. Wouldn't it be wonderful to go to America one day? It would be exciting meeting his family, discovering all about him and the beautiful city she'd seen in films.

The music had changed again, to 'Whispering Grass'.

Trixie spotted Hen clasped so close to a young man she was sure a cigarette paper couldn't fit between them. She was gazing up into his eyes as if he was the only man in the room. Trixie hadn't seen him before. She wondered what had happened to Ken and Tom.

Vaguely, Trixie remembered Hen telling the girls that Malcolm and she were getting serious. Malcolm? Trixie really couldn't keep up with Hen's frantic love-life.

Trixie's feet were killing her and the heat was making her thirsty again. 'Do you mind if we sit the next one out?' she asked.

'Of course not,' Ben said. She was glad of his arm now around her waist, supporting her.

As they made their way back to the bench, the musicians had moved on to 'Don't Sit Under The Apple Tree'.

'Go, girl, GO!'

Trixie held on to Ben. She was feeling a little unsteady but the voices raised in excitement made her turn to the dancers. A space had opened up in the centre of the floor and two dancers, happy about the fast tempo of the music, were engaged in a quick and very energetic jive.

Trixie gasped. The girl being tossed into the air over her partner's shoulders, landing lightly, being caught and pulled between his legs to an upright position to continue dancing, without missing even a beat of the music, was Dolly! Around the couple, onlookers were now whooping and cheering.

'I never knew she could dance like that,' said Vi, now standing at Trixie's shoulder.

'My God, she's good,' agreed Trixie, 'So light on her feet.' She wiped perspiration from her forehead. She badly wanted to sit down. They weren't that far from their bench but she couldn't bear to miss a moment of the fantastic performance being played out in front of her. She suddenly remembered Dolly finding a ladder and climbing it to brash trees and Alf shouting at her. Dolly was a girl who did what she wanted and liked the limelight.

'Are you all right?' The whisper came from Ben.

'I think so,' Trixie said.

'Here, drink this,' Ben said. He held out a glass of orangeade to her and Trixie drank it thankfully.

'I think some fresh air would do you good,' Ben said.

He gathered her to him and turned towards the door. Trixie was happy to rely on Ben's arms and help: her head was swimming and her legs didn't feel as if they belonged to her. She peered into the crowd hoping to see Vi to tell her she was going outside but Vi seemed to have been swallowed into the onlookers watching and cheering on Dolly and her partner.

'Whew! That feels a little better,' she said, breathing in the cold, fresh air. 'Don't you let go of me,' she begged. Her head was reeling.

It wasn't dark but fast becoming so, and Trixie was glad no one was about to witness her stumbling towards a wooden seat at the end of the yard. She kicked off her shoes.

'I don't know what's made me so ill . . .' she began, very much aware that she was slurring her words as she sat down heavily in an ungainly position.

'What are you doing?'

Instead of helping her to sit up on the seat, Ben was pushing her down so she was almost lying on the damp wood.

Trixie wanted to raise her arm and hands, wanted to slap him so he would stop crawling on her, which was what he was attempting to do now. But it was as if she had no strength in her body. Even her head felt too heavy for her neck to support it. It was too much of an effort even to scream at him.

'You know what I'm doing, Trixie, and I know you're begging me for it.'

She could feel his fingers at her knicker-legs, tearing at the elastic. The smell of his greasy Brylcreemed hair made her want to vomit and she knew she had to get out from underneath him because she didn't want him to do what he seemed determined to do, with or without her consent. But his writhing body was heavy and she seemed to have lost all power in her limbs.

And then his head suddenly jammed itself down with force against her neck. A gasp came from his mouth, like air escaping from a balloon, and he was rolled unceremoniously onto the grass.

'Pig!' Vi barked.

Trixie swallowed the bile that was fast rising inside her

and managed to scramble up on the bench to see Vi still holding the heavy metal watering can with which she had just walloped Ben.

Trixie had no choice in what happened next. Although she turned her head away, she was promptly sick over the bench, the grass, her shoes and Ben's trousers, which were hugging his ankles.

Vi had dropped the can to hold back Trixie's hair.

Trixie, having rid herself of her stomach contents and gained some of her wits, said, 'Thank you, Vi.' She wiped her mouth with her hand. 'How did you know I was out here?'

'I'll tell you in a minute,' Vi said. 'Let's get you down to the back of the pub so you can wash in Donnie's kitchen. He needs to know there's something in his garden that needs clearing up before anyone else comes out here.'

Chapter Thirteen

'You're going to have to get a door supervisor, Donnie. That piece of scum could come back and attack another girl.' Vi remonstrated.

'What? Do you nae mean a chucker-out?'

Vi rounded on him, 'You can't be taking money for tickets and beer and letting blokes molest—'

'He didn't molest me,' Trixie said.

Vi wasn't about to let her have her say. 'Only because I belted him one with the waterin' can!' She turned towards Trixie, who was sitting in a threadbare armchair before the fire in the homely stone-flagged kitchen of the Yellow Duck. 'Don't you try to deny what I saw with my own eyes.' Then she added, 'You've got to tell the police, when they arrive, exactly what happened.'

'That'll do nae good at all!' said Donnie, who was pouring

thick black tea into tin mugs. 'They won't catch him. By the time ye came tae me an' I went tae the yard, the man had gone!'

Vi added, 'We know his name, and we can give a description of him, can't we, Trixie?'

Trixie shook her head. 'How many men are about six feet tall, have blond hair smeared with Brylcreem and are in the air force?'

Safe now from her seducer, having thrown up again, downed a mug of tea and tried to make herself believe her head wasn't throbbing fit to bust, Trixie knew there really was little chance that the man could be apprehended. Not only did she feel ashamed of herself for allowing him to dupe her, she wanted to pretend the whole affair hadn't happened.

Donnie stood in front of her. 'Will you be all right here while I finish locking up?' He bent down closer. 'Lassie, you must know how sick my heart is that something like this happened to you here at my pub. I want to make amends as best I can. You know that, don't you?'

Trixie nodded, and he left the kitchen, shoulders slumped like an old man's.

'His name's Ben Tate, don't forget,' added Vi.

'That was probably a lie,' said Trixie. She was thoughtful.

'I believe now he planned everything beforehand. He decided I was ripe for the picking and went all out to get me alone somewhere. With everyone inside the hut, watching Dolly and her partner jiving, he took his chance.' She paused. 'But you knew he was going to try something, didn't you, Vi?'

'I thought he'd put whisky in your drinks,' she said, 'but I couldn't accuse him until I was sure. I needed to be certain it wasn't all in my head.' She sat down on a kitchen chair and began drumming her fingers on the oilcloth covering the table.

'What made you think that way?'

Vi stood up again and began to pace across the rag rug. It was like she couldn't sit still and needed to get something off her mind, thought Trixie.

'When he brought back the drinks from the bar and passed a glass of orangeade to you, I thought I could smell spirits as it went by me. And there must have been a hefty nip in your drink, not simply a normal single or a double. I was immediately suspicious. To make sure I was correct, when you got up to dance with him, I asked which drink was mine. He fell straight into the trap and moved a certain glass towards me.' She paused. 'Had all the drinks been only orangeade, he would have said, "Take any." But he didn't. When you were dancing, I took sips and realized my drinks were pure orangeade and yours weren't.' Vi looked at Trixie. 'Didn't you think the orange tasted different?'

Trixie couldn't shake her head as it was thumping so much. 'Nothing tastes the same as it did before the war. Not food or drink. I'm not a drinker. I can't distinguish between the taste or smell of different spirits. I asked Ben for orangeade. I believed he'd bought what I asked for . . .'

For a moment there was silence between the two friends. Trixie could see the flames from the fire burning orange and red. Its warmth comforted her. She was suddenly glad that Donnie was out of the room. It would do him no good to worry that Fiona had unwittingly poured the drink that had made her lose control.

She knew she was lucky that Vi had acted swiftly when she discovered Ben had led her from the hut. But she was angry she'd allowed herself to be tricked by the man. She'd felt ill and believed him when he'd suggested fresh air would do her good. At no time did she imagine she was drunk.

But she'd sobered up now. She was still in one piece, not hurt, and she would survive. She wanted nothing more than to get back to Shandford Lodge and wash herself until she had scrubbed off all memory of that man. She knew that wouldn't be possible: memories couldn't be swirled down the sink with the dirty water. She would always remember his hands on her, his breath, his strength, her own inadequacies and utter helplessness.

A thought struck her.

'How did you know it was whisky?' she asked Vi.

Vi's eyes darkened. For a while Trixie thought she wasn't going to answer but then Vi stood in front of her, laid a hand on Trixie's arm and squeezed gently, 'Don't make me talk about it now,' she said quietly. 'I'll tell you another time, I promise.'

Trixie stared into the girl's eyes. Vi was smiling at her. But Trixie wasn't fooled. She could see, behind the smile, the pain, that Vi was broken inside.

Vi let her hand drop.

'I was keeping my eyes on you all the time,' she added, 'but when Dolly started her fancy footwork, the crowd got in the way. That was when he took his chance.'

For a while nothing in the kitchen could be heard except the ticking of the clock on the mantelpiece, the crackle of the fire and the sound of Donnie's keys settling on the table. He had returned and was making fresh tea.

'Thank you, Vi,' Trixie said. 'You saved me. I'll always be grateful for that.'

Vi sat down on the chair again and, after glancing at the time, addressed Donnie, who was now slipping a knitted cosy over the earthenware teapot. 'Please could you take us back to Shandford Lodge? We'll get into trouble if we're late back – and I'm sure Trixie doesn't want to have to tell them what's happened.'

'There's been nae trouble like this before,' he said. Trixie thought the poor man looked worn to a frazzle. It was obvious he didn't want people knowing about the incident. Neither did she, for she was sure she wouldn't be able to stand the stares and comments that would be bandied about back at the Lodge.

'And there won't be trouble again if you arrange for a big beefy feller to stand at the door and keep an eye on things,' Vi persisted.

Trixie knew Vi liked Donnie, and the Yellow Duck was the only place with any life in it in the evenings. There had to be some kind of compromise. Vi was determined that safety for the girls who attended the dances was paramount. And she was quite right. An idea started to form inside Trixie's head.

'What about we don't call the police?' As the words fell from Trixie's mouth, Donnie breathed a sigh of relief.

After all, Trixie thought, the chances of finding the so-called Ben were negligible. She had been frightened and felt shaken, but because of Vi's well-timed intervention Ben hadn't raped her, which was a blessing.

However, if someone was looking out for the girls, whose one aim was to have a happy evening dancing, without fear of being attacked, and she could make that happen, then why not? Perhaps one day it might be possible for women to go wherever they wanted, day or night, without predators on the prowl, but until then a door supervisor at Donnie's hut could only be an improvement, couldn't it?

Trixie repeated: 'What if we don't involve the police, this time,' she added, 'on the condition you hire a big beefy door supervisor?'

She could almost see Donnie's brain working. She picked up the mug of tea he'd left on the small table at the side of her chair and drank. She had a bit more to say that she thought would seal the bargain but she left it a while before she added, 'I love playing your piano and I know you appreciate the extra trade it brings in. I had hoped I could go on playing for you, right up to the time I'm transferred by the Forestry Commission, Donnie, but tonight I've had a terrible shock . . .'

Donnie narrowed his eyes. 'I'm sorry for what you went through, I truly am.' He sighed but went on, 'You're a canny lass, and I think I know just the person to do the job. A big mannie from the village, who lost his job because he wouldnae leave his wife to be looked after by neighbours when she was dying. He stayed with her until the very end. Could be a new lease of life for him,' he added. A smile crept across his lips. 'I cleaned your spewed-on high-heeled suede shoes. Vi told me they're your favourites.' He paused long enough to let her know he understood her terms. That he'd cleaned her shoes told her he really cared about her and appreciated her playing the piano in the bar. 'Aye, you're a canny lass and you've got a deal!'

Chapter Fourteen

'You're quiet this morning,' Hen said. Trixie looked at her across the breakfast table. Hen wasn't her usual beaming self today either, she thought. But Trixie had woken with a bad head, probably the after-effects of the whisky. 'Have some porridge. It tastes really good today,' Hen added. 'Then you can tell us why you two nearly got locked out last night.'

Beneath the table Vi squeezed Trixie's hand, then spoke up before Trixie could utter a word. 'Donnie was chatting to Trixie, in his kitchen, about her playing the piano more because it brings in customers, and the time just seemed to fly.'

Trixie nodded. 'Luckily he gave us a lift back,' she added. She looked gratefully at Vi for taking the pressure off her. Vi had tucked her hair up beneath a scarf. It didn't do her any favours, Trixie thought, but she wasn't going to tell her that.

'I thought you'd gone off with that airman you were dancing with.' Hen helped herself to a doorstep of crusty bread and margarine and attacked it as if she'd never had anything to eat in her life. She was, as usual, scrubbed and healthy-looking. She plastered make-up on with a trowel when she went out in the evenings, made a good job of it and looked like a screen goddess. But no matter how late she came back she always washed off every scrap, then worked a dollop of Pond's cold cream into her skin before she slept. She never wore make-up during the day when she was working in the forest.

Trixie would have liked to think she looked after her skin, too, because she kept her face, like the rest of her, scrupulously clean, but her downfall was never washing off her make-up before she tumbled into bed. Consequently, she woke in the mornings looking like a panda because her mascara had smudged all around her eyes.

Trixie wondered why Hen was eating so heartily – usually she picked at her food to keep her figure.

Vi caught Trixie's eye and mouthed silently, 'You all right?'

Trixie gave her a quick nod and a smile, then said, so everyone could hear, 'I danced with him but I've got my Cy and I don't fancy anyone else.'

Trixie hadn't wanted to go with them for breakfast this

morning. Food was the last thing on her mind after what had happened the previous evening, especially after the sleepless night she'd had, tossing and turning. When she'd finally woken, she knew she had to carry on as usual if she didn't want the girls asking questions.

Again, Vi broke in. 'Usually, you're the one who's last in, Hen. What's the matter? Got chucked by your Malcolm?'

Jo spluttered into her mug. It was almost as if Vi's words had hit a chord with her. Hen and Jo sometimes shared secrets, as did Trixie and Vi.

Trixie hadn't missed the glisten of tears in Hen's eyes that were almost, but not quite blinked away, as she spat back at Vi, 'He didn't chuck me, I chucked him!'

There was a sudden silence between the four friends. Trixie could see immediately that Hen was trying to disguise very real hurt, which was probably quite new to her. Hen threw back her head defiantly and said, 'I found out he was married.'

'The bounder!' Vi exclaimed. She was staring at Hen with great interest. 'How did you find out?'

Hen dabbed at her eyes with her handkerchief. 'We were sitting out a dance last night, just after Dolly had stunned us with her footwork. Malcolm needed a piece of paper to write down a different phone number where I'd be able to contact him when we leave here after finishing our training. A photo fell from his wallet.' She took a deep breath. 'It was of a dark-haired woman with two little girls. He went bright red, and as he snatched it up, he tried to tell me it was his sister and her children.'

'You didn't believe him?' asked Vi. Her gaze was steady as she stared at Hen.

'If it was his sister, why would he bother to grab at it? Surely he'd have said, "This is my sister." No, he tried to hide it.' Her voice faltered. 'I'm not so dim that I don't know when a man is lying to me.'

Trixie knew that nothing any of them could say would ease the hurt Hen was experiencing.

'Just be grateful you found out before you got too entangled with him,' said Vi.

Hen began to cry. She used the heel of her hand to wipe the skin below her eyes, and when that didn't work, she blew her nose into her handkerchief.

Vi frowned. 'You weren't sleeping with him?'

Hen put her hand to her forehead, leant forward with her elbow on the table and sobbed.

'Tell me you weren't!' Jo insisted.

But instead of answering Jo, Hen leant sideways, buried her face in Trixie's neck and cried harder. Trixie put her arms around her friend, who was shaking with misery. Hen needed comforting but Trixie winced when the other girl's face touched the flesh where last night she'd been subjected to Ben's ill-treatment.

Trixie patted Hen's back and managed to move slightly thus enabling her to ignore her own discomfort. 'I think this war brings out the worst in some people,' she said softly to Hen. 'It makes people do things they'd never normally consider.'

Trixie could feel Vi's eyes on her. She caught the merest shake of Vi's head warning her against confiding her own trauma. Of course Vi was right. After all, how would her own revelations help Hen? And, more to the point, did she really want anyone else besides Vi to know? 'Did you and he argue about it?' Trixie asked.

Hen moved away. 'Not really,' she said. Her face was swollen with tears. 'I looked him in the eye and said, very calmly, "Your wife is waiting for you and loving you, while you're treating her like this. You won't do it to me."' Then I got up and walked away. That's how I got back here before anyone else.'

'You did right,' Trixie said softly. She didn't have to think about it, she would have done exactly the same. Who knew? Maybe the man who called himself Ben was also married with children. Trixie shuddered.

'Malcolm's nothing but a rotter,' said Vi. 'He got what he wanted from you and would have gone on getting it, if you hadn't seen that photo.'

'Not all men are bad,' Jo broke in. 'You just have to find the right one.' Her voice was soft. No one commented.

'I cared about him,' was all Hen said. She was about to say more when a huge burst of laughter came from a nearby table.

'They're talking about Dolly and her dancing,' said Jo. 'And you said something about her footwork, Hen. Did I miss something last night?'

'Well, if you must go to bed early instead of coming out with us . . .' Trixie had taken her own handkerchief from her pocket and was trying to wipe away Hen's tears.

Hen took the hanky and carried on mopping her face. 'Dolly never told anyone how professional she was at dancing, and when a piece of fast music was played, she had everyone watching her and her partner jiving.'

'Really?' Jo was curious.

'Really,' answered Hen, 'I've never seen fancy footwork like it before.'

Trixie saw Vi smile at her and they both knew that, for the moment at least, Hen was back on an even keel as she explained to Jo the complexities of Dolly's dance steps.

The tables began to empty as the girls finished eating and cleared away their cutlery and plates. They collected their packed lunches and left the dining room to return to the huts to assemble the clothing and anything else they'd need for that day's work in the forest. If they'd taken their things to breakfast with them, they went straight to their waiting transport.

Trixie hung back, allowing Hen and Jo, arm in arm, to carry on ahead out of earshot. She had something to ask Vi and didn't want anyone to overhear. 'Vi?'

Vi looked at her. 'If it's about Hen, I think she'll make a speedy recovery, don't you? Malcolm's not the first bloke she's had hanging around her in the short time we've been here. Men are like moths to a flame with our Hen, so he certainly won't be the last.'

'It's not that. It's not about Hen.'

'What is it, then?'

'If it hadn't been for you intervening when you did last night, things could have been very much worse for me than they were.'

Vi stopped walking. She looked as if she wanted to stem the flow of words coming from Trixie but Trixie put up her hand. 'It was as if you had some idea of what Ben was up to, long before he took me outside . . . You were very perceptive about him spiking my orangeade with whisky.'

By now they had reached the hut and Trixie stepped aside as Maisie came through the doorway in her boots, carrying her lunchbox. Maisie grinned at them. 'Me an' Dolly are with you four today, so Alf says. He told me to tell you to get a move on – he ain't got all day!' Maisie flounced off.

Trixie watched her walk swiftly towards the main gate where Alf was standing next to the cart, stroking Lulubelle's nose and smoking his pipe. Already Hen, Dolly and Jo were on the cart, sitting among stooks of straw.

Vi went to speak but Trixie hushed her. 'Let me finish. When we first met, on the train, you were covered with bruises and trying to hide them.' Vi sighed, but slowly nodded assent. Trixie carried on: 'I believe you've been badly hurt by someone, probably a man.'

This time Vi did speak, but sharply, 'I'm not going to get into this now. You, Trixie, are the best mate I could wish for. You're like the sister I never had.' Her eyes grew hard, her voice bitter. 'I've known men like that bastard.' Suddenly she shook her head, as though deflecting bad thoughts. 'I'll tell you everything when we get back to Gosport, I promise.'

And before Trixie could say another word, Vi had slipped through the door and away, and the moment had gone. Trixie followed to collect what she needed to take to work for the day.

A few moments later, as the pair hurried to their transport, Trixie heard Alf shout, 'This ain't a bleedin' charabanc taking you girls out for the day! Come an' get on this cart now, you two!'

Vi threw her bag to Hen, who caught it. She put one foot on the wheel, hoisting herself up onto the wagon. She put out her hand to pull Trixie up. 'Our carriage awaits us!'

Chapter Fifteen

It seemed no time at all to Trixie that she, Jo, Vi, Dolly and Maisie had been dropped in the forest clearing, along with tools, their belongings for the day, a billy-can, and their sandwiches.

'I'll not be long,' said Alf, smiling, showing yellowed teeth. 'Don't start without me. I'm dropping off the straw at a house yonder,' he waved an arm expansively, 'and depositing Hen with the other measurers, so she can go further into the forest. Get the billy on for tea. I'll be back before you've missed me.' He clicked the reins so Lulubelle picked up her heavy hoofs and moved on, after a whinny and a toss of her head that sent her thick mane flying. 'If you're scaredy cats in the woods on your own, don't be. There's another team not too far away,' he called back, with another smile.

Trixie watched the cart, Hen on board, move out of the glade and down the muddy lane. Hen gave them a final wave.

Trixie listened hard and, sure enough, she could hear muffled shouts and the sounds of crashing timber not too far away. A movement caught her eye and she looked upwards to see, hovering in the blue sky, a large bird that she was sure could only be an eagle. Then it was gone, and she wondered how anyone could be scared with all this beauty around them.

Fourteen-pound axes, cant-hooks to roll the logs, bill-hooks for pruning or lopping vegetation, which Trixie thought vicious-looking, were honed and ready for use, lying on the pine needles. Cross-cut saws that required two to use them, one girl at either end, were not as heavy as they first appeared. Spokeshaves, for fine-smoothing the wood, and fretsaws, for snedding and brashing to remove the shoots and young branches from the trunks.

All the tools they might need for the day's work were at their disposal. A few weeks ago, Trixie had never set eyes on any of them, much less learnt what they were used for. She looked with pride at the enormous stack of timber ready for removal from the forest either by horse and cart, or tractor and trailer, to the local railway station or sawmill.

They'd worked hard to build that log-pile. Trixie realized

she'd had a hand in preparing almost every huge tree trunk. Yes, it was tiring work. However, she'd learnt more than she'd thought possible about forests and timber in a couple of weeks and she was happy and proud of herself.

Alf had been muttering about sawmills and charcoal this morning so she guessed they were soon to be moved on to learn other skills.

'Hen didn't speak much on the journey from the Lodge, did she?' Jo said to her, breaking into Trixie's thoughts.

'She probably didn't want everyone knowing her business.' Vi nodded towards Dolly and Maisie, meaning that the more people knew, the more they would gossip. 'I get the idea that she's not had a lot to do with fellas.'

Trixie smiled. 'Don't be silly. With her looks she's a magnet to men.'

'You can smile, Trixie, but what you see with Hen isn't the whole story,' Vi said mysteriously. 'I get the feeling she's kicking over the traces, trying to make up for lost time with blokes.'

'D'you know something I don't?' Trixie asked, picking up the billycan. She often thought Vi was very astute in her thinking. She, too, thought Hen likened men to sweeties in glass jars: she wanted to taste as many as possible.

Now, she made for the fast-running burn, where she knelt

down at the edge among the moss and stones and allowed the icy water to run over her hands and into the billy-can. It had amazed Trixie that the water from the taps in the Lodge's washroom, was tinged brown. She'd been told it was because of Scotland's peaty soil and that the water was probably purer than any found in England's reservoirs, and it certainly produced a fine cup of tea!

She liked making a drink before they started work. Alf wouldn't leave them alone for too long but a brew now would be more than welcome. Besides, the girls usually worked in pairs and today there were five instead of four so Alf wouldn't have reason to moan about the amount of work they eventually got through. Not that he moaned constantly. He didn't. He had the knack of telling and showing them exactly what he required of them. He smoked his pipe and watched. To their credit the girls tried to please him. Praise from Alf meant everything.

Trixie looked up into the branches of the tall trees. She never tired of listening to the forest's soothing sounds. The tranquillity of her surroundings, with the late-summer sun piercing warmly through the branches, made her feel calm and almost free of the strong emotions she'd experienced last night at the Yellow Duck. How fortunate and how alive the forest made her feel.

Jo had the fire going by the time she returned from the burn. Dolly and Maisie were sitting together on a tree stump a little apart from the others, deep in conversation, and every so often Dolly threw back her head and laughed. She wasn't a particularly pretty girl, thought Trixie, but she was liked and a hard worker, not backwards in coming forwards. Trixie guessed she, like Maisie, hadn't had an easy life in Birmingham so they were open to job opportunities, like the Women's Timber Corps, and relished working together in the fresh air. And why not?

Trixie would never forget the happiness and pride Dolly had shown last night while she was executing the complicated dance steps. She had captured everybody's attention. It had been Dolly's big moment of glory, thought Trixie, and she had deserved it.

'We've a fair few trees to cut down today,' said Jo, looking about her. She had built up the fire, with a good flat surface for the billy-can to settle on. She'd also set out the tin mugs but turned them upside-down in case insects decided to crawl into them.

Trixie giggled to herself. The first time a grasshopper had found its way into her sandwiches she'd screamed. Now she simply picked out the bugs, set them free on the grass and carried on eating. She glanced at the pine trees they would be chopping down today. Jo had said there were many to be felled because she'd seen the red markings.

Trees considered ready for cutting had their trunks marked with red lines. The height of the markings denoted where the axe-cuts should start. Leaving the mark visible after the tree had been felled indicated that the correct tree had been cut. Blue markings signified boundary lines and the trees that bore them had to be left uncut. Unmarked trees were not to be touched at all. The measurers had a hand in marking trees.

Trixie heard the sound of an axe hitting hardwood. She looked about her. Dolly and Maisie had decided to start work.

'They're keen to get going,' she said. She didn't blame them. It could be boring, sitting around, waiting.

The midges were out in force today. She checked her sleeves were pulled down and fastened at the cuffs and that her top shirt buttons were done up to her neck. Bare skin was like an aphrodisiac to the little blighters.

When Dolly and Maisie had been sitting on the tree trunk, chatting in the stillness of the forest, wearing shirts with their sleeves rolled up, they must have been eaten alive, she thought. Midges, tiny biting insects that loved the damp, boggy soil, would bite anything in sight, leaving irritating red weals on skin that itched and itched. They loved human blood but animals weren't immune to their attacks. Usually, the girls tried to cover as much flesh as possible when they were working in still, muggy places. Amazingly, even a slight breeze caused the insects to disappear.

'Bloody things,' Vi said, flapping a hand in front of her face. 'Maisie and Dolly have obviously decided to move around, do some work, instead of being sitting targets for the little devils.'

'That's not what Alf told us to do, though,' said Trixie.

'I'll take their tea over to them when it's brewed,' said Jo, the peacemaker, ever helpful.

'The midges will be gone by next month,' said Vi. 'I read up about them. From May to September, they're out in force, and then it's reasonably clear for the next six months or so. I wouldn't mind betting midges are the reason the Scottish Highlands are so sparsely populated. Who wants to live where they're going to drive you mad?'

'You're daft, you are,' said Trixie. 'But in that case we shouldn't be bombing Germany. We ought to gather up all the midges and send them over to ol' Adolf. We'd soon win the war, then.'

Vi stopped laughing long enough to add, 'Alf was moaning about them yesterday. He said, "You kill one damned midge and a hundred comes to its funeral!"'

'That's the kind of thing he would say,' Trixie said, a smile lighting her face again. She looked down at the billy-can. It was beginning to bubble at last. 'Come on, water, hurry up. We could all use a cuppa,' she implored.

Something in the rhythm of the chopping sounds echoing through the trees made Trixie glance up from the fresh packet of Brooke Bond Dividend tea she'd taken from the haversack and was attempting to open.

She gasped, dropped the packet and it upended itself, spilling a mound of tiny brown leaves onto the damp earth, 'What's Dolly doing with ... ?'

Trixie's voice petered out as she saw the head on a fourteen-pound axe descend from Dolly's body height. Dolly didn't have a hand at either end of the wooden handle so she was unable to slide it to meet the downwards swing.

Trixie felt as if she was watching a scene from a horror film as Dolly lost control of the axe: the sharp blade made contact with the tree's hard wood then slid, seemingly with a life of its own, and rebounded back towards Dolly's lower left leg.

How many times had Alf told them stance was crucial? A hit that partly misses and doesn't have full force or a wrong swing could glance off the wood and veer in any direction, possibly back towards the axe-wielder.

The axe had done that, all right, before it fell to the ground where it lay, bloodied and embedded in the pine needles.

For a moment there was not a single sound.

Then came the scream, an unearthly piercing sound that cut through the forest's stillness and turned into Dolly's strangled sobbing.

A multitude of startled birds had already risen, practically as one, into the sky, their flapping wings almost louder than Dolly's anguished cries.

Chapter Sixteen

'Jesus!' said Trixie, and began to run towards Dolly, who had collapsed to the ground.

'Come on!' she cried to Jo, who hadn't moved but whose face had lost every vestige of colour.

'We need help!' cried Vi. 'Transport! Move, Jo!'

'I can't go to Dolly. I can't!' Then Jo seemed to pull herself out of her stupor. 'I'll run down the lane after Alf – he can't be far, might even be on his way back. And didn't he say there was another team nearby?'

Trixie, running fleet-footed across the grass, saw Maisie standing horror-struck, her hand across her mouth, doing no more than staring down at Dolly on the ground.

'Take Maisie with you, Jo,' Trixie yelled. Aside to Vi, she said breathlessly, 'Maisie's like a wet weekend in Southsea! Absolutely no use at all! She's gone to pieces!'

Trixie pondered Jo's words: 'I can't go to Dolly.' It seemed an odd thing for her to say but there was no time to worry about that. 'Grab the first person with a vehicle you see, Jo. Find someone – anyone!' Her voice was almost at screaming pitch and the last thing Dolly needed to know was that they didn't have everything under control. Another thought entered her mind. 'I should have kicked earth over the fire!' she said to Vi. 'It won't do to cause a bloody forest blaze on top of everything else, will it?'

'I already thought of that,' Vi said. 'I emptied the billy on it.'

Dolly was lying on her side. Her eyes were closed, but she was sobbing pitifully. Blood was pumping onto the gaping lower-leg material of her dungarees. The wet red stain was growing larger and darker by the second. Trixie could see torn flesh, and something hacked, shattered, possibly bone, below her left knee. She turned her head away, determined not to vomit. It wouldn't do to show Dolly how much her injury disgusted her.

'It hurts,' Dolly cried, in a tiny voice, and Trixie's heart went out to her.

'We'll soon get it sorted out,' said Vi, briskly, falling to her knees next to the girl. Trixie wondered how Vi could feel so confident when she was pretty sure neither of them had ever come across an injury of this magnitude. 'We're going to get you to a doctor as quickly as possible, Dolly,' Vi continued. 'Look at me!' Dolly opened her eyes. 'This forest is full of working people and, who knows, you might get a handsome bloke to whisk you off!'

Trixie saw, at Vi's words, the brief lift of Dolly's lips into a smile. Her admiration for Vi was growing at the ease she seemed to have in dealing with the situation. She wished she had even a scrap of Vi's calm attitude. Trixie could hardly bear to look at Dolly's mangled leg.

Vi's next words were firm. 'I promise I'll try not to hurt you but we can't let this dirty cloth stick to the wound.' With her fingertips, gently and without touching the shredded skin, Vi began to pull the fabric from the gaping gash. Trixie busied herself searching through Dolly's bag for a cardigan or jumper to lay over her for warmth and to keep off the worst of the midges.

When she turned back to lay the cardigan over Dolly, she saw the girl's eyes were filled with terror. 'It hurts,' she repeated, in a whispery voice.

Trixie tried to think of something to say that could possibly ease the tension of the atmosphere. Nothing came except the realization that she still wanted to vomit. Again, she swallowed it and groped for Dolly's hand, holding it to comfort her and forget about herself.

'We've got to stop this bleeding, Dolly,' Vi said, with authority. She sat back on her heels and stared at Trixie. 'It's got to be several inches above the wound.' Then she pulled at the turban covering her hair. It slipped off, still knotted. Vi untied it, shook out the cotton material until it was in its usual square shape, then twisted it deftly, while saying to Dolly, 'I'm going to try not to hurt you as I raise your leg and tie the most God-awful-looking garter as tight as I possibly can above your knee. It's to help stop the bleeding.'

Dolly's eyes were wet with tears of pain and fear. Trixie couldn't tell which was worse, but she held Dolly's hand and whispered, 'Vi's got everything under control until help comes, Dolly.' And Trixie knew Vi did. The quiet girl she'd met on the train was a puzzling enigma.

The knot in the scarf above Dolly's knee looked so unyielding that Trixie felt she, not Dolly, might pass out with the pain. And still Vi pulled tighter. Trixie felt Dolly's hand slip from her fingers as she lost consciousness.

Wordlessly but deftly, Vi tied a knot in the scarf, then settled back on the earth with a sigh. 'I don't think it'll hurt her to be out of it for a while,' she said. 'And thank God the wound's stopped bleeding.' She peered carefully at Dolly, then sat back and looked at Trixie. 'I couldn't have done this without your help,' she said. 'Thanks.' She picked up the pieces of bloodstained material that had been stuck to Dolly's skin and threw them into the undergrowth. Trixie saw that Dolly's blood had stained Vi's clothes and her skin. Vi caught her observing her. 'I wish I hadn't kicked over the hot water to put out the fire,' she said. 'I could use a cuppa just now, couldn't you? And a wash.' Without waiting for Trixie to answer, she added, 'Please, God, let the girls come soon with help. I hope they've found someone.'

All the energy seemed to have evaporated from her and she began to cry, her shoulders heaving. She turned away from the prone form of Dolly, scrambled up and stumbled a few steps towards a pine tree marked with a red line. She continued to cry, her head leaning against the bark as though its very stillness could comfort her.

Trixie had seen just how much effort Vi had put into appearing capable and efficient. She was the one needing support now. Within moments Trixie had jumped up and put her arm around Vi's shoulders gathered her towards herself and allowed her friend to cry unrestrained. After a while she said, 'You did good work, Vi. I could never in a million years have acted in such a clear-headed way, even if I'd known what to do.'

'But it's not over yet, she needs to be in a hospital, Trix.' Vi's words were muffled by her tears.

And then, like an answer to a prayer, thought Trixie, the

sound of an engine, came grumbling through the trees to the clearing.

'It's a bleedin' jeep!' Vi's tear-stained face split into a wide smile. The vehicle crunched over the brushwood and undergrowth and halted. Two tall Canadian airmen jumped out of the front, both dressed smartly in blue. They were so fresh-faced and clean-cut they looked as if they'd stepped out of Burton's men's outfitters' window, marvelled Trixie. She almost cried with happiness at seeing them and their transport.

Jo and Maisie, Maisie chattering inanely, climbed out of the back. The smell of petrol from the vehicle was at odds with the fragrant pine of the trees.

'How is she?' called Jo, worry etched on her face.

Trixie put her finger to her lips to signal that Dolly was asleep. Jo nodded, understanding perfectly.

The girls watched as one airman foraged on the flatbed of the vehicle and pulled out a rolled-up stretcher.

'Morning, ma'am,' said the other, now at her and Vi's side, looking down at the inert figure of Dolly. Around Dolly the grass and pine needles were stained with blood – it seemed to have got everywhere, not just on her and Vi's clothing.

'We're going to transport the patient to the Stracathro Wartime Emergency Hospital in Brechin, ma'am. They're expecting us. Atkinson and Boucher at your service.' Trixie assumed he was Atkinson but before either she or Vi could say anything the stretcher was placed on the pine needles, then unrolled, and the two men lifted Dolly carefully onto it as though she were a child. Dolly opened her eyes. A moan escaped her lips.

'Don't worry, sweetie,' said Atkinson, softly, kindly, to her. 'We're taking you to get fixed.'

'Can we go with her?' Vi asked, pointing to herself and Trixie. 'She might be terrified on her own.'

The man, Boucher, answered, 'Of course! That'd be just dandy. You're from Shandford?'

Vi nodded.

'It's relatively easy to get back there from the Stracathro.' He grinned at Vi, showing very white teeth.

The stretcher, lifted carefully but swiftly by both men, was carried towards the jeep and settled in the back. Maisie, watching, chimed in, 'We waved these two down just after catching up with Alf. He's on his way back here. Lulubelle's not as fast as a jeep. We're to pack up all the tools and belongings and wait for him. No more work for us today, he says.'

'I'll explain back at the Lodge you've gone with Dolly,' said Jo, cutting off the flow of words from Maisie. 'And don't worry about any of your things. We'll see they get back to the hut.'

Trixie gave her a grateful smile, 'Thanks,' she said.

In the back of the jeep with the stretcher, Trixie watched as Boucher placed a grey blanket over Dolly. She searched for Dolly's hand, squeezing her fingers lightly, then holding them reassuringly.

The jeep set off. Trixie turned to Vi, who was staring at Dolly. 'Perhaps Dolly would prefer to have Maisie with her.'

'Maisie doesn't know what day it is,' Vi answered.

'Where did you learn all that stuff, Vi?'

Vi tucked strands of limp hair that had come adrift, back behind her ear. Her voice was a whisper, 'I come from a bad area in Gosport so I've picked up all sorts.' She shook her head. 'Best not to talk now.' Her voice tailed off as she turned away.

Trixie gazed out of the window at the Scottish landscape. Now they were away from the forest, it was composed of heather and short grass that was being nibbled by sheep, which wandered alongside the narrow road, dangerously close to the traffic. Trixie realized there was probably much more to be seen of Brechin than she had thought.

But, then, what did she know? She'd been living in the hut at Shandford Lodge for such a short time and wasn't there to sightsee but to learn about forestry. Her evenings, after she'd had dinner, washed and prepared for the next day, had been mainly taken up by walking down to the Yellow Duck.

Playing the piano in the pub made her think of the Alma back home in Gosport. That reminded her of her mum. She missed Rose and Des more than she'd ever thought she would. She knew then she was really looking forward to going home for a while before being sent Heaven knew where in Scotland when her training was completed. But, for now, she was relieved Dolly was on her way to being cared for professionally.

'It looks new!' Vi had interrupted Trixie's thoughts.

Through the jeep's windows the hospital did indeed look modern. Atkinson gave a quick glance back from the driving seat and added, 'It was built in 1939 for war casualties. When it opened its wards, the first patients were the victims of a Montrose air-raid in 1940.'

'Dolly's going to be in very good hands, then,' said Trixie, not that Dolly knew what was happening. The jeep stopped outside the main entrance.

'Follow us in so you'll be able to speak to someone. They're waiting for us to arrive. They might allow you to stay, maybe not.' Both men had left the front seats and were carefully lifting the stretcher from the rear of the vehicle. Trixie and Vi now waited alongside them.

'We have to report back to base immediately,' Atkinson

said. 'We wouldn't leave you if we didn't know you can get back to Shandford quite easily from here.'

'Thank you both for everything,' said Vi.

'You've been marvellous,' added Trixie, and saw Atkinson colour.

Two nurses stepped from the doors to meet them, and while the Canadians spoke to one briefly, then disappeared down a white-painted corridor, carrying their charge on the stretcher, the other nurse ushered the girls into a small office. She motioned for them to sit down, then seated herself behind the desk.

Trixie thought it was no wonder patients fell in love with their nurses. Her white cap showed blonde hair peeking around it, curling softly. Her skin was like the bloom on a peach. Her starched white apron over her blue dress made her eyes seem even bluer than they were. She looked clean and wholesome. Even her spectacles made her seem virtuous. Trixie was intensely aware of her own grubby, blood-marked clothing that smelt of chopped wood and sweat. She glanced at Vi, who shrugged her shoulders and smiled at her as though she knew exactly what she was thinking.

The nurse asked them to give as many details of the accident as they could.

'It all happened so quickly,' said Trixie.

'We tried to make her comfortable,' Vi added, as the nurse adjusted her spectacles.

'You acted speedily and that's what matters,' the nurse said. Then, 'Those two Samaritans telephoned that they'd be bringing Dolly in.' Trixie guessed she meant the Canadians and admired their calmness and quick-thinking.

'Sorry we know so little about her,' Vi said. 'You see, we're an intake of girls living at Shandford Lodge and scarcely know each other.'

'Don't worry, no doubt the authorities there have all the relevant information.' She smiled at them both, then scribbled on a tablet of paper.

Trixie asked, 'Will we be able to say cheerio to Dolly?'

With a shake of her head, 'Probably best not to,' the nurse said. 'She might even be in theatre now.' Vi and Trixie looked at each other. 'What I will do when I contact Shandford Lodge is ask them to let you know how she's getting on.'

'So, we wait to hear from you?' Trixie asked.

The nurse smiled and nodded. She rose and Trixie understood that they were expected to leave.

'Please give Dolly our love,' Vi said, as she got to her feet.

'Thank you,' Trixie added.

From the corridor they stepped through the doors into the late August sunshine. Trixie breathed a sigh of relief.

She hadn't noticed before but a rectangular garden alongside the driveway hosted white petalled roses with their fragrance perfuming the air.

'Do you really think she'll be all right?' she asked Vi, who looked exhausted. 'You were marvellous today,' she added.

Vi blushed beneath the grime and flecks of dried blood on her face. She fiddled in her pocket and drew out some coins. 'We'll catch a bus back,' she said quickly. 'There's always bus stops near hospitals.'

'We won't know which way to go.'

'We got tongues in our heads,' Vi said, slipping her arm through Trixie's. 'Tonight we'll go to the Yellow Duck.'

'That's the last thing I need,' Trixie said. 'I feel like I've been pulled through a hedge backwards. I want sleep and plenty of it.'

'You made a promise to Donnie,' insisted Vi. 'You won't get any sleep in the hut. Dolly's accident will be the main topic of conversation and everyone will keep us awake asking questions.'

Trixie knew her words made sense. She was also reminded that Donnie had promised her that, if she played the piano nightly for the remainder of the time she was at Shandford, he'd employ a door manager. Trixie suddenly realized that Dolly's accident had taken precedence over everything today and she'd not had time to dwell on her own misfortune of last night. 'It's an ill wind that blows nobody some good,' as her mother would say. So Rose was quite right about that, wasn't she? A man keeping an eye open for predators meant a lot to her after her own awful experience.

Vi was right, too. Trixie couldn't go back on her promise. Besides, playing tunes might take her mind off what had happened today. At least, she hoped it would. Music usually worked its magic on her.

Outside the hospital gates Vi elbowed her good-naturedly and nodded towards the bus stops at either side of the road, which was flanked by shops and people going about their daily business.

'You asked me if I thought Dolly will be all right,' said Vi. 'My answer is probably, eventually. But I'm glad that last night, dancing, she had her moment of glory. It could be a long while before she dances like that again. So, Trixie Smith, if all you have to moan about is being tired, you should think yourself lucky.'

Trixie watched as Vi left her side to approach a young woman in a headscarf with a pushchair, a crying child strapped inside. Vi walked back towards her saying, 'Bus due in five minutes, this side of the road. My throat's dry. I could murder a cup of tea, couldn't you?'

Chapter Seventeen

'Play somethin' for me, darlin', please? I'm sad and a long way from home.'

The young freckled auburn-haired English airman she'd never noticed before in the pub held on to the top of the piano as he leant down to whisper in Trixie's ear. Cigarette smoke swirled in the air and mixed with his beery breath as he breathed into her face. The last notes of 'Amapola', a song she loved to play, echoed throughout the bar.

'I got the news today that my older brother's aircraft didn't make it back from Operation Jubilee. That swine Hitler got him over German-occupied Dieppe. I should be home comforting my ma. We should be comforting each other.' His blue eyes were damp with tears and bloodshot, and threatened to overflow once again. He couldn't have been much older than herself. What a vile war it was. He'd be remembering his older brother as someone to look up to, someone who probably took the lead. Someone who had protected him, perhaps shared his confidences. Times that were now gone for ever. He was certainly a lad who needed consoling, Trixie thought.

The pub was packed with couples chatting and clamped together in an imitation of dancing. It was a bit like taking solace from each other, she thought. Not a bad thing when no one knew what the next day would bring.

Big Al was staring protectively across at her from his place at the bar where he could keep an eye on what was going on. He had a pint in front of him that would last him all night because he wasn't a drinker. Big Al, Alasdair Anderson, six feet of muscle and sinew, red hair and beard to match, was the latest addition to the staff of the Yellow Duck. He was the new door supervisor. She smiled at him to show him the lad was no trouble. He reluctantly turned his attention to Vi, who was waiting for Fiona to refill glasses with lemonade to bring back to the piano and a thirsty Trixie.

She had heard the news on the wireless about the amphibious attack on the occupied French port. At least half of the six hundred infantrymen had been killed, wounded or taken prisoner, and the RAF had lost more than a hundred aircraft. No doubt the awful news was worse than the announcer's careful wording, Trixie thought, and listeners were being spared the whole truth. Sometimes it took a while for it to filter through. Like the terrible sinking earlier in the month of HMS *Eagle*, the aircraft carrier, on her way to Malta, by a German submarine. More than a hundred men had been lost.

Trixie was beginning to understand that it was important to try not to dwell on what was already in the past but to cherish every new day. Her mind went back to her half-finished letter to Cy. She had no idea where he or his ship was. She prayed every day to hear from him. Sometimes she wondered if she had dreamed their meeting but then her heart told her that he and his love were real, very real indeed.

The Dieppe raid had given the girls in the hut something else to talk about besides Dolly's unfortunate accident. But Vi had been right, the questions had been relentless, and Trixie was relieved to be sitting at the piano and allowing the music to sweep through her mind, washing away, at least temporarily, the horror of the day.

'You got a favourite song?' Trixie asked. 'I'll play it if I know it.'

'It was Archie's favourite song,' he said. 'We had a good few laughs about it when we were young. Laughter was in my brother's nature. "If you can't laugh at yourself, it's a pretty poor show," he used to say.' He leant across and whispered in her ear.

'I can't play that.' She giggled. 'It's not very respectful. Those words were frowned upon when Marie Lloyd first sang them!'

'No, but just remembering made you smile, didn't it? Marie changed the last word to 'leeks' but everyone knew what she meant. I want to imagine Archie listening and smiling,' he said.

Big Al, followed by Vi, parted the customers and set down the tray containing lemonade and packets of crisps on a small table nearby. He grinned at Trixie, who picked up her drink and took a swallow. She knew he had come across to the piano in case her new drunken friend became argumentative. Donnie had hired the hulk of a man to work nightly, not just for the dances held in the hut, but because her piano playing brought in more custom. Donnie had kept to his part of the bargain and Trixie was more than happy to fulfil her promise to play in the evenings until she left the area after her training was completed at Shandford Lodge.

Big Al looked the young airman up and down. 'All right?' he asked. His voice was like coarse sand washing up on gravel.

'I'm playing a request for my friend here, who's had bad news,' Trixie said, before the airman could answer. She hadn't been slow to realize that, after one look at Big Al when they'd first met, he was ready to lay down his life, if anyone dared to put a finger on her. Trixie began playing the Marie Lloyd music hall song, 'She Sits Among the Cabbages And Peas'.

Even she smiled, albeit with a tear in her eye, when her 'friend' added, 'Ma used to chase us round the table when we sang it.' Trixie could imagine the lads finding the words excruciatingly funny! And now, despite his inebriation he squatted and nearly fell over in a parody of the song's lyrics!

Later, tucked into the back of Donnie's ancient car trundling along the pot-holed lane, Vi said, 'It's a nice night, and we wouldn't have minded walking back to Shandford Lodge. It's a shame to waste your petrol.'

'I dinna mind. It's nae trouble. I'm only too pleased you both turned up at the pub. I was wondering whether, Trixie, you might have been too shaken up after what happened. I wouldnae have blamed you if you'd stayed away.'

'I couldn't break my promise when I knew you'd keep yours,' Trixie said. Besides, she thought, the moment she had entered the bar tonight, lifted the lid of the piano and pressed her fingers to the keys, it was as though the music helped wash away the awfulness of the day and the bad memories of Ben Tate.

'Aye. You're a grand lass – you both are,' he added. 'I heard about the dancin' girl and her accident. Stracathro's a good hospital, so she'll be well looked after.' He cleared his throat. 'When I first heard Brechin was going to host lasses to chop down trees to help the war effort I thought we were about to be overrun by fancy young things with painted nails frightened to dirty their hands. Aye, I've seen a few of those and they've not lasted long, I can tell you.' His voice seemed to take on volume as he said, 'My niece is a nurse at Stracathro. She told me what you did for that girl, Dolly. You're grand lasses, the pair of you,' he repeated. 'I'll miss you when you move on.'

Trixie was aware of the sudden silence between them his words had caused.

Vi was the first to speak. 'That's a lovely thing to say,' she said. 'Thank you.'

Donnie cleared this throat again, 'Aye, even Fiona likes you two, and that's a first,' he added. Then he gave a big belly laugh. 'An' my Fiona, aye, she a good barmaid, but she cannae abide the lumberjills. She doesnae agree with women doing men's jobs.'

They waved goodnight to Donnie and watched the car rattle down the lane.

A couple of lamps were still burning when Trixie pushed open the hut door. A few of the girls were sitting on beds, smoking and chatting, but as usual most were asleep. The blackout curtains were pulled across the windows and the fireguard around the pot-bellied stove was hung about with clothes and socks drying.

'Smells like a blinkin' laundry in here,' said Vi.

Trixie glanced across to Jo's bed where she was curled up and fast asleep, as usual. Vi made a bee-line for the wash-room after mouthing, 'Hello,' to Hen, who was sitting up in bed reading. Hen, looking like a freshly scrubbed angel with her blonde hair newly washed and hanging across her shoulders, put down the letter she was reading. 'In case you were wondering why I wasn't at the pub tonight it was because I don't feel ready to face Malcolm yet,' she said.

'The place, as usual, was packed so I don't know if he was there or not,' Trixie said. 'But you can't put your life on hold because of that snake.' She looked along the line of beds and immediately noticed the two empty ones where Dolly and Maisie slept. 'Where's Maisie?' she asked, sitting on the edge of Hen's bed and pulling off her shoes. She used her toes to push them beneath her own bed.

'Maisie's been missing since lunch-time,' Hen said. 'She was in a bit of a state.' She shrugged. 'I heard you and Vi were regular Florence Nightingales today.' Trixie could smell Gibbs dentifrice on Hen's breath from when she'd cleaned her teeth. 'You're probably sick of talking about it, but I'm so proud of you two.'

Momentarily Trixie had forgotten that Hen, as a measurer, had already been dropped off to another working party this morning, before the accident had occurred.

'I didn't do much at all, Hen. It was Vi. I can't believe how she's changing in the short time she's been here.'

'Perhaps this place has given her a new outlook on life.'

Trixie was thoughtful for a moment. 'I think we're all changing, in one way or another.'

Hen lowered her voice so it was hardly more than a whisper. She looked towards Jo's bed. 'Not all of us, Trixie. I wish I knew what's eating her up inside.'

Trixie was about to answer her when a voice from inside the hut called, 'It's lights-out time. If you want to go on reading your letters it'll have to be by candles, girls.'

Moans and groans could be heard amid the rustle of envelopes and paper.

'Aren't you going to look at your letters, Trixie?' Hen

asked. 'When the post was brought round, I put yours on your locker.'

Trixie's eyes swerved towards the neat pile of envelopes sitting next to her washbag. Her heart felt as if it had suddenly sprouted wings.

Chapter Eighteen

My Darling

We have a beautiful future ahead of us once this war is over. We came together, you and I, through forces beyond our control and I know you are the girl I've waited my whole life to meet. When I saw you sitting alone in the cabin on that ferry something clicked inside my heart and, like it happens in films or in books, I fell for you, hook, line and sinker. In fact, my heart is swimming in an ocean of love for you.

I've written to my ma about you and she's longing to meet the girl I've fallen for. I've shared with her some of the stories you've told me about your school-days and childhood. I want to know all about you, Trixie. I've written several letters to you, hoping you'll at least get one of them. I can't tell you where I'm going or why, that's not allowed. I can tell you I share a bunkroom with other guys, among them Hobo, who plays the harmonica all the time. Sometimes it drives me mad but he's my pal and I love music so I don't complain too much. Bruno is the pretty one. He's Italian, from New York. His family own a Pizza Place. Hobo's always saying his dad should have sent a pizza to join the Navy. It would be more use than Bruno! Seriously, though, they are nice guys. I have a request to make. Could you send me a photograph to pin above my bunk so I can see you when I close my eyes and when I wake up?

Yours Cy xxx

Trixie, now in bed and reading by the light of a candle stuck in a saucer, refolded the pages and tucked them beneath her pillow. She couldn't believe Cy had written her so many letters but she was ecstatic that he had. She wiped a tear of happiness from her cheek. After all the bad things that had happened during the past couple of days, she was almost scared to allow herself the contentment and happiness his written words gave her.

She looked around. Some of the girls were still reading. Vi, at the end of the hut, was a sleeping mound in her bed.

Grunts and sighs could be heard from other girls already asleep.

She was aware of the sharp sting of rain beating against the windows. In Gosport when it rained it was a minor nuisance that required a headscarf to keep her hair dry after she'd carefully styled it. Scotland's rain was relentless, poking freezing fingers into unprotected skin. The forest would be cold and wet tomorrow, Trixie thought. She wasn't looking forward to returning to the clearing, which had been the scene of so much angst today. She looked at Hen, who was sharing the light of her candle to read a paperback with a lurid cover.

'Have you any idea where we're going tomorrow?' Her voice was a whisper so as not to disturb anyone.

Hen smoothed back her hair and put her book, pages down, on her blanket. 'Remembering the list of skills we were told to expect to learn, I'm sure sawmills and charcoal burning haven't been covered yet. Alf'll tell you what's happening in the morning. I'm not often in the same working party as you, am I?'

'That's true,' whispered Trixie. She yawned, tiredness catching up on her. 'That's because you're a clever clogs,' she added.

After a short silence, Hen said thoughtfully, 'But you're

the one who's had the opportunities, Trix, and I envy that.' Before Trixie had time to work out what she meant, Hen's voice changed and she said brightly, 'Good letters?'

Trixie dismissed Hen's previous cryptic remark about opportunities and said sleepily, 'Wonderful letters.'

Immaculate in full Timber Corps dress, Maud Styles entered the dining room while breakfast was in operation and stood at the front. The noise stopped. Even the homely smells of cooked food seemed to disappear. Trixie replaced her cup in her saucer. Vi put down her cutlery and waited.

'It'll be news of Dolly,' Trixie whispered to Jo.

'Let's hope it's good, then,' Jo said, replacing a doorstep of bread on her plate.

Hen stared at Trixie.

Maud Styles cleared her throat and, once she was certain she had the full attention of the room, began to speak. 'Good morning, everyone. Some of you may be aware of a distressing accident that occurred yesterday. To put your minds at rest, the girl concerned was quickly dispatched to hospital and was operated on forthwith. It is hoped she will recover.' The brief words received applause. 'On a lighter note, the travel warrants have arrived for those of you who have requested them and will be handed out before your final day here at Shandford Lodge. Details of your next posting with the Forestry Commission will be given upon your return.' A brief smile lifted her lips, as she added, 'I'll leave you to finish your breakfast in peace. Any questions, I'll be in my office.'

And then she melted away.

'Short and sweet,' announced Hen, before she lifted her mug of tea.

'If you've changed your mind about coming back to Gosport to visit your family, I expect she could still sort out your warrant, Jo,' said Trixie. She was hoping Jo wanted to see her family after all. 'Once we're scattered all over the place it might be more difficult to travel home.'

Jo shook her head. 'There's nothing for me down south,' she said. 'And I wish you'd stop trying to make me change my mind.'

Her elbow caught her half-filled mug of tea, which skittered across the table as she rose quickly and clambered from the bench. Trixie watched Jo's resolute back as she stalked out of the room. She looked at Hen. 'That's me told to mind my own business,' she said, using the half-eaten crust that Jo had left on her plate to soak up the liquid.

Hen said, 'The closer we get to going back to Gosport the quieter Jo's becoming. When we first arrived, she was full of hopes and dreams about Scotland and the work we were expected to do, but as the weeks have passed, she's withdrawn into herself more and more.'

'She's never once come along to the Yellow Duck,' said Vi.

'She's bloody good at felling trees,' announced Trixie, in defence of her friend. She flicked her fingers after depositing the soggy bread on Jo's abandoned plate. 'She's a kind person, thoughtful. A really hard worker.'

A uniformed young woman had approached the table behind Trixie and bent down to whisper in her ear. After Trixie's surprise at being singled out, she muttered, 'Thank you.' She watched as the girl walked away. She looked at her friends, her eyes settling on Vi. 'We've been summoned to the Holy of Holies, you and me, Vi. Maud Styles wants to see us in her office.'

'What, now?'

'I don't expect she'll mind if we finish our breakfast first,' said Trixie.

Nevertheless, she quickly drank her tea, then stood up. Hen was staring at her, open-mouthed. 'I'll tell you all about it when we get back.' Trixie put her hand on Vi's shoulder, 'C'mon, you, let's go.'

As the pair left the room, Trixie could feel myriad eyes following her. She shuddered as she caught sight of the stags' heads, with antlers, decorating the walls of the gloomy hallway.

'Come in,' they heard, after Trixie knocked tentatively on the office door.

They stood at the desk. Trixie's heart was banging inside her chest so fiercely she thought at any moment it would explode.

Maud Styles left her seat and came around to the front of her desk, facing them. 'Thank you for coming,' she said. 'This is an informal chat.' Trixie could smell the faint aroma of violets. 'And I expect you know why you're here?' She paused. Vi shook her head.

'Not really,' admitted Trixie. 'Is it about yesterday?' Her heart was sinking into her work-boots. Had she and Vi taken on too much in deciding their course of action when Dolly had hurt herself? What should they have done differently?

'Yes, it's about the accident yesterday. Without your intervention the girl would almost certainly have died. You make a good team. You are, both of you, an asset to the Women's Timber Corps.'

The moment Vi knew they were being congratulated, not castigated she burst out, 'You said Dolly'll be all right. Can we go and see her?'

The answer came swiftly, 'That won't be possible. She

was operated on but is being transferred to a hospital in Birmingham. Her family are there. Rehabilitation will take some considerable time. Have either of you any more questions?'

'I have,' said Trixie. 'What about Maisie, her friend, who was with her in the forest? Her bed wasn't slept in.'

'Maisie left the Lodge yesterday afternoon. She said that, regrettably, forestry work was not for her. I believe she too has returned to Birmingham.'

Trixie listened to the silence that followed. Maud Styles was obviously not going to take her or Vi any further into her confidence. The older woman looked at her watch. 'Duty calls, and time is of the essence.'

Trixie was taken aback when Maud Styles leant forward, reached out and vigorously shook her hand, then did the same to Vi. 'Well done, the pair of you,' she said firmly and clearly.

Outside in the corridor, once the office door had closed on them, Vi looked at Trixie, 'Fancy that!' she said.

Trixie grinned at her. 'Fancy that, indeed, team-mate,' she answered.

Chapter Nineteen

'This is one of the more important jobs for you to be involved in, apart from chopping down trees.' Alf took off his flat cap, rubbed his glistening forehead, replaced the cap and stared hard at the girls. 'Can anyone tell me why we badly need charcoal?'

Trixie shuffled her feet so that pine needles stuck to her wet boots. Vi stared first into the forest, then back at the large metal containers in the clearing. The previous night's rain had been torrential, leaving a chill in the air, and the ground was mushy underfoot. Most of the girls had dressed for further wet weather and some could hardly move freely in their waterproofs.

'You have no idea, have you?' whispered Trixie.

Vi answered her, 'And I suppose you have?'

Trixie shook her head. None of the girls answered Alf,

so he said, 'I thought as much. Charcoal is used in gas-mask filters. Necessary during the First World War when mustard gas, which has practically no odour, was added to shells for the most devastating effects on our men. The government has issued gas masks to everyone in case the German buggers do it again. Charcoal absorbs poisons, you see.'

He pointed to the huge metal containers.

'Them's the kilns and I'm going to show you lot how to make charcoal.' A few groans were heard from the twenty or so girls huddled together listening and watching the old man. 'Oh, so you're all excited about that, are you? To keep you happy then, afterwards I'll tell you how to mix the blasting agent for explosives used for firearms, artillery, mining and quarrying.'

'We usually have a billy-can of tea before we start,' came a voice from the back of the gathering.

'Do we now?' mocked Alf. 'Well, today we ain't having tea until we've done some work!' This time big sighs came from the girls with groans.

Alf was clearly enjoying himself as he said, 'And that's because for a while we're free of midges so we got to take advantage of the little buggers not bein' around. Now, I want two of them metal containers filled tightly to the brim with waste timber you'll find lying about.'

He waved his arms in his tattered coat-sleeves encompassing the woodland around them. 'Pick up the seasoned lumber, the bigger branches left from brashing, the drier the better and stack 'em inside the kilns as tight as you can. Them are big kilns and they'll need a lot of filling.' He moved nearer to a kiln and pointed a crooked finger. 'See them filters, them pipes, sticking up from the ovens? Try not to get any bits of wood stuck in them. They're vents and they need to be kept clear. If you notices any wet muck in them vents use your fingers to poke it out.'

Vi moved off with Trixie and began picking up the bigger branches. Some were practically log-like. Jo caught them both up. She was carrying three bill-hooks and handed one each to Trixie and Vi.

'If Alf wants the rubbishy twigs shaved off, we might be needing these,' she said.

'Clever of you to realize that,' said Vi. 'But I should think it's more difficult to chop dead ends off bits of branches that have already been lopped off trees. I wouldn't know how to hold the branch and cut it at the same time.'

Trixie caught her eye and knew she was remembering what had happened to Dolly due to her own carelessness. She didn't intend to allow a similar thing to happen to herself.

Jo looked sheepish. 'I didn't think about that,' she said. 'I had an ulterior motive in collecting these from the back of Lulubelle's cart. I thought we might curry favour with Alf in thinking for ourselves.' She paused. 'I see now it's a stupid and dangerous idea to do something without asking whether or not it's safe.' She stopped. Then her words toppled over themselves: 'I'm sorry about this morning when I had a little tantrum in the dining room.'

Vi stuck her free arm through Jo's and said, 'Forget it, Jo. We're all allowed to say what we feel from time to time.'

'And I promise I won't mention Gosport again.' Trixie felt herself blush. 'Whoops! Sorry,' she said.

Jo gave a small laugh. Then she became serious again. 'I will go back to Gosport. But not just yet. If we're lucky enough to be billeted together, wherever the Forestry Commission is going to send us, I'd really like it if you'd ask me again.'

'Of course,' said Trixie. 'I wonder where we'll end up.'

Alf's raspy voice cut through the trees, as did the smell of his pipe. 'You three collecting wood or standing there gassing? The war'll be over if you aren't careful and we'll have lost it because you couldn't be bothered to do as you was asked!'

'Oh dear!' said Vi. 'We're for it now. He's not in a very

good mood today. I expect he's upset about Dolly's accident happening on his patch.'

'He shouldn't be!' snapped Jo. 'I remember Alf telling us not to start work until he returned. Dolly took no notice of him, did she?' Then she added, 'And I was going to do the same!'

'Quite so!' admitted Vi. 'You're not often wrong but you're right there!'

Jo gave a mock-cough. 'And we're supposed to be collecting wood, aren't we?'

A short while later Alf gave them a yellow-toothed smile as they packed wood into every available space in the waist-high metal containers. All the girls stood back surveying the fruit of their efforts.

'Right,' he said. He pointed to a small fire burning happily near an area where the girls had left their sandwiches and other belongings while they worked, and where cut tree trunks and logs gave them somewhere to sit. 'I've put two billy-cans on, so when we've lit the ovens and you've listened a bit to me, we'll all have a nice cuppa.' Alf used the back of his hand to wipe his nose. Then he pulled out a burning twig from the fire, took it to the first kiln, and used it to light the contents. The girls, who'd matched him step by step, huddled around him, watching.

'It needs to be heated slowly, so the wood dries out but its capacity for burning ain't lost. We need to restrict the oxygen so the wood doesn't catch fire. We don't want ash. Now, in a bit, we'll put the metal lids on top of the containers and then we'll seal all the air holes except the vents. How we gonna do that? You may well ask.'

No one had asked, thought Trixie. She guessed the girls were more interested in when the billy-cans would be boiling to make the tea. It seemed Alf, too, had decided that, for he added, 'Some of you might be thinking, I'll never need to know all the tripe this silly old bugger's spouting, but one day you just might, and this is why Shandford Lodge tries to instil in you all the right ways to go about things.'

Vi, who had obviously been taking in every word Alf was saying, asked, 'How can we make sure the only air that goes in the kiln is what's needed?'

Alf's rheumy eyes lit on Vi like she was an angel sent from Heaven. 'We packs up every unnecessary gap we can find in the metal with earth.'

The smell of burning wood and its smoke was drifting into the atmosphere.

'Earth?' exclaimed Jo.

'It's a dirty, smoky job making charcoal!' came a voice from the crowd.

'Yes, it's a filthy job,' said Alf, treating everyone to another gappy yellow-toothed smile. 'But it keeps the bleedin' midges away. C'mon, get your hands dirty!' He picked up a clod of wet turf and pressed it between the lid and the canister, sealing part of the top. He motioned for the girls to start doing the same.

'How long will it take before the wood turns into charcoal?' Vi asked.

'Shortest time maybe twelve hours, longest time, twenty-four.'

Trixie noticed his limp was more pronounced the longer he was walking around the clearing, checking they were sealing the huge canisters before they became too hot to touch. She wondered how old he was. Seventies, perhaps?

At last, the kilns were sealed and burning to his satisfaction. 'That's it now, ladies. Go and wash yourselves in the stream. I reckon you've all earned a cuppa.' Alf looked at his silver pocket watch 'Might as well stop now for your sandwiches an' all,' he said. Then he smiled at Trixie. 'Nice to see you using your right hand, Trixie gal!'

Trixie glared at him, embarrassed because he'd reminded her of her blunder.

The mumbling from the crowd grew to joyful chatter as sandwich tins were rescued from personal belongings or collected from Alf's cart. Lulubelle had been presented with a nosebag, and was munching contentedly.

Trixie said, examining her sandwich, 'Does anyone want to do a swap? I can't stand pilchard and cucumber.'

'I've got banana sandwiches. You can have them if you like,' said a voice.

'Real bananas?' Trixie was excited. 'I can't remember when I last ate a banana!'

'It's mock banana made from boiled mashed parsnips, a smidgeon of sugar and banana essence!'

Trixie passed her packet of sandwiches along and received the 'banana' ones. Anything was better than pilchards, which she hated. Sitting astride a big log, she could feel the warmth from the fire as she gulped some tea. It was black and thick like tar, as Alf always made it. He was now settled on a tree stump with his legs stretched out in front of him. She could see the bowl of his pipe sticking out of his jacket's top pocket.

'Thought you were going to tell us about gunpowder, Alf,' Trixie said.

Jo, sitting on the damp grass at her feet, turned and glared at her, obviously not interested in listening to another of Alf's lectures.

'So I was!' His face lit up with elation before he set down

his empty tin mug and pulled his pipe from his pocket with a small string bag. He filled the bowl and tamped it, then lit it with a Swan Vesta. He drew on it contentedly. Trixie thought she would forever after associate the smell of a pipe with Alf and the girls sitting in a damp Scottish glade.

'What's that tobacco you're smoking?' she asked.

He removed the pipe stem from his mouth and said, 'Condor, when I can get it, because of the war. When I can't I smokes old socks!'

Trixie laughed and he smiled with her. Then he stood up and said, loudly enough for everyone sitting about to hear, 'Pay attention, you girls. I'd be shirking my duty if I didn't tell you about how carbon, that's your charcoal, is mixed with sulphur and saltpetre, that's potassium nitrate, to make a blasting agent, or black powder as it's often called, for explosives, in artillery, firearms, mining and quarry work. Carbon from these pine trees gives the spark, but willow, alder, beech and grape vines makes the best black powder.' He saw he had their attention and shook his head. 'Don't worry I ain't going to get you scrambling about the forest looking for that little lot because here in Scotland, in Ardeer, we got one of the largest dynamite plants in the world.' He sucked on his pipe, then added, 'I knows about Ardeer, and now you knows about Ardeer. Thirteen thousand people work at Ardeer, but let's keep that secret in case ol' Adolf finds out about the dynamite factory and sends his Flying Pencils over to bomb it.'

Voices started up but Alf quietened them with his next words. 'Some of you will be back cutting down trees tomorrow. Some will go on to different work. Some will come back here. I decided a break away would take your minds off what happened to the Birmingham lass.' His voice was practically a croak as he added, 'You've got to look after yourselves.'

He gripped his pipe and knocked the ash from the bowl by tapping it against a nearby tree trunk. 'I'll give you time to get yourselves together,' he said, 'but the rest of today will be yours to do as you like. Those that want a lift back to the Lodge, come with me. If you want to make your own way back, you can.'

Claps and whistles started up, causing consternation among the birds in the tall trees. Alf sat back down again.

'What about the kilns, Alf? Surely we can't just pack up and leave them burning?'

He looked at Vi, then shook his head. 'Normally I'd agree with you but we'll not be leaving here until the prisoners arrive from the Shielhill PoW camp to take over.' He looked at his watch, and it was as if that was a signal for two covered lorries to trundle into the clearing. They drew up near the kilns a short distance away from where the girls and Alf were huddled about the fire.

'I've never seen an enemy prisoner before,' said Vi. She was leaning forward, aiming for a good view. From the cab of the first lorry two guards jumped down as soon as it stopped. They stood at the rear and watched as a dozen or so young men clambered out.

'They're just lads!' exclaimed Vi.

'Yes,' said Alf, using his red neckerchief to wipe moisture from his neck. 'Italian lads. They got to work for their keep, same as you. What did you expect to come from the back of that lorry? Wild animals?'

Trixie saw Vi glare at Alf. The second lorry was discharging its prisoners now. One noticed Trixie and Vi, and waved, a big grin spanning his handsome face. The prisoners all wore serge battle-dress with distinctive large red spots on the trousers and jackets.

Alf coughed dramatically. 'I'd hoped to have you girls away from here before they arrived,' he said, getting up. He looked down at the fire and kicked the surrounding earth so it covered the burning twigs. Then, with his heavy boots, he stamped on the remaining embers so the fire was well and truly extinguished.

'Get yourselves in the wagon if you want a lift back,' Alf said. 'Don't think you can hang about here talking to them Italians because the guards'll soon shift you,' he called, loud enough for everyone, including the prisoners, to hear.

Girls, many of them still in wet-weather outfits, were standing around eyeing the young men. Jo was clearing away mugs already rinsed in the stream and Trixie watched as she carried them and the bill-hooks back to the cart. It was painfully obvious, thought Trixie, that Alf didn't want to encourage contact between his girls and the prisoners.

It was clear, too, that the old man had sympathy for the Italians, who were, thought Trixie, like our own young men, fighting a war they probably didn't understand or want.

Vi was insistent: 'But we won't see the end product of the wood we packed in the kilns.'

Alf stood in front of her. 'Maybe not this time, girly. But if you thinks that's the only time you'll have a hand in making charcoal, you're mistaken.' He gave her a grin. 'I ain't sure where I'm taking you lot tomorrow but if we gets a chance to come back here we will,' he said, walking towards Lulubelle and the cart.

Trixie could see his leg was troubling him because his hesitant steps took a while to develop into a sure-footed gait.

Trixie began to relax on the drive along the lanes back

to Shandford Lodge. She decided she would wash her hair when she got to the hut, write another letter to Cy, and reread some of his letters to her. It was amazing the things she'd discovered about him and his friend Hobo. They'd gone to school together and got into all kinds of scrapes, both good and bad. The Mississippi river was their playground for fishing, paddling, but Cy had never learnt to swim. Hobo swam like a fish, he wrote. She'd already decided she wanted to write and tell her mother everything. It went without saying that she'd walk down to the Yellow Duck to play the piano in the evening.

She decided the day had turned out well, after all. She, like Vi, would have preferred to witness the end result of the charcoal burning but Alf had dug in his vast pockets, drawn out burnt sticks and passed them around.

'Eventually your wood will end up like this,' he'd said. The hard sticks were black and marked the skin on their fingers. Trixie glanced back to the scene they'd just left. A few of the girls were still hanging about, chatting to the young men. And why not? If she hadn't met Cy maybe she'd be among them. Human nature, she thought. The young men were eyeing up the girls, who were pretending they weren't really bothered. It was a natural enough game to play, wasn't it? But she noticed the guards watching them all, every second.

'Your mate's doing well at her measuring,' Alf said, Lulubelle's reins held loosely in his hands.

Trixie, sitting behind him, was pleased to hear it. 'I wondered how she'd take to it,' she replied.

'Like a duck to water,' he added. 'She's soaked up a lot of information in a short while and I wouldn't be a bit surprised if the powers that be don't have her travelling about buying up acres of trees from private landowners.'

'Will she really have to do that? It sounds very important.' Trixie was impressed.

'If she's capable enough and I've heard she is.'

Trixie's heart plummeted. She wanted the four of them to stay together, not for Hen to be sent God knew where.

It seemed to Trixie that such a lot was happening in a short time. Of course she wanted Hen to do well but she didn't want the four friendships to end: being separated might mean losing touch. It was bad enough they were hardly ever all together nowadays. Trixie looked to where Jo was sitting, idly watching the countryside roll by. It took her but a few seconds to wriggle in beside her.

'Earlier on you apologized for being a bit narky with me this morning at breakfast. Today you've got no excuse that you're tired because we've hardly done any work and we're going back early. Please, please, come down to the Yellow

Duck with me and Vi, tonight. I'd really like us all to be together.'

Jo seemed to consider her words carefully. But when she spoke, she asked, 'What about Hen, will she come?'

Trixie remembered Hen hadn't set foot in the place since her argument with Malcolm. Hen and Jo were close so if she gave any indication that Hen mightn't come tonight, Jo might back out.

Behind her back, Trixie crossed her fingers and said, 'Course she will!'

Chapter Twenty

Bursting through the hut door, Trixie saw the new letters piled on her bedside locker.

'Who's a lucky girl, then?' said Vi, who was close behind her and had also spotted the envelopes. 'Bags I the washroom while you read them!'

Trixie was aware that Vi was happy for her relationship with Cy but she tried not to talk about him too much. Vi didn't receive letters. As far as she knew Vi's mother hadn't written to her since she'd arrived at Brechin. It didn't seem fair to keep reminding Vi that Cy had fallen for her like a ton of bricks and wrote constantly.

It wasn't long before the hut was alive with the chatter of the girls who had been allowed time off. The gramophone was soon spinning, the strains of 'Amapola' adding to their well-being, while mail was read and tea brewed on the pot-bellied stove.

Jo was another girl who didn't receive letters.

Trixie sat down and kicked off her work-boots. She'd already pushed her wet-weather clothing under the bed, and watched her friend haul out her suitcase. After delving among her things, Jo pulled out a pair of grey slacks and a long-sleeved strawberry-coloured jumper with puffed sleeves and shoulder-pads. 'Will these do for tonight?' she asked.

Trixie's heart leapt. So, Jo was keeping her promise to accompany them to the Yellow Duck. 'You'll look smashing!' she said, her eyes straying to Cy's letters.

'Go on, see what lover-boy has to say. I know you're longing to read them.' Jo smiled at her as she picked up her towel. 'I'm going to take my chances in the queue for the washroom.'

Trixie's fingers trembled as she tore open the first envelope. She loved it that Cy spent so much of his free time writing to her but felt a little guilty that her own output of letters didn't match up to his. She curled her legs beneath her, and as soon as Jo had left, she leant back on her pillow and read:

Hello, Honey

I got the photo you sent. All the guys are envious when they catch a glance at it pinned above my pillow. They say you are cute. Well, let me tell you you're the cutest girl I ever met. I remember your eyes sparkling when I saw you that day on the ferry and you looked at me for that first time. We are destined to be together when this doggone war is over and I will do everything in my power to make sure I stay safe for you. I will also pray you stay safe for me. You said in your last letter that I am very brave to tell you I love you after only one meeting. I have only one answer to that: what's brave about knowing something for certain?

I had a letter from my ma. She's told all the regulars in the shop that her Cy has a girl. I know when you meet her you will love her. Did I tell you she has a tiny corner shop near the French Quarter? She's very spiritual and sells prayer cards, ancient books, crystals, herbs, oils, rosary beads, candles and a whole lot more, and she's set in high regard.

I love it when you tell me things about your childhood and school. I guess I just want to know everything about you and what makes you the wonderful gal you are. I was sunbathing up on deck today. I love the sun, do you?

Our ship is designed to be fast and to escort larger vessels, so we're not alone in keeping an eye out for the enemy. I can't tell you more but I love reading about what you do in Scotland. I also worry about you so please, please, please take care, my darling.

Hobo is glaring at me now. I told him I'd join them to play cards. This seems to be a nightly occurrence now as things are pretty quiet here.

I thought you might like this picture of me and Hobo taken on shore leave when we first joined SS *Ready*. I'm the good-looking one.

You are me and I am you and I love you.

Cy

Trixie sat gazing at the black-and-white photograph. It was a head-and-shoulders print of the two men taken in a doorway. They had their arms about each other and were grinning into the camera like lunatics. In Hobo's top pocket she could just see part of his beloved harmonica. She looked closely at the face of the young man who in such a short time had come to mean so much to her . . .

'If you want to wash and tidy yourself up, Trix, I'd go now before the rest of the girls arrive back at the hut from work.'

She heard Jo's words and smiled at her, putting down the letter on top of the others that had arrived that day. Then she scooped them up and stuffed them beneath her pillow. She'd so look forward to reading them later.

The gramophone had been rewound and the record changed to 'I Don't Want To Set The World On Fire' as Trixie gathered together her flannel, shampoo, soap, tooth-brush and towel, and set off to the washroom. She liked the music that was playing now but not the scratchiness of the record. The needle probably wanted changing in the arm of the gramophone but, like everything else, due to war shortages, they were probably impossible to buy.

'You're back early!' Hen's words shook Trixie's mind away from gramophones and needles.

'Alf gave us time off because of what happened to Dolly,' she said.

Hen grinned at her and stepped aside so she could pass her on her way to the washroom. Her cheeks were rosy with being outside. She put her hand on Trixie's and said, 'It's getting cold out there now. I'm frozen,' and made for the stove.

'Don't rush off, Hen,' began Trixie. 'Alf told me you're really getting good at what you're doing. I'm ever so happy for you. I've managed to persuade Jo to come to the Yellow

Duck tonight and I want you to come as well. It would be lovely if we could all be together, don't you think? I know you don't want to set eyes on Malcolm but he hasn't been in for a while and, anyway, you'll be with me at the piano and he won't bother you—'

'Yes, that would be nice,' said Hen, cutting off her long speech.

For a moment Trixie was silent. Then, 'You will?' She hadn't thought it would be so easy to persuade Hen to come to the pub.

'I've just said so, haven't I?' Hen was smiling.

'I'd throw my arms around you, I'm so pleased,' said Trixie, 'but if I did I'd drop all the stuff I'm holding, wouldn't I?'

Hen was laughing at her now. 'Go and make yourself beautiful and hurry up about it. I'd like to wash as well, and it'll be time for dinner soon.'

Trixie pushed open the washroom door and made her way to a basin that wasn't being used. She looked in the mirror above it, surprised that she looked so well and healthy. She was enjoying the hard work she did each day and all the time she was learning different things about forestry and what would be expected of her when she left the Lodge. She'd write and tell Cy about that, she decided. There were a few things she wouldn't and couldn't share with him. She definitely wouldn't tell him about Ben putting whisky in her drinks and trying to do stuff to her she hadn't wanted. She didn't want Cy worrying about her. Ben Tate hadn't been seen in the Yellow Duck since that night and she didn't have much longer at Shandford Lodge so, hopefully, she'd never set eyes on him again.

Now that Donnie employed Big Al to keep an eye open for any unsavoury characters in the bar and at the dances, there should be no further trouble. As for Ben, Trixie firmly believed in karma. She was sure he'd get his comeuppance one way or another: what goes around comes around.

Neither would she dwell on what had happened to Dolly. Dolly had had a total disregard for her own safety and the result had caused an accident. She wouldn't tell Cy about that either, she decided. He had enough to think about, keeping himself and his mates safe on USS *Ready*.

Trixie opened the sachet of Amami shampoo, filled the sink with water and began to wash her hair. She was looking forward to tonight.

Chapter Twenty-one

Cy was amazed at the speed the enemy aircraft were coming in, torpedo-blasting the ships about USS *Ready*. The noise was ear-shattering and flaming smoke billowed from the stricken ships, engulfing the screaming men. It was like watching a movie, he thought, only it was all for real and he didn't feel like any film star.

And there were so many planes. They had come from nowhere, attacking the convoy. USS *Ready*'s gunners couldn't make much of an impact on them, for the planes varied their flying heights, some low, some high, but all very fast.

'Get to the boiler room.'

The order from the Tannoy system was clear. Cy looked at Hobo, who shrugged. The order must be obeyed.

The awkwardness of his bulky Mae West, a khaki-coloured cotton life preserver with inflatable rubber panels, made progress difficult in the confines of the ship's passageways, as he ran with Hobo to help fix the problem.

'Are we the only ones obeying orders?' Cy yelled, in the empty corridors.

The next explosion was deafening. The lights blew, leaving the corridor in darkness. There was a sudden silence. No shouting, nothing. Until another two explosions followed, smaller this time and close together. The ship bounced in the sea, like a rubber ball in water.

When they reached the boiler room the men were dead. Cy knew if they had arrived sooner, they, too, would have been killed.

Hobo grabbed at his arm. 'They've all had it. Let's go.' There was little point in staying. The place was a mess of blood and limbs, and water fast gushing in, covering the bodies.

Another disembodied voice came to them from the bridge: 'Prepare to abandon ship.' There were no warning whistle blasts.

Now Cy could smell burning and feel the extreme heat approaching.

'You'd think the water coming in would put out the fire!' he yelled at Hobo.

Hobo looked at him fearfully. It was like his friend had

never seen him before. His gaze reminded Cy momentarily of the eyes of the skinned dead rabbit his ma had hung in the outhouse. He shook his mate's shoulder, hard.

Hobo became Hobo again. 'Let's get the hell out of here,' he said.

Cy let out a deep breath of gratitude.

Smoke filled the corridors.

Everything up on deck was chaos. Men were being mown down by aircraft guns. Despite the smoke stinging Cy's eyes, he peered across the water towards the supply ship they'd been accompanying; it was going down fast and the sea around it was mostly a bed of flaming oil. Men without life preservers were jumping into the burning waves around it. So many were leaping into the ocean from the supply ship and USS *Ready* that they were falling onto men who were already floundering. Couldn't they see how useless it was?

He thought of Trixie and patted his pocket. He'd grabbed her photograph from above his bed before he'd left his cabin and gone on deck. Wherever he was going, she was coming with him, always. He blinked hard: he could barely see.

The smell of cordite hung over everything. Shrapnel fell and the screams from the wounded and dying men on the deck filled the air.

'We can't leave them like this,' Cy cried, smoke scorching his throat.

Hobo's voice was guttural. 'We're not fuckin' joinin' them, not if I can help it.'

The damaged handrail burnt to Cy's touch as he looked down into the water. The sea below was roiling but oil free. Instead, it was red. There were bodies. Alive and dead. Had they drowned in their own blood?

'I can't swim,' he cried. Growing up next to the Mississippi he'd paddled, fished, sailed, even worked on the river. Swimming had never come into it.

'That's what your Mae West's for.'

He felt the hard push of Hobo's hand into his back and then he was falling. He could see the wine-coloured water coming up to meet him. He hit the waves and was sucked under. Water filled his ears, his mouth. He flailed as he hit the surface again. And felt someone grab at his life preserver.

Trixie pulled the blanket up around her ears and tried to blot out the snuffling noises issuing from the sleeping girls. She was tired but in a good way. The evening in the Yellow Duck seemed to have cemented the friendship between the four of them and she was very happy.

She doubted she would ever understand what went on

in Jo's head that enabled her to keep a part of herself back from her friends but that didn't really matter: friendships evolved and needed to be worked at, she told herself.

The four of them were so different that they were never going to fit like pieces of a jigsaw, were they? In spite or because of this, Trixie said a little prayer that Fate would smile on them and they'd be billeted within meeting distance of each other. Deep down she knew Fate would need to laugh, not just smile, for that to happen.

'Trix! You still awake?'

'I am,' she murmured.

She turned in her cot, grabbing more tightly at her bed-clothes to keep their warmth in, and faced the small expanse between her bed and Jo's. Already the nights were colder now, especially when the pot-bellied stove was allowed to burn down. The interior of the hut smelt of wood smoke and last year's peat turf that had been dug from the moun-tainside and left to dry in the summer sun and wind by some enterprising lumberjills. Scotland was beautiful, Trixie had decided, but Gosport was definitely warmer.

'I just wanted to say thank you for letting me come with you tonight.'

'You're very welcome,' Trixie answered.

As soon as they'd arrived at the pub Jo had found a chair

and placed it next to the piano so she'd be near Trixie. Fiona had brought over drinks and Jo hadn't moved all night, remembered Trixie. She'd hardly spoken, except when pressed by Trixie to name a tune she'd like played. Her reply had been, 'Anything by Billie Holiday,' so Trixie had begun playing 'God Bless The Child'.

While playing Jo's request she could have sworn she'd seen the brightness of tears in Jo's eyes but she'd dismissed that. Her own eyes were smarting from the thick cigarette smoke that hung in the bar like winter fog. At least, thought Trixie, she was a tiny step nearer to understanding Jo, who was obviously a fan of Billie Holiday.

'It's not a case of letting you come to the pub with us. I love it when we do things, besides work, together,' Trixie said. 'And I'm pleased that Hen feels she can show her face in the place again.'

She got no further for Jo stifled a laugh. 'Even though she danced with two different men and disappeared out the back with that local chap for ages . . .'

'Yeah, well, that's our glamour girl! On to pastures new!' answered Trixie.

'Why didn't you dance with that young Canadian when he asked you?'

'I couldn't!' whispered Jo, 'He was too young for me.'

Trixie thought she caught a hint of regret in Jo's voice.

'Jo, he only wanted to dance, not set up home, with you!' she said.

She thought she heard an intake of breath from the direction of Jo's bed but before she had a chance to question her, a voice from out of the darkness chided, 'Shut up, you two! Some of us want to sleep!'

'Sorry,' murmured Trixie. Nothing more came from Jo.

Trixie lay awake, listening to external night sounds. A wind had risen. The gentle brushing of the gorse bush outside the window on the glass sounded like a wooden floor being swept. It reminded her of the Virginia creeper being tossed by the wind against the tin roof of the outside lavatory at her mother's Gosport home. Her bedroom was at the back of the terraced house and overlooked the garden. She gave a little smile. It wouldn't be long before she'd be sleeping in her own bed, would it? And how lovely it would be to see her mum.

Trixie remembered how apprehensive she'd been about coming to Shandford Lodge to learn about forestry. These past weeks had been some of the happiest she'd ever known. The amount she'd learnt about trees seemed incredible, and the episode with Ben had taught her that some men were not as nice as they made out, so good had come from that experience, hadn't it?

And tomorrow? Tomorrow, she had heard, while playing the piano in the Yellow Duck where gossip abounded, they would find out what happened to the trees when they reached a sawmill.

Would they be ferried there by Alf and Lulubelle? Trixie knew how fortunate she was to have Alf keeping an eye on her and the other girls. It was quite usual, she had discovered, to travel to the places where they were working, or being taught, under their own steam, which meant walking, using the local bus service, or even borrowing one of the elderly bicycles that Shandford Lodge owned. When eventually she knew of her final destination, she might find it necessary to save up and buy a second-hand bicycle of her own, especially if her lodgings were some distance from her work. The future was certainly full of possibilities.

Trixie slipped her hand beneath her pillow. Her fingers found Cy's letters. She caressed the envelopes knowing that at some time, before she finally received them, Cy had touched the sheets of paper and licked the envelopes. It made her feel as though a little part of him was with her.

She slept.

Chapter Twenty-two

'I'm not hanging about here. I got places to go and work to do. You girls'll be all right with Lachlan. Take your things with you and I'll be back later.'

Trixie and the other girls jumped down from the cart, carrying their lunches, bags and spare clothing. She watched as Alf, Lulubelle and the cart turned in the forest clearing near a collection of wooden huts and trundled back along the sawdust-covered lane they'd just come from. She'd miss him and his fatherly advice; there seemed to be no end to the old man's knowledge about the forest. Then she brightened. Today they'd be learning something different, partly indoors, she hoped, away from the still air, the biting midges and the rain that threatened.

A square board proclaimed 'Lachlan MacLeod, Proprietor, Sawmill', and was nailed to a tree. The extreme and persistent high-pitched sound of sawing equipment made it difficult to hear anything else around her, and Trixie, after working in the forest, found it unnerving. A strong smell of wood shavings filled the air.

'What d'you think about this place?' Vi's voice was practically a shout.

'Noisy. We should have earplugs,' said Jo, pulling a headsquare from her coat pocket, shaking it out, folding it across her hair and tying it beneath her chin. Bits of sawdust flew about, competing with the midges for landing spots. Jo's eyes moved heavenwards. She sighed. 'Looks and feels like rain.'

'We'd better let someone know we're here,' said one of the girls Trixie knew vaguely.

'Shall we find the office?' chimed in another. Trixie agreed with everything that was being said, and as anything was better than becoming food for flying, biting objects, she took it upon herself to walk up to the first hut and bang on the door.

She realized immediately how futile that was, with the din of the whining saw.

The hut said 'Office', the white paint barely legible. She pushed against the door. Unlocked, it creaked open. Trixie took in a wood-burning stove, a desk covered with papers, a black Bakelite telephone, a chair, and a stack of metal filing cabinets. On top of the papers a large orange cat was curled up, fast asleep. It woke, raised its head, yawned, stared, considered she was of no consequence and went back to sleep.

Closing the door and looking back at the waiting girls she shrugged her shoulders and moved on.

Through the gaps between the buildings, she could see logs piled in huge stacks, lumber in pit-prop lengths, stacked high, cut into planks, reaching towards the heavens, lumber long enough to become telegraph poles. She recognized the Scots pine, the spruce. She'd never before seen so much wood in one place.

Despite the sound of the saw, which dominated everything, Trixie thought she could now make out voices. She started walking towards the biggest shed. It seemed to be where most of the noise was coming from but she paused to peer through the window of another hut, almost identical to the one marked 'Office'.

This one contained wooden benches and a couple of old chairs, a large table on which lay assorted bags, newspapers, items of men's clothing, a couple of flat caps and waterproof gear, and a large greasy-looking kettle. There was a stained stone sink with scummy crockery filling it to the brim. A lit stove and shelves with tea-making materials and assorted stained metal mugs completed the furnishings. Trixie guessed that hut was used for meal and tea-breaks. It, too, was deserted.

'Do you think they've forgotten we're coming today?'

Vi had appeared beside her. Trixie hadn't heard her approach. 'We're not special, Vi. The men are probably too busy to come looking for a load of girls they probably don't really want to be bothered with.'

'I bet it's the big shed they're in,' Vi answered, ignoring her sarcasm.

'Well, they aren't going to hear us shouting with all that noise going on, are they?'

Trixie began walking towards the other girls, who seemed content to stand around and chat, every so often slapping away midges. She turned back to Vi. 'We'll investigate together. I'll ask the others not to wander off.' There didn't seem to be much likelihood of them doing that, from the laughter and loud chatter coming from the group.

Trixie moved quickly to catch up with Vi, who had now reached the largest wooden building.

'There's windows but no door,' called Vi, frowning.

'I think we've arrived at the back of the shed,' shouted Trixie, 'but this is definitely where all the action is.' Her words fell on deaf ears because Vi had moved on and was now gesticulating wildly for her to join her.

Trixie tutted crossly, but when she caught up with Vi, she found her talking to a tall young fair-haired chap in overalls. He was wearing horn-rimmed spectacles that made him look like a professor.

'You don't make it easy to find a proper way into this place, or anyone for us to talk to, do you?' Trixie said snappily.

The man didn't reply to her questions but said warily, 'You're from the band of girls we're supposed to show around, aren't you? My name's Lachlan MacLeod.'

She nodded, then said airily, 'I was expecting someone older.' She was put out at having to search for him, but remembered seeing that name on the sawmill's sign.

'There is someone older. My dad,' he replied. 'I'm named after him but he's retired now and simply keeps a fatherly eye on things, not that he needs to. I grew up learning this business.' In a softer tone he added, 'And you play the piano in the Yellow Duck each night.' His next words tumbled over themselves, 'I've seen you in there. You're Trixie. You play really well. I like listening to you.'

Trixie stared at him. She wasn't sure how to deal with his sudden praise after being put in her place because she'd spoken out of turn. But one look at his crestfallen face told her he really was sorry that he hadn't been there to welcome them when they'd first arrived.

A big sigh escaped her. 'Thank you, I enjoy it. But our time at Shandford ends soon. We'll be moving on, so no more pub piano for me.'

'Oh!' was all he said. Trixie thought he looked disappointed. Patiently, she added, 'That's why we need to know what happens to the trees after we've cut them down. Some of us might be assigned to sawmills.'

Trixie felt Vi's elbow dig into her side, reminding her she, too, was present.

'This is Vi,' Trixie said. 'My workmate and friend. You met her but I don't suppose she told you who she was.'

Vi gave a small giggle. 'I'll go and get the girls, shall I?' She didn't wait for an answer but left with a smirk on her face.

Trixie could now see that the back of the building, which was the front, was the heart of the business and men were working at various jobs. From the lane it appeared that the buildings had been constructed the wrong way around.

The huge shed opened wide its enormous doors onto a railway track that snaked into the forest, disappearing out of sight beyond the trees. A huge flat-bed wagon piled high with timber was at a standstill on the line, needing either to be unloaded or sent somewhere else. A steam engine, gently huffing away, was uncoupled, standing on a nearby spur of track.

Lachlan said, 'The rail line dictates the loading area, the actual entrance. Some of my men are in the process of unloading stock and reversing the engine before we collect lumber from another supplier. Others are in the actual sawmill.'

Trixie thought of the backbreaking work involved in being part of a team of lumberjills who carried the heavy tree trunks they'd chopped down on their shoulders through the forest to a waiting trailer hitched to the back of a tractor, or to a patiently waiting team of horses. That was only the first part of the lumber's journey. There was much more to follow.

'So, the logs reach you via a road trailer, horse and cart, or,' she waved towards the track, 'train, and need to be unloaded again?'

He nodded. 'That's right. Loading, unloading it's a never-ending process. We need all the help we can get for this.' He nodded at the gaggle of girls, Vi and Jo leading them, approaching. He smiled and Trixie saw his teeth were large and very white. 'You've seen the posters, like "Your Country

Needs You". This country needs all the lumber we can provide. We deal mostly with large-diameter timber here – well, all kinds, really – and we also have prisoners of war from Shielhill camp working for us. They're a great help and there are some good men among them.'

Trixie felt drops of rain fall on her skin. 'You certainly have lots of timber stacked up,' she said.

'It's all at different stages of maturation,' he said. 'It needs to dry properly before it can be sent out. We air-dry the timber here. That is, stack the wood, expose it to the environment so that air can flow easily around it and allow the moisture in it to evaporate. That can take up to a year,' he said, pushing his spectacles up higher on the bridge of his nose. Trixie was sure his glasses hadn't moved and yet, somehow, she found the gesture strangely endearing. 'That's why there are so many stacks at various stages of the process and why we need an everlasting supply to keep up with demand,' he added.

Trixie was aware, from the way he was relating all these facts to her, that not only was he extremely proud of his sawmill, and the work that went on there, but probably thought she'd be able to repeat what he was telling her later to the rest of the girls.

'Will you look at that!' One of the girls was pointing

towards the inside of the shed where the huge circular saw, the cause of the ear-shattering noise, was spinning madly. Some of the men, mostly the younger ones, began wolf-whistling the girls and calling out suggestively, while the saw carried on slicing a tree trunk.

'Look at him, you mean,' said another girl, nodding towards one man in particular. Trixie realized he was the Italian who'd had some of the lumberjills drooling over him yesterday in the forest. His dark curly hair fell glossily across his forehead. His aquiline nose reminded Trixie of a carved statue and his full lips were raised mockingly at the corners. Trixie saw his eyes dart among the girls and rest briefly on Vi before he looked away. It was almost as if he was appraising her, she thought, but had found Vi wanting. Something about him reminded her of Ben Tate and Trixie shuddered.

'You'd better gather your girls up, Trixie, before the men get so excited it takes their attention away from what they're doing,' said Lachlan, with a broad smile. Then, loudly enough for them all to hear, and as if to remind them of his superiority, he shouted, 'I'm really sorry I wasn't around to meet you all but if you'd like to come with me to the tea hut I'll provide a cuppa, run over some of the facts I've been discussing with Trixie, then tell you about what we achieve in this sawmill and what I'll expect of you workwise.' Trixie breathed a sigh of relief that he was going to talk to the girls.

She heard a few groans at the word 'work'. Had they forgotten, she wondered, that they were here to see how a sawmill operated because it was likely some of them might end up employed in one?

She also realized Lachlan had decided she was in charge of the group. She thought now wasn't the time to tell him otherwise and a cup of tea would be just the thing to settle everyone, especially as they could get inside a hut, away from the midges and out of the rain that was now coming down heavily.

To whistles and cat calls from the men, the girls, some of them in their waterproofs, followed Lachlan and Trixie from the barn. Trixie, brushing away tiny flying objects, marvelled that midges disappeared during a light breeze, were hearty enough to withstand a shower, and enjoyed a party when the rain stopped.

With the rain lashing against the hut's windows, Trixie sipped her tea, so grateful for a hot drink that she didn't mind the chipped mug.

She looked across to the sink where a couple of the girls were showing off their domestic skills by wading through the dirty crockery, washing up as though it might be part of working in a sawmill. The hut was warm, dry and smelt of unwashed bodies but was a lot better than being out in the storm.

Jo sat on her own, staring out of a window at the rain coming down in sheets. Trixie wondered why she hadn't joined her and Vi, but there were times when Jo preferred to be alone and perhaps this was one of them. It hadn't escaped Trixie's notice that Jo had been extremely interested in the sawmill and what went on there.

'He likes you,' said Vi, shattering Trixie's thoughts.

'Shut up! You don't know what you're talking about!' snapped Trixie. Then she tutted and dismissed Vi's words with a shake of her head.

'You can tut all you want but I got eyes and I know what I see,' said Vi, not at all perturbed.

Trixie glanced across the room to where Lachlan MacLeod was sitting at the table poring over some papers. He must have felt her eyes upon him for he suddenly looked up. He smiled. He had an honest, comfortably lived-in face, she thought. She looked away but not until she'd returned his smile.

'I don't like sawmills,' said Trixie.

'That don't mean to say you can't like the men who own them,' Vi returned.

'He must be a nice bloke – that cat hasn't left his side. Cats aren't wrong – they know good people from bad ones.'

'Has anyone ever told you you talk some right drivel at times?' Trixie said. She remembered seeing the cat in the office, yet it had deserted that dry hut, braving the elements, to find Lachlan and was now sitting on the table among the detritus, washing itself. 'I hope there's letters waiting for me when we get back to the Lodge,' she said.

'Letters from Cy?'

Trixie smiled at Vi. 'Who else?' She sighed, then drank some tea. 'Don't you have anyone, Vi?' It wasn't that she'd forgotten the bruising Vi had tried so hard to disguise on their first meetings but there was so much she wanted to understand about her friend and why she was reluctant to talk about her past life in Gosport.

'I don't want anyone!' The four words were practically toxic. 'And I saw that Italian, who thinks he's God's gift to women, eyeing me, thinking I'd certainly be up for it. Afterwards I'd be spat out before he moved on to someone else.'

Trixie stared at Vi. 'I'm sorry,' she said. 'I didn't mean—'

Vi didn't let her finish. 'Forget it,' she said. Her voice was softer now. 'I know you mean well. But some men . . . I just happen to think that man sitting at the table *is* a good one.'

'You're probably right,' said Trixie. She swallowed the last of her tea, put down the mug and continued looking out of the window at the tumultuous rain. 'I don't think we'll get much more of a tour of this place, today, do you?'

Almost as though he'd read her mind, Lachlan shuffled through the papers he held, then stood up. 'I'm sorry your first visit to my sawmill is a wash-out, and not just because of the rain!' There were a few laughs and amazingly the group had stopped chattering to find seats and listen to him.

'My men can go on working in the sawmill during bad weather but they'll not get much done if we're all in there together. Due to the severity of the rain, I can't take you on a proper tour. However, I can,' he moved his spectacles further up the bridge of his nose, 'explain what happens to the timber before it leaves here.'

A few groans were heard but he quickly added, 'I have contacted the Lodge and shortly they'll be expecting you back at Shandford, transported in one of my lorries.' He paused, looked around the room and added, 'I told them not to send the horse and cart. It's much too open to the elements. I hope that meets with your satisfaction?'

The noise of clapping and happy voices assured him it was.

'I like the sound of that,' whispered Vi.

'Let's get on, then, shall we?' Lachlan said. 'The saw we were using today is called a head saw, or primary saw. It cuts the logs into cants and flitches, or unfinished planks. These are then trimmed, edged, planed—'

He was interrupted by Jo, who asked, 'Is that after the logs are dried, or before?'

Lachlan looked extremely pleased that she was listening and had taken in enough information to ask that question. 'May I have your name?' he asked.

'I'm Jo,' she answered.

'Well, Jo, that happens after drying. Dried wood shouldn't buckle or warp when it's to be used for furniture, other household items, doors, frames, fencing, construction. You get the idea?'

Some of the girls nodded, including Jo. Lachlan again looked pleased.

'We use different saws for different jobs. Generally, the wider the blade, the straighter the cut.'

Again, Jo's voice was heard. 'What about the sawdust? I see it gets everywhere. Do you use it for anything?'

Lachlan smiled openly at her. 'Yes, Jo, we do. We turn the sawdust into wood pulp and board. It's used in the making of lino and Bakelite, which as you all know is what our telephones are made of. Animal bedding, powering heat in furnaces and kilns, it has many uses and we waste nothing here – but it does tend to blow about a lot!' The girls laughed. Lachlan opened his mouth to continue but the sound of a vehicle's horn cut him off.

Outside, through the window, Trixie could see a lorry, engine turning over. It was obviously waiting for them.

'I guess that's it, ladies,' said Lachlan, rising from his chair. 'Outside is your lift back, so the sooner you board, the sooner you'll arrive at base. If time permits perhaps another visit might possibly be arranged. Goodbye, everyone.'

Trixie, gathering her things together, saw Lachlan approach Jo. They spoke briefly.

'Wonder what he wants with her?' asked Vi, her voice tinged with nosiness.

'We'll find out later,' said Trixie. She decided it wouldn't be prudent to interrupt them while they were talking so she shuffled towards the door, ready to climb, with the other girls, into the back of the lorry. As she reached the doorway, Lachlan called, 'Bye, Trixie. I'll see you in the Yellow Duck before you leave.'

Trixie waved and smiled, and saw that Jo too was joining the crush to leave. Her face was inscrutable.

What, Trixie wondered, was going on?

Chapter Twenty-three

He opened his eyes to darkness and the sound of an engine throbbing. The smell sickened him. He was lying on bare boards. Cy turned his head and the vomit gushed out of his mouth. He took another breath. He could taste sweat, faeces, the stale stink of rot and death. He turned his head and retched again, feeling the warmth of his emptied stomach swirl against his ear, his head, his neck.

The stink wasn't simply of his own making: he'd merely added to it. He could hear whimpering, low cries of suffering. Confused, he tried to think, to remember. The heat was oppressive. His throat was parched. With a dry tongue he attempted to lick his lips and felt sore, flaking skin.

'You're back with us, then?' It was Hobo's voice, hoarse, almost unrecognizable, but it was his friend. Cy felt his head being raised; he was able to peer into the dullness. Overhead he could make out wooden girders, beams intersecting them. Men lay on shelf-like wooden structures, some moving, others not. Most, like him and Hobo, occupied the floor. The engine was still reverberating. He thought he might be in the hold of a ship. Was that possible?

What he saw was misery. Men, bloodied, burnt, covered with oil, packed together, frightened eyes staring into the gloom, men twisting, writhing, reminding him of worms in a bait box.

This wasn't real, Cy thought. It couldn't be. He was in the middle of some hideous dream. Yes, that had to be it. He managed now, unaided, to turn his head, to see Hobo's face. And the livid, weeping, dirty red gash that ran from beneath an eye to his chin.

'I got in the way of a bayonet,' rasped Hobo. His lips, too, were parched, cracked and Cy saw the effort it took for him to talk. His hand went to his breast pocket. 'I still got my buddy, though.' Cy knew he meant his harmonica.

His own hand twisted and wriggled towards his own breast pocket and he felt the papery softness there. It didn't matter what condition it was in. It was Trixie's photograph. Trixie, his girl. Memories were returning. He couldn't expect her picture to be the same, not after his stint in the water, but she was still with him.

He looked at Hobo. 'You pushed me.' More memories came rushing in. He'd had a life preserver, hadn't he? 'You saved my life.'

'And got you into this shit,' Hobo said. Cy saw the brightness of his eyes that, without moisture, couldn't make a tear.

'Does it hurt?'

Hobo would know what he meant. 'Only when I fuckin' laugh!' his friend returned.

Cy felt vast relief. No matter what had happened his friend was the same, a rock, his rock. Hobo slipped his arm away from Cy's neck. 'Sorry,' he said. 'I need to move.'

'Is there water?' Cy's throat burnt.

'No water.'

It took a little while for him to assimilate the answer.

'Where are we?'

'We're on a Japanese boat. In the hold.' He paused, and Cy heard Hobo try to swallow to enable him to speak more clearly. 'In the Great War they called these hell ships. Never thought I'd end up in one. We're prisoners. Lot of men in here. We've been here a couple of days and you've been out of it . . .'

'Out of it?'

'Unconscious. I think something hit you in the sea but a Jap pulled you out of the water.' Hobo stared at him. 'Don't you remember?'

'No.' He stretched a hand to his head.

'Jap said you'd live. Dumped us in this cargo ship. *Havana Maru*. Little air, no ventilation, no food or water and lying in our own piss and dysentery. We're the lucky ones. Six from USS *Ready*. Other guys been here longer. Some dead.' Hobo's voice weakened, cracked.

'You're exhausted,' said Cy. God, he needed a drink. Even to wet his mouth somehow would help.

'The Japs on board are bastards.'

Cy tried to incline his head to hear Hobo better. 'Where are we?' he asked him.

Hobo's eyes met his. Cy knew that look. He didn't know. 'Where're we going?'

There was the merest shake of Hobo's head. 'It don't matter,' he whispered. 'We'll be attacked by Allied subs, ships or aircraft before we get there. They won't know this Japanese ship's full of prisoners. Friendly fire,' he said. 'It'll sink us. Be over then, all over.'

'Here she is! Here's the lassie!' Donnie's voice rang through the crowd the moment Trixie, with Big Al's help, disentangled herself from the blackout curtain covering the entrance to the Yellow Duck.

'Trixie,' said Big Al, 'before Donnie grabs you, I'd like to say how I appreciate you and your friend Vi playing a big part in getting me this job. There's nae much work around here, unless you're in the forces. It's good to be of use again.'

He didn't get to say any more for Donnie had pushed through the drinkers in the smoky bar and enveloped Trixie in his arms. 'Got a surprise for you,' he bellowed and, noticing her friends, added, 'The more the merrier!'

Trixie looked back at Al, winked and followed that up with a smile.

Then, closely followed by Hen, Jo and Vi, she allowed herself to be led through the throng towards the bar where Donnie called to his barmaid who was serving a customer, 'Sort these lassies out with drinks when you're finished there, Fiona.' Then he lifted up the wooden bar flap with one hand and hauled Trixie through to the back, leaving her three friends on the customer side.

'What's going on?' gasped Trixie. 'I came down to play the piano for you, same as usual.'

'Aha!' said Donnie. 'That's as may be and I'm happy about it, but I'm aware you'll soon be gone from Shandford Lodge and you've aye been an asset to this place over the last few weeks. I wanted to do something to show my appreciation, lassie.'

Fiona set glasses of their preferred drinks on the counter in front of Trixie, Hen, Vi and Jo.

'But you letting me play means so much to me.'

'Wheesht!' he said, silencing her, then much louder, because the customers' noise had heightened once more, 'Listen, everyone!'

Donnie picked up a dimpled glass mug and banged it on the bar to gain attention. The liquid in the full glasses on the counter shot into the air, then wetly settled again. When he was satisfied everyone was looking towards him, he put a hand beneath the counter and took out a long parcel untidily wrapped in newspaper. 'Open it, lassie,' he demanded.

It didn't take much opening as the crumpled paper practically fell away to reveal a glass-covered wooden plaque that she didn't have time to study because, overflowing with emotion, Donnie suddenly crushed her to his apron enveloping her in the smells of beer, food, sweat and, strangely, a hint of men's cologne. He whispered to her gruffly, 'I want to hang it at the back of the bar so people will ask me what it means,' he said, with great pride in his voice. 'You'll not be forgotten in this place.'

He let her go and again banged on the counter with the beer mug. All eyes, including Trixie's, were on Donnie as he bellowed, 'This young lass will shortly be leaving us, as will the current intake of lumberjills completing their training at the Lodge.' He paused and cheers erupted. When the noise abated, he turned to Trixie and said, in a theatrical voice quite unlike his own, 'I present this to you in return for the happiness you've brought me and Fiona.' Trixie took a quick glance at Fiona whose face was blank. Undeterred Donnie carried on, 'I'll read the dedication in case ye lot cannae see the words from that side of the bar.'

The plaque left Trixie's hands as Donnie held it in front of his eyes. '"Dedicated to Trixie Smith. The lumberjill who released this threepenny joey and brought back music to the Yellow Duck."'

And now Trixie could see that the inscription was burnt in neat copperplate script onto the wood at the bottom of the frame and dated 'September 1942'. The coin had been polished so the silver glittered as it nestled beneath the glass on a bed of black velvet. Queen Victoria's crown was surrounded by its wreath of oak leaves.

The plaque had been made with enormous care. The thought behind the crafting of the plaque was making Trixie feel even more emotional as she thought back to how she had tried to play the piano and the thud-thud of the jammed notes spoilt the tune. She remembered borrowing a hairpin from Hen and eventually, painstakingly, releasing the trapped coin from between the ivory keys.

She wanted to speak but the words wouldn't come.

Trixie looked towards the piano. Making music was her love, her salvation. It made her feel happy, yet this dear man was congratulating and thanking her for it. 'Thank you,' she finally mumbled. 'Thank you.' And promptly burst into tears.

It took quite a while for Trixie, with help from Vi, Jo and Hen, to calm down enough to ask Donnie what song he'd like her to play that evening.

'"Amapola". It's my favourite,' he said, his face red as a beetroot. Trixie wasn't sure if he was blushing because he'd told her he liked the song, or if it was the effort of nailing the plaque at the back of the bar where it would be permanently on show. 'But make it the first tune you play as I wouldnae like Fiona to start serving the wee bits of shortbread and sandwiches I had her make especially for tonight and interrupting everything while you're in the middle of it!'

'Food as well? You're so kind, Donnie,' she said.

Before she made her way to the piano she asked, 'Why's the coin called a "joey"?'

'Aha!' Donnie said, 'Probably only a Scot could tell you that. It's all tied up to the thrifty streak we're supposed to be known for.' He laughed. 'A groat, fourpence, went out of circulation around 1830. The physician and Scottish Tory MP Joseph Hume campaigned for its reintroduction because he was fed up with London cabbies saying they'd no change and keeping the remainder of a sixpence as a tip. The new groat became known as a joey, after Hume, and the name passed on to the silver coin we know today.'

'Fancy that,' Trixie said. 'I've always wondered.' She took a sip of her drink. Already Vi and Jo had bagged chairs near the piano and were chatting with some of the regulars. Hen was talking earnestly to a sailor in uniform, who was hanging on her every word.

'Now tell me, lassie,' asked Donnie, 'do you know the date you'll be leaving? I've heard the authorities are giving you travel warrants to spend a few days with your families before you're sent to your final destinations.'

Trixie shrugged. 'We could have them any day soon,' she said. 'Can I ask you something?'

'Aye.'

Amid the noise, Trixie heard the persistent tap-tap of a coin on the bar top and Donnie, frowning, said, 'Ask me whatever you want after I've served this customer who cannae wait!'

Within moments he was beside her again and Trixie asked, as if there had been no interruption, 'Why is this place called the Yellow Duck?'

He grinned at her. 'I believe you're asking because

ducklings are yellow as chicks, lassie, but when adult, become white?'

'Yes! That's it exactly,' she answered.

'Fiona!' he bellowed. 'Can you cope for a minute or two while I tell a story to this lassie?' Fiona, who had both elbows on the bar and was chatting, looked over and nodded. Trixie turned away fearing a glare the barmaid might throw in her direction.

'Good lass!' Donnie called to Fiona.

'You're going away, but I wouldnae like you to tell.'

'My lips are sealed,' she said.

'Good, because I cannae have people think I'm a sentimental fool!'

Trixie took a swallow of her drink while Donnie began, 'I come from a small place in the north of Scotland called Bettyhill.' His eyes seemed to mist at the name. 'In Sutherland, there's no many people and everyone knows everyone else. I'm the son of a crofter and when I came of age, I married Jeannie McKay . . .' He must have seen her raise her eyebrows at Jeannie's surname for he quickly added, 'McKay is a common clan name, so every other person has that name in Sutherland.' Trixie nodded and he carried on, 'She was my childhood sweetheart. I came from a big family but Jeannie was an only child. My Jeannie was so full of love for everyone and everything she couldnae bear to swat a fly, and when she found wee creatures inside the house, she'd never tread on them but would carry them outside.' He looked away but already Trixie noticed he had tears in his eyes. 'We were happy in our croft. Sheep on the hillside and ducks flapping about the burn running at the bottom of the wee house. Aye, Jeannie loved those ducks, always shooshing them oot the house, mind. She loved it that the wee bits of yellow fluffy ducklings changed to the purest white of adult ducks.' He sighed, 'But came a year, one didnae change colour. She grew into a yellow adult. Damn duck!'

He might have sworn an oath about the duck but Trixie could tell that talking about it brought back soul-stirring memories for Donnie.

'This duck, she called it Daisy, followed my Jeannie everywhere – it would have slept in the bedroom, if I hadnae put my foot down.' Donnie gave a long sigh. 'She didnae fall for a bairn for a long time, and when she did, we were the happiest couple in Bettyhill. Of course, Daisy had long gone to the farm in the sky by then.'

Then Trixie saw him do something quite unusual. He picked up a glass and a bottle of whisky. When he'd poured a dram, he said, '*Uisge beatha*, the water of life.' He drank the contents straight down in one gulp and set the glass on the bar. Until then Trixie had thought he was a teetotaller. It was obvious he was finding it difficult to confide in her. 'I dinna ken you've been to Sutherland?'

Trixie shook her head.

'It's nothing but mountains that roll to the sea, lochs that sparkle blue as the sky. No trees, because the wind willnae let them grow except on the estates where they're planted and cultivated. But the few people who live there are the hardiest and kindest because they need to depend on each other.' He paused, then began again: 'Snow was on the ground when the bairn was born. Ma neighbour couldnae get through to the midwife. The wee bairn died first and Jeannie soon after.'

Trixie felt herself go cold all over. Donnie's voice was low as he continued, 'I left after the funeral, simply shut the door and come away, leaving my loves buried together in the churchyard by the sea. After a long while I ended up here.

'There's never been another lass who matched up to my Jeannie, but when I saw this pub for sale, not called the Dirty Duck, not the Duck and Drake, not even the Yellow Duckling, I knew it was ma Jeannie's way of telling me to stop my wandering and put down roots. So I took her canny advice and I'm happy. Well, as happy as I can be without her at my side.' He wiped his hand across his eyes, then placed his hand to his heart. 'But ma Jeannie lives on in here,' he said. 'And now you know the story of the Yellow Duck! I didnae name this place but Fate brought me here.'

For a moment she stared at him. Then she said, 'You really did love her, didn't you?'

'Aye, I did,' he answered. 'The first love is the deepest.'

Trixie leant forward and kissed his grizzled cheek. Then she sat down on the piano stool and began to play 'Amapola'. And as she did, the music spoke to her, reminding her of how fortunate she was.

Chapter Twenty-four

She couldn't sleep. So much was going on in Trixie's mind that she was tempted to get out of bed and wander down to the washroom for a mug of water. But she really didn't want to wake any of the other girls in the hut who'd no doubt worked much harder than she had today and needed sleep.

She turned over in her bed and the crackle of Cy's letters beneath her pillow made her smile. He and his written messages were such a comfort to her. She'd never had so much correspondence from anyone before and, although they had met only that one time, she felt she was getting to know the real person inside him.

Cy's childhood, his upbringing, his whole lifestyle were completely different from hers. Their one similarity, that they were born to mothers who fiercely loved them, seemed to cement their love for each other. She never felt unsure about writing what was in her heart. It was truly wonderful to love and be loved in return.

He'd said he wanted to take her to America, to his home in New Orleans. At first she was thrilled by this. Now she wasn't so sure.

'Can't you sleep?' The soft words came from Jo in the bed next to hers.

'Too much going on in my head,' she answered.

'D'you want to pull your coat over your nightie and come outside to walk with me? It's not raining but I expect it's wet underfoot.'

Trixie didn't have to think too hard about her answer.

Moments later, in wellington boots and thick greatcoats, part of their uniform, they were congratulating themselves on escaping the hut without a telling-off for disturbing anyone. The night was cold and clear with a slight breeze that kept the midges away, and the stars hung like diamonds in the sky. Arm in arm the two friends wandered in the moonlight towards the trees, the pine needles crackling beneath their feet.

'I noticed earlier a Douglas fir had fallen,' said Jo. 'If it hasn't been cut and hauled away, it'll give us somewhere to sit.'

Trixie was well aware of Jo's solitary rambles in the woods

about the grounds of the Lodge. It was not often she liked company.

After a few minutes' walking, watching out for stray low branches or brambles that might trip them, and listening to the cry of a vixen calling for a mate, Jo motioned towards a large tree that lay with its roots exposed. 'There's the snag,' she said.

'What did you call it?' Trixie hadn't heard the word before.

'Snag,' said Jo. 'A tree that's fallen spontaneously and been allowed to decompose naturally. Though I doubt this tree will be left here.'

'Didn't know I'd left my bed for another lesson about trees.' Trixie laughed.

Jo sat down on the gnarled bark. 'Don't take any notice of me,' she said. 'I've done a lot of extra reading on working for the Forestry Commission. I couldn't bear it if I got turned down and was sent back to Gosport permanently after our training.'

'It never really entered my head that some of us might not make the grade,' Trixie said. She stared at the trees about them. 'That's a Sitka spruce, and there's a Scots pine.' She nodded into the near darkness.

'Pack it in, clever clogs, you'll pass with flying colours,' Jo said. She fumbled in the pockets of her thick coat and drew out two bottles of Coca-Cola. She passed one to Trixie, who looked at her in utter amazement. Ignoring Trixie, Jo returned to her pocket for a bottle opener. 'I've developed a taste for the stuff. Thirsty work, walking,' she added. 'Brenda gets it from her Canadian boyfriend and I did a swap with some clothing coupons.'

Trixie drank thankfully and sighed as Jo said, 'Are you going to tell me what's bothering you or are we going to sit here in the dark until morning, talking about trees?'

'All right,' Trixie said. 'I'm head over heels in love with a man I've known less than a month. He feels the same way about me. We've barely kissed more than a couple of times but I feel I know him inside out. He's asked me to go and stay with him in New Orleans when the war's over. I've done a lot of reading up on the discrimination against Black people in America and we would never be allowed to be together like any other couple.'

'Has he asked you to marry him?'

'No, not yet. But because of the war everything seems to be moving so fast that I feel he soon might.' Trixie gave a sigh that seemed to rock her whole body.

'If he returns to England, there's nothing stopping you two getting married here,' Jo said. 'There will, no doubt, be people who'll turn their noses up, probably gossip about you, but those kinds of folks aren't worth bothering about. Times are changing. At least you'll be together.'

'You'll think I'm stupid to be worrying about this . . .' Tears welled in Trixie's eyes.

'I think you're sensible looking at problems that might arise before they do.'

Jo pulled Trixie around so they were facing each other. 'But you have to grab happiness, when it comes, with both hands. You never know when it'll be taken from you . . . Please, please, Trixie, don't complicate the present by thinking too hard about the future. Enjoy each day now! This bloody war has to run its course and who knows what the end of it might bring?'

Jo folded her arms around Trixie, whose thoughts were whirling. She could smell smoke in Jo's hair; the Yellow Duck had reeked of cigarettes tonight. Then her mind cleared and she disentangled her reasoning.

'And that answer is what makes you so bleedin' clever, isn't it, Jo?'

Jo laughed. Then she put her finger to her lips and said softly, 'Ssh!'

Trixie could see Jo was listening hard to the rustling sounds coming from mounds of nearby leaves. Snuffling noises followed, then stopped. Trixie held her breath.

Whatever was moving on the forest floor was very close. Jo spotted the creature before she did. The long snout and the white stripe down its face showed up clearly in the moonlight. The large badger stared at Trixie, not sure if she was friend or foe. Trixie was entranced. Her mother, when Trixie next wrote, would find it difficult to believe she had been so close. Then the sturdy creature took fright and scuttled quickly away.

'That was a badger, wasn't it?' Trixie needed confirmation.

Jo laughed, 'Yes, it was. I can tell you've not seen one before.'

'No, there's not many in Gosport.'

'Actually, you're wrong. Brockhurst is named after badgers but the ones living there are clever enough to keep away from us humans. When the streets are quiet and night falls, that's when the animals appear. Not only badgers and foxes, deer too.'

'Really?'

'Really,' confirmed Jo. 'I've often walked late at night. It's another world in Gosport, after dark.' She nodded to where the badger had disappeared. 'And it's said if a badger crosses your path, as that one has, it will bring good luck. All the more reason for you to accept your good fortune now and let the future take care of itself.'

Trixie realized that Jo, whom she'd thought of as quiet and often moody, was probably battling her own demons, which had followed her from Gosport. Shandford Lodge, with its rules and regulations, the hard manual and mental work the lumberjills were set, was helping to heal Jo. And not just Jo, herself too. It wasn't only her body that had changed. Yes, she was physically stronger now, after chopping down trees and hauling logs, but she had also been taught to rationalize her thinking, to decide which was the right way to approach problems. Before, she'd done the first thing that had come into her head. She smiled to herself, remembering how she'd blithely copied the left-handed Maisie when being taught brashing.

What was it Jo had said to her? 'Accept your good fortune and let the future take care of itself.' Trixie could go on worrying, or she could accept her own motto of 'What goes around comes around', couldn't she? Because, first, this war needed to be won.

Trixie watched Jo's eyes searching the undergrowth for the badger's re-appearance. 'You love being in the forest, don't you?' She didn't wait for an answer. 'It's not just the actual work, it's the trees, the wildness, isn't it?'

'You've discovered my secret, then?'

'Not all of it, but maybe some day I will.' Trixie's words

made Jo frown, but she carried on talking, 'You couldn't sleep either tonight, and I'm guessing it wasn't because of all the fuss about me at the Yellow Duck, was it? So now it's your turn to talk.'

Jo sighed. 'You're right. My problem is, I don't think I want to leave this place.'

Trixie's forehead creased. 'But isn't this just a stepping stone to moving on? I know sometimes the work we've been given has been hurried and incomplete. I took that as a sign we'd find out more when we were actually doing the job. Some young women who sign up are sent straight out into the forests and sawmills without instruction. At least we know what to expect. The lectures have been helpful, though.'

'No!' interrupted Jo, 'That's not what I mean. I feel I'm up to doing the work, but I don't want to leave this place.'

That made Trixie think. She remembered how Lachlan MacLeod had called Jo back to talk to her. 'You've not fallen for the sawmill owner?'

For a moment there was silence, then Jo shook her head. 'No! Definitely not. If he fancied any one of us, it was you. Though, if I did stay here, I'd be assured of a job. He picked up on my interest in what was going on.'

'You wouldn't want to work in that noisy place.'

'It's not noisy all the time, silly.' She paused. 'He needs someone in the office, and I can type. He needs someone who understands the business, and I'm a quick learner. Most of all, I won't have to leave this place.'

'So, he did sort of offer you a job? I don't understand why you're not excited about moving on to pastures new, to more exciting times, to new experiences.'

'I don't want more changes in my life than I can cope with. I came away from Gosport to forget, to start a new life, and it's within my grasp.'

Trixie saw, in the moonlight, the pain on Jo's face. There was something else, too. Something she couldn't define that made Jo look even wearier and much, much older.

As though reading her mind, Jo added, 'And please don't ask me to come back down south with you, before I make up my own mind. I have no desire to go back to Gosport. There's nothing there for me now.'

Chapter Twenty-five

Trixie opened the brown-paper parcel her mother had sent in the post. There were no letters for her today.

Some of the girls were lounging on their beds talking, and Brenda's gramophone was playing 'Summertime' by Billie Holiday, which was quite cheering as it was cold outside. Trixie had sat through a lecture on tree diseases, which she'd found informative though the speaker's voice was monotonous. She'd made notes, in case she ever needed the information.

She wound up the parcel's string and put it safely in the drawer of her bedside locker. It didn't do to waste anything that might come in handy. War shortages had taught her that. Waste not, want not.

She picked up the tin of Condor pipe tobacco. Her mother was brilliant! Trixie had walked into every local shop that purported to sell cigarettes and tobacco only to be told, 'Sorry, sold out!'

She wanted to buy Alf something she knew he'd appreciate as a thank-you for his kindness to her during her training period. There was a short note tucked in with the tin she'd asked Rose to track down and buy:

We're looking forward to seeing you, and your friends. I'm counting the days. Des managed to get this off a "friend" who owed him a favour. Don't you dare offer to pay him for it, he'll get very cross! The shops and houses opposite the Criterion picture house had a direct hit last night. Longing to hear all your news about Cy and the forestry work. See you soon.

Mum X

Trixie sniffed away a tear. Her mum was well aware that out of the forty-six shillings she was paid per week during the training period, the authorities subtracted board and lodging. Hen did marginally better, with fifty shillings a week, but board money was still deducted. Thank God, she thought, Shandford Lodge provided almost everything they needed and they'd certainly never gone hungry. She could buy personal things in the village, except when, due to the war shortages, the shops had little in stock.

She thought about the cottages and shops opposite the Criterion. Her mother hadn't said whether there were any casualties. She'd almost forgotten what it was like to have enemy aircraft coming over constantly. Her mother usually kept her up to date with what was happening in Gosport but she didn't dwell on it and for this Trixie was grateful. She didn't doubt that after the four weeks she'd been here in Scotland, she would find Gosport greatly disfigured by German bombers when she went home.

'Had a parcel?'

Trixie looked up to see Hen smiling at her. Her cheeks were rosy from the cold wind, she wore her work jumper and jodhpurs, and she smelt of pine trees. She looked like an angel, thought Trixie. She wondered if Hen knew how pretty she was, then immediately dismissed that idea. Of course she did. Didn't every man's eyes swerve towards her whenever they set foot out of the Lodge?

'You've not taken to smoking that?' Hen waved towards the tobacco. Now she was frowning at Trixie.

Trixie laughed. 'Don't be daft! It's a goodbye gift for Alf.'

'Of course! You being his favourite protégée!'

Trixie sighed, why did Hen sometimes use words the rest

of them had to think about? But Hen had had an entirely different education from her, and being sarcastic wasn't one of her failings.

'You don't think I'm being silly, then?' Trixie asked.

'Good Lord, no! I think he'll be pleased as Punch.'

Trixie smiled with relief. 'I need to get hold of an apple or something for Lulubelle. I can't leave her out. You know how Alf dotes on his horse.'

'I've got apples.'

Trixie looked at Hen in amazement.

'Cast your mind back to when we came up on the train and I handed apples around? I've still got some left.' Hen was smiling at her.

'But that was nearly four weeks ago. Surely they've gone bad by now.'

'Not these. Remember I told you we had orchards at the back of the house in Western Way?' She didn't wait for an answer. 'My father supplies shops in Alverstoke with fruit. Our apples, kept at the right temperature, last for ages. I have two left and they certainly won't give Lulubelle a stomach ache.'

Hen jumped up from where she'd been sitting on her bed and went to her locker. From the bottom drawer she took out a cardboard box. Inside were two paper-wrapped parcels. She unrolled one and out fell a fresh apple. Trixie picked it up, it was unblemished and looked so good she almost took a bite out of it.

'I've grown up at home eating an apple a day, which keeps the doctor away,' she parroted. 'We keep apples cold, and it's only warm in this hut when the stove is lit. But my locker is ideal for storage,' she said. Hen had unwrapped the remaining apple and handed it to Trixie.

'Are you sure? It's very kind of you.'

'We're going home soon and then I can eat all the apples I want. When are you going to give the gifts to Alf? Better wrap the apples up again if—'

'Soon as possible,' said Trixie. 'I don't want to leave it for too long in case I have to leave without seeing him.'

'Alf's cart was outside the Lodge a while ago when I came in. I think he's gone to see Maud Styles.' She moved towards the door, opened it and looked out. A draught of cold air swept in. 'The cart's still there,' she said excitedly. 'If you're going now, can I come with you?'

How could Trixie say no? She joined Hen at the door. Then she paused, looked at the apples and the tin in her hand. 'Do you think I should wrap everything?'

'Don't be daft! He might have gone by then!'

Of course Hen was right. Besides, she had only the brown

paper, with her name and address printed all over it, that her mother had used to post the tobacco to her.

The old man was climbing onto the cart when Hen called to him. He sat down on his seat wearily, stared at them running towards him, and waved.

Lulubelle was snorting in the cold air, warm breath steaming from her nostrils. She stepped from one hoof to the other, as if she was dancing on the spot.

'Hello,' he said. 'To what do I owe this pleasure?'

Trixie stood looking up at him. This might be one of the last times she'd ever see him. She swallowed, choked with emotion. He'd been so kind to her, patiently answering her questions.

Lulubelle whinnied and the noise jolted some sense into Trixie. That and the dig in the ribs from Hen.

'I – I just wanted to say thank you.' Her words were hesitant and said in a small voice that could hardly be heard.

'What she means is,' said Hen, taking over in a clear, firm tone, 'that she will miss you and she'd like you to accept these small gifts in appreciation for all you've taught her.' Then Hen put out her arm and nudged Trixie's hands containing the apples and tobacco so that Trixie raised them and Alf could bend down easily and take them from her. He stared at the bounty and gently touched one of the apples.

His voice was like scraped rust as he said, 'Oh, my dearie, you've thought about my Lulubelle. I thank you kindly. You're a very special young lady to remember this is my favourite smoke. Difficult to get hold of, too.' He swallowed and blinked. He laid the gifts beside him on the seat and wiped a hand across his eyes. 'The pair of you are a credit to this place.' His eyes met Trixie's and she saw the glint of tears. 'You'll do well, girlie,' he said. 'You've got a feeling for the trees.' He jiggled the reins and Lulubelle stopped dancing on the spot. 'Just you remember to go on using your right hand,' he said, and smiled.

Trixie's mind flashed back to the brashing when she'd tried to copy Maisie who was left-handed. She looked into his eyes and saw the kindness in them. She knew Alf had exhausted his repertoire of thanks and good wishes and was now as eager to be on his way as she was. He raised his eyes skywards and said, 'You'd best get inside, looks like rain.'

Trixie and Hen watched until the cart turned out of the main gate. Hen slipped her arm through Trixie's. 'C'mon, it's freezing, let's get inside. It'll soon be time to eat.'

'Thanks,' said Trixie. 'I sort of dried up, didn't know what to say.'

Hen grinned at her. 'You did all right,' she said.

'Do you think he was pleased?' asked Trixie.

Hen nodded. 'I think he was very moved,' she said.

Chapter Twenty-six

Cy blinked as the brightness of the light from the opened hatch cut through the darkness, hurting his eyes. He shook Hobo's arm hoping he'd succumbed to sleep, not death.

Cy squinted and managed to fix his eyes on the silhouette stepping down the stairway. A rush of air from the bright opening made his head whirl with the unexpected freshness. A second figure followed.

'Water! Please, water!' The plea came from a figure lying at the foot of the steps.

Both men wore Japanese drab uniforms, caps, trousers with puttees wrapped to their boots, and carried rifles with long bayonets attached.

The two guards now stood in the hold among the dying prisoners. The first looked down at the man who had asked for water. Then he jabbed down hard several times with his bayonet. The man's flesh tore and blood ran.

Cy's heart was sickened. He knew that unless he desired a similar fate, he must do and say nothing.

The guard kicked the prisoner aside and, in halting English, announced, 'You all climb to deck and wait. You leave nobody in here.'

He turned and followed the second man back up the stairs. Cy wondered why two guards were needed to impart that message and to mindlessly injure a dying man. He realized that if his reasoning was functioning it meant he still had some of his wits about him.

The hatch door had been left open. Cy hauled himself to a kneeling position and, in the shaft of sunlight dropping into the stinking hold, breathed deeply of the fresh air. Then he grabbed Hobo and dragged him into the square of light.

'We're to get out of this hole.' His voice shook. 'C'mon.'

Hobo opened his eyes with difficulty. They were crusted slits in his ruined face.

Cy allowed him a couple of breaths and a hint of the sun on his cheeks, then took Hobo's arm and pinched the flesh, hard. Men were moving like slugs towards the ladder.

'Ow! What the fuck . . .'

'So, you're in there, then?' Cy watched Hobo rub his arm,

at first weakly, then with more vigour. His face, which until now had been the colour of putty except for the wound, had an angry glow.

'Take it easy!' This time Cy was rasping at a fellow prisoner whose feet were staggering, treading on bodies to reach the ladder, the escape route.

The man, in ragged clothing, hauled a dead body that hit each metal step on the way to air and sunlight. In the cloying heat, disturbed insects flew about. Cy swatted at his face. The noise from the engines had stopped. He could hear voices up on deck.

The man, pulling the cadaver, breathing hard, must have felt Cy's eyes on him. 'Them bastards want this hold cleared. They won't touch dead bodies.'

In a quavering voice, Hobo agreed. 'He's right. Best not go empty-handed. Them Japs are fond of their bayonets.' He raised himself to his knees. 'You American?'

The man with the corpse paused. 'Canadian flier from Leuchars in Scotland. Ben Tate's the name. Shot down over the sea and rescued by this bloody shower.'

Hobo nodded. 'Americans, off USS *Ready*. I'm Hobo,' he looked towards Cy,, 'and this is Cy Davis.'

Ben Tate resumed dragging the dead man.

'Help me.' The voice belonged to an English man, whose

arm hung loosely at an awkward angle. He was upright and leaning against the cabin's wall.

'We'll help each other,' Hobo said, and moved towards him.

Cy was mentally thanking God that in attempting to help the sailor towards the stairs for their climb Hobo seemed invigorated. They were all damaged, he thought, in some way or another, and needing help.

The man who had been bayoneted was no longer on the floor. Only congealed blood remained.

A steady stream of injured, dead and dying men was rising towards the deck. Cy felt sick watching their suffering. Man's inhumanity to man, he thought, but a sailor's words dragged him back to the present. The young man could hardly stand. He was sweating and shaking, his forehead running with perspiration.

'Take me, please?' he asked.

'Grab hold and we'll go together,' Cy said, putting his arm around the man's waist. He felt the terrible heat of his body as he climbed, half staggering, half dragging him up to the sunlight.

Cy heard the whooshing water before he saw or felt it.

The wooden deck was awash with the scrambling bodies of weakened men being swept off their feet, over and over by the gigantic force of sea water from a heavy industrial hose that needed several laughing guards to direct its flow. The prisoners rolled and slithered on the slippery deck trying to gain purchase. Cy felt the young man's fingers slide from his grip. He made a fruitless lunge at the empty air.

The strongest, those who survived the onslaught of water, managed to grab and hold on to any secure object on deck that would keep them from falling and sliding or being washed overboard.

Other guards, when the command for the water to be turned off was heard, moved among the men on deck who showed no or little sign of life. They were rolled and kicked into the sea by Japanese boots.

Cy had been washed towards railings he now clung to. His breath had been knocked from him. The onslaught of water had been freezing and his teeth were chattering, his hands gripping the metal rods that numbed his fingers, yet he knew he must not let go. Through slitted eyes he stared across the deck, searching for Hobo. To his intense relief he saw him sitting upright and wedged against a large coil of rope. The Canadian was sitting next to him. Tate hawked onto the deck, then ran a hand through his blond hair.

Cy scanned the survivors for the young man he'd brought up the steps but didn't see him. Only about a third of the men who had come up into the sunlight now remained. He also knew that if he and Hobo had been in the ship's hold any longer, they too would have perished.

The sun was hot overhead. It shimmered on blue sea that stretched into the distance, meeting an azure sky. His skin burnt, not just from the sun's rays but from the salt in the seawater drying on his scraped and broken flesh. Strangely, the sea water had also energized him.

The *Havana Maru* was moored to a well-made, hastily repaired wooden jetty. Concrete buildings faded into the distance, shimmering in the sun's heat. Made-up roads, not dirt tracks, disappeared into the horizon. There was evidence of bombing but also reparation. Billboards and signs hung about shops that hadn't been razed to the ground. 'Smart Women Everywhere Swear by Revlon', 'Mars are Marvellous', 'Old Gold Cigarettes'.

The nearest, a slogan covering a wall opposite the jetty where the *Havana Maru* was docked, showed a box of Coca-Cola and yellow roses, and the slogan 'Hospitality is an Art. Coca-Cola makes it easy . . .' Cy reckoned that if he didn't feel so shit, he could almost laugh. But where the hell were they? Where had the ship brought them? Those were American posters, weren't they? Surely the Japanese hadn't conquered his homeland.

Japanese soldiers were on the pontoon, holding weapons and enjoying watching the scenes unfolding on the deck of the *Havana Maru*. Cy's half-formed idea of making a run for it at the earliest opportunity faded. He wouldn't stand a chance: he'd be shot immediately.

More men climbed out of the hold to meet the hose, which had been turned on again. It was a sickening sight. He turned his head away. And felt bile rise: he was ashamed that he would not, could not, do anything. He knew this was war, but lives were being violently, needlessly, wasted in front of him. What kind of people could do this?

He was still thirsty and he could see steam rising from the remnants of his clothing drying on his skin in the heat. He patted his top pocket and hoped Trixie's photograph would dry out so he could see her beloved face once more.

But he was alive! And when he looked across at Hobo and saw him looking back, Cy felt a measure of hope.

Chapter Twenty-seven

'It doesn't seem possible our training's over, does it?' Hen said, facing Vi, who was standing behind her in the queue to receive their travel documents.

Before Vi could answer, Trixie broke in: 'Well, it isn't officially over until Saturday, when we leave, is it? But tomorrow will be the last day we'll be in the forest chopping down trees.'

She shuffled along slowly as the line of girls summoned by Maud Styles moved forward. 'One thing I won't miss,' she said, 'is this horrible menagerie of stuffed animal heads staring down at me every time I walk along this corridor.'

'What's the matter with our Trixie? She's not her usual happy self tonight, is she?' quipped Vi.

'Are you going to tell Vi why you've got the miseries, or shall I?' Hen asked. 'Though personally I don't think you've got the slightest reason to moan and it's probably the post office playing silly beggars.'

Trixie clamped her mouth tightly shut.

Hen sighed. 'You know all those piles of letters she's been getting from lover-boy?'

'Yes,' said Vi.

'Well, today, no post at all from him. Again!' said Hen.

'Well, I expect the postman's got a bad back from delivering all that lovey-dovey stuff and didn't turn up today . . .'

Vi's words petered out when she saw Trixie's glare. She glared right back.

'Two days without hearing from him,' said Hen.

'Look,' Vi said, 'he's on a ship, God knows where, but up until now you've had more letters from Cy than the whole of the hut's occupants have received from anyone. There aren't any post boxes in the middle of the ocean, you know.'

'It doesn't feel right,' protested Trixie. 'I'm sure something's wrong.'

'If you're starting in on that karma nonsense, I'm moving to the back of the queue,' said Hen. 'And Vi's right. You should think yourself lucky that you've someone who writes you letters. In the time we've been here, Jo's never had any post at all.'

'She's not moaned about it,' added Vi. 'And I only get a letter from my mum once in a blue moon.'

Trixie looked first at Hen, by her side, then back at Vi. Now she felt ashamed because her friends' explanations were plausible. The main thing was she didn't doubt Cy's love for her.

Again, the queue moved. Soon they'd be standing in front of Maud Styles in her office to receive their travel warrants. A few more days and she'd see her mum and Des, who would be able to meet Hen and Vi, the friends who meant so much to her. Her mum would ask how she'd felt about learning new skills and she'd be able to tell her that signing on to become a lumberjill was one of the best things she'd ever done. Rose would want to know where the Forestry Commission was sending her but she wouldn't know until she returned to Shandford Lodge.

They'd been advised to clear their lockers and the huts of personal items. A new intake of girls could soon be occupying their premises. Trixie had already decided to take Cy's letters home to Alma Street. They'd be safe with her mother, and were too precious to cart around the country in a suitcase. And his words were engraved on her heart, weren't they? Maybe she'd take a couple of his letters with her. She'd be able to show her mum and Des his photo. They'd see how handsome he was. Already, the girls had been advised that letters arriving for them, after they'd left the Lodge, would be forwarded to their new addresses. She felt relieved that letters from Cy would eventually reach her.

Vi and Hen were right. She had nothing to worry about. Nothing at all.

'As we've so little time left, I think I'd like to go to the Yellow Duck tonight.' Trixie said.

'Thought you'd never suggest it,' said Hen. Her face lit with a huge smile.

'Jo said earlier she was hoping you'd say that,' replied Vi. 'Count me in.'

'Good! That's settled, then.' Trixie thought of the night she and Jo had sat on the log in the forest, talking. She wondered if Jo would become more outgoing if she stayed in the village and worked at the sawmill. She also wondered how Jo would fare, staying in the hut without her friends for the short time they'd be down in Gosport. Trixie had since discovered not everyone was taking advantage of the break, so Jo wouldn't be totally alone.

Slowly the queue moved along until Trixie stood in front of Maud Styles's desk. She smiled at the trim, severe-looking woman in her smart uniform, and received a smile in return.

'Thank you,' Trixie said, her hand stretched out to receive the envelope containing her travel documents.

'Don't thank me now, Trixie Smith, thank me or complain

when, upon your return, you discover your final destination.' Maud Styles's smile hadn't wavered.

'I'm sure I'll be sent where I'm needed,' Trixie replied. She raised her head and looked into the deep brown eyes staring back at her.

'Quite so,' Maud Styles said. If the woman knew Trixie's destination, or if she'd been deemed inadequate for the lumberjills, she was giving nothing away. The woman glanced at her watch. 'Have a good break.'

Trixie, knowing she was dismissed and clutching her treasured envelope, left the office to wait for Hen and Vi in the hall, beneath a particularly sad-looking stag's head with the most enormous antlers.

Battling through the Yellow Duck's blackout curtain Trixie practically fell into Big Al's arms.

'You look bonny tonight,' he said. 'I didn't think we'd be seeing you again.'

'I'm going home Saturday.' She shrugged, 'I wanted to say goodbye tonight.' She began pulling off a headsquare and patting her hair, which she'd taken great care in curling and combing to look like Veronica Lake's style. As Trixie's hair wasn't naturally blonde she'd spent a long time trying to disguise her mousy roots. The village shop hadn't stocked the peroxide and ammonia she mixed into a paste and patted along her partings to bleach it. She'd already decided she'd make bleaching her hair one of her first chores when she got home.

The girls had walked to the pub from the Lodge and she hoped her head-covering had kept the damp from making her hair droop. It was comforting to think Big Al had noticed she'd made an effort.

She wore grey slacks and a knitted grey jumper beneath her greatcoat. It was amazing how quickly the weather had changed from summer mildness to autumn cold. Trixie had intended to wear her flowered dirndl skirt with the grey jumper that her mum had knitted for her, but Vi had begged to borrow the skirt and Trixie didn't have the heart to refuse.

Hen was wearing a blue woollen dress with front pleats. She always dressed well. Trixie could tell by the stitching and the material that her clothes weren't cheap.

'You can borrow whatever takes your fancy,' was Hen's persistent message but the thought of dropping something that stained one of Hen's expensive dresses filled Trixie with alarm. Jo had borrowed Vi's button-through dress and had used Trixie's curling tongs heated on the pot-bellied stove in the hut. The ends of her hair were all curled under and for once she was wearing lipstick, cherry red, borrowed from Hen, and Trixie had to keep staring at her because she looked so pretty.

'Give me your coats. You can collect them from me when you leave,' Big Al said.

Trixie shrugged out of hers, leant forward and kissed his cheek. He smelt of tobacco and mints and blushed furiously.

'That's a goodbye kiss in case I forget later, and thank you for looking out for the girls,' she said.

'It's me who should be thanking you. If it wasn't for you and Vi, I'd still be alone in my wee house, moping. I like being here at the Yellow Du—'

'Get away with you,' broke in Trixie. She didn't want to remember why Big Al was employed by Donnie. The last person she needed to think about tonight was Ben Tate. She breathed in the cigarette smoke, beer and assorted perfumes that permeated the air as she pushed through the noisy customers to stand at the bar.

The plaque commemorating her feat of removing the coin from the piano keys caught her eye. As did the yellow cloth next to the bottle of Snowbird wood polish on the shelf below. A warm feeling enveloped her: Fiona must have been polishing the plaque. The Yellow Duck was a lovely place to be, she thought. She'd miss it when she moved on.

Trixie spied Donnie at the far end of the room, talking

to an elderly man. He looked up, smiled, held up his hand to tell her he'd be a while, and called to Fiona who was putting money in the till.

The woman snapped the drawer shut, looked to where Trixie stood, and smiled. A smile from Fiona was indeed a bonus. Trixie motioned towards the piano and Fiona nodded. Fiona also mimed drinking, so Trixie nodded back, knowing she meant she'd bring over some drinks when she had time.

Passing customers on her way to play, she saw Vi had, as usual, set chairs out for herself and Jo, and dragged the stool in front of the piano. Jo never wandered off, chatting to people: she was content to sit near the piano all evening. Looking around for Hen, Trixie spotted her laughing with a sailor, her head thrown back and her hand on his shoulder.

Everything was the same, yet it wasn't, she thought.

'Play "We'll Meet Again", dear, please?' asked an elderly woman, sitting at a table with another beside her who just had to be her twin. Trixie sat down, lifted the lid and was consumed with a great sadness because she knew that, after tonight, she'd never sit here playing again. Then she blinked, took a deep breath and allowed her fingers to move over the keys. She was doing something she loved and wouldn't allow negative feelings to spoil it.

'Over the Rainbow' followed. A voice from the crowd shouted, '"You Are My Sunshine", please!' Trixie played on and on until she felt a hand on her shoulder.

'Tonight's my last night, Donnie,' she said. She couldn't bear to look up at him.

'I came over to tell you I shall miss you, that I will, but if ever you need a place to be,' he said, 'you're to come to me, do you understand?'

'Thank you,' she said, her eyes quite damp.

Before he left her, he added, 'I'll take you and your mates back to the Lodge later, lassie.'

Trixie allowed the music to run through her fingers and calm her. She was playing 'String Of Pearls' when Fiona brought over a tray with four drinks and a plate of sugary shortbread nestling on it. 'Try not to stop playing, love, but I need to tell you something. Two things, actually.'

As she took the shortbread and lifted the plate from the tray to the table, Trixie saw her hand was shaking. 'I heard you'd all received your travel warrants and I knew you'd not leave without a final goodbye. Now, this recipe won me first prize at the Scottish Women's Institute. I made it especially for you.' She took a breath. 'I might not have shown it, but I do care for you.' She was silent for a moment, then added, 'Second thing, Donnie thought it better coming from me than him. You know what men are like.' She sighed.

'I have a friend who works in the canteen at Leuchars air base. She's a young bit of a thing, like you. A while ago a Canadian airman had a go at her.' Fiona stopped, then added, 'You know what I mean by that?'

Trixie went on playing 'String Of Pearls'. She knew exactly what Fiona meant.

'She said his name was Ben Tate. She didn't know he'd got a bit of a name for himself, not taking no for an answer from the lasses.'

Trixie went on playing. She'd begun the introduction to 'String Of Pearls' all over again. Oh, well, she thought, perhaps the crowd in the pub might not notice her playing it twice.

'Why did you say his name *was* Ben Tate?' Trixie asked, her heart beating very fast.

'The airman went out on a night raid. Apparently, he was shot down over the sea. Missing, presumed dead.'

Trixie looked up from the piano keys into Fiona's eyes. She didn't know what to say. Her fingers paused. She said, as loudly as she could so everyone would hear, 'Thank you, everyone, for listening to me play these past weeks. I'm dedicating this last tune to Donnie for letting me loose at this keyboard. Playing has helped me come to terms with being away from home and, well . . . with life, really.'

Ignoring the calls and clapping and whistles, Trixie played 'Amapola'.

After closing the piano lid, her eyes travelled towards the bar, looking for Donnie. When she found him, he nodded, and an understanding needing no words passed between them.

Chapter Twenty-eight

'Don't seem right to have all this beauty around us, us being prisoners and not able to touch it,' said Hobo. 'Will ya take a look at that, Cy?' He inclined his head to where red hibiscus, pikake, and plumeria entwined their fragrant scented blossoms among the fan-shaped travellers' palms. Hobo had read books. He knew all about plants and growing stuff.

Cy had been told time and time again that Hobo's daddy had been a gardener at an antebellum home in Natchez and would walk to work with Hobo sitting on his shoulders. Hobo was nine when his daddy ran off with one of the helpers, a girl just seven years older than Hobo. It didn't stop Hobo loving the feel of the soil between his fingers, though, and reading about gardening, all sorts, not just flowers. The big dope had even kept pot plants on board the USS *Ready*.

Hobo quoted his daddy often: 'All things come from the

earth, and all things end by becoming earth.' He said he thanked his daddy for his love of the soil, because it was pretty near all he had to remember him by.

Tall palm trees either side of the road offered little shade to the men marching along wearily in the heat. It wasn't an easy or comfortable walk as most were without shoes, Cy included. Not only was the bare earth hot but the sharp flints cut his skin to ribbons.

'We could be nearly there. That barbed-wire fence running alongside the road must mean something,' said Cy. He'd noticed it perhaps a mile or so back but hadn't thought to say anything. The intense heat wasn't conducive to conversation. Nobody answered him.

Until Ben Tate grumbled, 'I can't be bothered to look at anything while my stomach thinks my throat's been cut.'

'We're all hungry,' came another voice.

'No talk!'

Cy hadn't noticed the guard creep up but he heard the order and saw the raised bayonet. And, with great relief, he watched from beneath lowered eyes as the guard retreated to continue jabbering with his Japanese cronies.

They'd been walking for some time, the remainder of the men from the *Havana Maru*'s hold, the fittest, the most resilient ones, though Cy likened them all to the walking dead. They weren't dead yet, but they were starving and, once more, dehydrated.

Cy thought longingly of the bucket of fresh water that a guard had shared among the hardy men back on the jetty. That was when he knew he wasn't going to die, at least not immediately. The enemy wouldn't have bothered to give them water if they were about to be killed, would they?

The men surviving the hosepipe massacre and left under guard to dry out on the pontoon numbered fifty or sixty.

'You march!' was the command, and they'd been walking ever since.

They'd passed billboards and more American advertising. Cy had no idea where he was, but it was pretty obvious his countrymen had been there and left their mark. The bomb craters and heavily damaged buildings made it quite apparent they didn't inhabit the place any longer. He was intrigued that one name cropped up time and time again on the roadside hoardings: Pan American Airways. And he remembered when he was newly out of the *Havana Maru*'s hold that he'd seen an airfield conning tower in the distance. He'd been unable to take it in at that moment but it was coming back to him slowly.

'Will ya look at that?' Hobo crowed.

Cy's eyes took in the remains of a roadside bar. Part of it still stood drunkenly to the right of them. Palm-roofed, what was left of it, and timber-walled. There were stools placed at the broken glass-topped bar as though waiting to be sat on, any moment, by ghostly customers. Cy could almost taste the bottles of beer shown on the tattered Coors advertisement trying its hardest to escape from the damaged wall. He heard the despondent murmurings from the marching men as they passed it.

And then the road veered off to show wooden buildings on stilts, palm-roofed and set about a large dirt rectangle. Cy was relieved to see men, other prisoners, he deduced, their ragged clothing the giveaway, standing in groups, sitting on wooden steps and watching as the newcomers approached the compound.

More guards unlocked the wooden-spiked and barb-wired gate. The men were herded inside to the accompaniment of ribald remarks from the prisoners.

Here, too, there was greenery and bright bougainvillaea climbing and covering the walls and roofs of the buildings. Cy looked at Hobo and they shared a smile. A tall watch-tower with searchlights overlooked the camp.

With the tips of their bayonets flicking skin, the Japanese guards manoeuvred and manipulated the newcomers into a square of close-knit rows, facing one particular large hut, painted white and visibly smarter than the rest.

The sun was unyielding.

From the hut, eventually, came a Japanese officer, surrounded by guards. He was the top dog, thought Cy, with that gold braid on his white uniform.

The officer stared at the men. Contempt distorted his face. 'I am prison commandant. You will bow.' His soft, unclear voice had no impact.

Cy was unsure what was required of him until he saw a fellow prisoner nudged with a rifle butt. Cy immediately followed everyone else as they bowed their heads as though the small man in the white suit was some deity. With his head bent towards the dirt, Cy listened as the commandant droned on and on, understanding little of what he said. The heat, thirst, tiredness and the unintelligible voice worked their magic. Cy passed out.

The first thing he noticed when he opened his eyes was that the long wound snaking down Hobo's face was beginning to pucker at the sides.

'It's healing,' he said. The second thing he noticed was water running from his mouth, making the rag that was all he had left of his shirt, extremely damp. He didn't feel as if he was choking but when he put a hand to his chest, it came away drenched. His fingers flew to his pocket. The photo was gone.

'Trixie's . . .'

'You looking for this?' Hobo waggled the dry but creased and forlorn-looking photograph in front of him. 'I took it from your pocket to keep it dry.'

Cy felt his love for Trixie well up inside him, and his overwhelming gratitude towards Hobo emerged with his next words. 'Thanks, pal! Were you trying to drown me?' Cy knew the opposite would be true. Hobo would always look after him.

His feet itched. He looked down and was amazed to see bands of clean cotton material wrapped around his freshly washed feet.

'I took the liberty of cleaning the cuts. The heat can make sores go septic,' Hobo said, 'and one of the men offered a pair of sneakers. They ain't new but . . .'

On the wooden boards near his mat was a pair of grubby and worn soft-soled canvas shoes.

'Have I died and gone to Heaven?'

'No, you're in a PoW camp on Pearlien Island, somewhere in the Pacific, we think. This tiny island belonged to the Americans. Pan Am Airways used it as a refuelling base, and when the Japs bombed Pearl Harbor they nipped over, bombed and claimed this island as well.'

Cy tried to make sense of what Hobo had said. He tried again: 'I'm wet. You gave me water?'

'Sure I gave you water!' Hobo brought his face very close. 'We got all the water we need! We got it coming out of a pesky tap! Courtesy of Pan Am!'

'But the Japs . . .'

'Tadamichi Yamamoto, camp commandant, Tad to his back and when he ain't listenin', don't want us dead, unless we do somethin' to annoy the bastard! Like try and escape.'

Cy was beginning to absorb the stream of information still coming from Hobo.

'He wants us to rebuild the airport and the runway. We gotta improve the island's defences, bunkers, fortifications . . .'

Cy scrambled to a sitting position. He saw he was lying on a rush mat on the floor of a wooden house. There was an electric light above him, its bulb shining down. Men were lying around him on straw mattresses. A couple nodded a welcome.

'Why am I on this mat on a hard floor, and they've got mattresses?' Cy broke into Hobo's stream of dialogue, which stopped immediately.

He warned, 'Don't start any trouble. They've been here longer. We'll get mattresses, eventually. You want any more water?' Hobo pointed to a tin cup next to the rush mat. Cy shook his head.

Again, he looked around at the thirty or so men sharing the floor. 'Why . . .'

'I know what you're gonna ask. Why are all these men lyin' around doing nothin'. Well, they're waiting to be fed after working all day. You been out of it so long the day's over.'

'Fed? What d'ya mean?'

'Bowl of rice, cup of miso soup, bread, maybe some pickles or vegetables.'

'You're making that up!'

'It's the truth, I tell you.' Hobo looked pleased with himself. 'I've been finding things out,' he said. 'We're the fittest men left from the *Havana Maru* and we'll be fed so we can work, like the other men here. We'll even be paid one yen a day!'

Cy had to look away. They'd be paid? Had Hobo even wondered where they would spend the wages, even supposing they were given them?

He looked around him again. The men seemed cheerful enough. A card game was going on in the corner. Good humour, laughter. So, what was the drawback? What was the snag? The fly in the ointment? What was it his mum always said? 'If it looks too good to be true, it usually is.'

He thought over everything Hobo had discovered and had now passed on to him.

The light-bulb moment finally came.

They, as prisoners, were to rebuild the airfield and

buildings, originally built by the Americans and razed to the ground by the Japanese, so they could use it themselves.

But this was wartime. When the good ol' USA got wind of what was going on, they'd fly over and bomb the crap out of little Pearlien Island to get rid of the Japanese, wouldn't they?

Bombs were bombs and couldn't tell the difference between Japs and Americans. They, as prisoners, would be sitting targets. With an endless flow of newly captured men arriving by hell ships to take their places.

No, he hadn't died and gone to Heaven. He'd gone to Hell instead.

Chapter Twenty-nine

On the train, Trixie looked at Hen sitting opposite her, chatting to a sailor. It seemed that she had known Hen for ever, not that they had first met only four weeks ago. Hen was gazing into the young man's eyes as if she could learn all there was to know about the secrets of the universe by hanging on to his every word. Her friend was in fine form today, Trixie decided. She'd squeezed herself into the silk costume she'd worn travelling up to Shandford but now it seemed to strain at the seams. Hen wore no blouse beneath her jacket and its buttons stretched across her ample breasts, only just stopping them escaping.

Vi sat next to her, reading *Mildred Pierce*, a new novel by James M. Cain, one of her favourite authors. Every so often Vi looked up and smiled at Trixie. Her personality had changed the most in that short time, thought Trixie. What bigger transformation could there have been, from timid girl to confident young woman? Hadn't Vi taken charge and decided exactly what to do when one of the lumberjills had injured herself? It had taken courage and guts to tie a tourniquet above Dolly's knee to stop her bleeding to death from her wound, hadn't it?

Trixie wondered if her mother might notice a change in herself. She didn't feel different and her clothes still fitted as well as ever. She hadn't lost her love of playing the piano. Possibly it was her attitude that had changed. When she'd lived at home, she'd felt unfulfilled, disenchanted with life. Now, when she awoke in the mornings, she looked forward with excitement to whatever the day might bring.

Her elation this past couple of days, though, had been tarnished by the lack of letters from Cy. She certainly wasn't going to voice any regret about it because she remembered only too well how last time the girls had teased her. She knew she was lucky to have Cy loving her, and when the hold-up in the mail was sorted out, she'd have so many letters to read that she might need spectacles when she'd finished.

A good, steady diet at the Lodge and loads of exercise had not only built muscle and decreased body fat but contributed to the girls' high energy levels, which showed in their glowing complexions and willingness to chat not only among themselves but to other people in the packed carriage on its way to London.

The last time Trixie had made this journey it had been in the opposite direction and it had been at night. She had seen nothing of the scenery. Now the mountains, the lochs, the heather, the Highland cattle and sheep were giving way to towns, stone and brick buildings, offices and the back-to-back houses she was more familiar with.

And there was the bomb damage. Gaps in rows of shops, like missing teeth. Piles of rubble that had once been cherished homes, and buildings propped up with wooden shoring.

Trixie sighed. This was the real world, she thought. It smelt of burnt wood, acrid sulphur and stale smoke, and it tasted of metal and scorched flesh. Gone for now was the scent of pine from the trees, the sharp, earthy smell after light rain, the freshness of Scotland.

Trixie didn't want to feel melancholy. She looked at Hen, asleep now with her head on the sailor's shoulder.

Vi was still reading.

Every seat in the carriage had been taken and the air was stuffy with cigarette smoke, sweat and assorted food smells. Outside in the corridor soldiers, some smoking, some asleep, used their kitbags as pillows. There wasn't an inch of space in their carriage that didn't have someone sitting in it or a suitcase or kitbag propped against it. Even the overhead luggage racks were dangerously full.

Trixie was hungry. She, Vi and Hen had long ago eaten the grated cheese and carrot sandwiches provided by the Lodge and Trixie was looking forward to arriving in London. They'd promised themselves, time permitting, that they'd eat in a café before catching the Portsmouth train home.

Hen would leave Trixie and Vi at Gosport ferry and catch a bus home to Alverstoke. Then, after a couple of days, Trixie and Vi would visit Hen at her parents' home in Western Way. They planned to travel back to Shandford Lodge together.

Trixie began thinking about the things she'd been pushing to the back of her mind ever since boarding the train. Now the clackety-clack of the wheels on the rails seemed to urge her to remember Ben Tate.

The man had tried to take advantage of her in the garden at the Yellow Duck. Ben Tate, so Fiona had told her, was not a good man. He had hurt other women.

All Trixie's life, so far, she had worked on the premise of cause and effect. It was important to her that she lived without hurting other people, that her intentions were decent and honest, and if they weren't she should expect retribution. A sort of do-as-you-would-be-done-by attitude to life.

Ben Tate: missing, believed dead. That was what Fiona had said, that his plane had been shot down by the enemy over the sea.

What goes around comes around, and he had tried to harm Trixie. For his misdeeds Ben Tate had paid the ultimate price: death. Was she, Trixie, partly to blame for that? It was something she was trying hard not to think about.

'This is getting to be a habit, Trixie, me waking you up on trains!' Vi stepped back from gently shaking her shoulder, then reached up and pulled the suitcase down from the overhead parcel shelf for her.

Trixie smiled a thank-you at Vi. 'I didn't think I'd sleep.' She rubbed her eyes, stifled a yawn, looked around the deserted carriage and asked, 'Where's Hen?'

'Outside saying goodbye to that sailor,' Vi said, and laughed. 'I'm sure every man she meets she thinks is the last man on earth and she'll never see another.'

Trixie stood up and stretched, glancing out of the carriage at the people on the platforms rushing to either board or alight from the trains. So many people, she thought, and so many men and women in uniform, all going about their business of trying to win this awful war.

'Ted says we've got a couple of hours to wait before the Portsmouth train leaves,' Hen said, tucking something into the pocket of her silk skirt while entering the carriage and grabbing hold of her case. 'He's given me his address so I can write to him.' She smiled from ear to ear. 'Let's go and get a cup of tea.'

The smell of smoke and oil wafted around them as they walked through the main part of the station. There were queues everywhere. People seemed to be waiting at every outlet selling tea and food. Children, fractious, were screaming. Fed up with being jostled, Trixie said, 'It'll take ages to get served in this station. I've had enough. Why don't we escape for a while?'

'What – leave the station?' Vi stopped walking and stared at Trixie.

'Hen's sailor said we've got a couple of hours to wait. We don't have to go far. We could leave our cases at the Left Luggage office so we don't have to cart them around. We could take a walk out in the fresh air . . .'

'Might find a fish and chip shop,' came Vi's excited voice.

Hen said, 'We might. We could look at the bridge.'

'What bridge?' Trixie was curious, but before Hen answered, Vi grabbed her arm.

'Left Luggage is over there,' she said, and strode away

towards a small queue of people waiting at a counter. The bald-headed man in the grimy overalls confirmed the leaving time of their southbound train, gave them tickets to reclaim their suitcases, and wished them a pleasant time in London.

'The chip shop is on the corner, girlies,' he added, 'opposite the taxi rank.'

Trixie gave him a friendly wave goodbye and they began walking along the concourse arm in arm.

'Much easier carrying just handbags,' said Hen, She had her gas mask slung over her shoulder, as did Trixie and Vi.

Once outside Trixie stood quite still. She took a deep breath. And promptly began coughing. From the piles of rubble that had once been shops, dust hovered in the air, covering everything with the smell of burnt wood. It immediately reminded her of Alf and the way he had shown them how to fill the kilns with twigs to make charcoal. She felt a pull of sadness as she remembered the old man and his smelly pipe. The rubble hadn't made a good job of hiding broken sheets of glass, shattered doors and the interiors of shops that wouldn't be trading anytime soon.

'I thought you said we'd breathe some fresh air outside the station,' Trixie grumbled to Vi.

Vi simply laughed at her and said, 'Can you smell that, then?'

She left Trixie and Hen to run ahead and claim their places in the queue that ran from the London Plaice and snaked along the pavement.

'What if we get to the counter and they say, "Sorry, sold out"?' asked Hen, when she reached Vi.

'Then we'll have to go without,' said Trixie. 'But fish and chips aren't on ration, so as long as they haven't run out we'll be fine.'

Trixie watched the basket of newly cooked chips being raised from the boiling fat in the fryer and tipped into the warm oven ready to be scooped up. The fish, already cooked and covered with golden batter, looked and smelt divine sitting in the glass-fronted warmer.

And then it was their turn to be served. Already Trixie's stomach was growling and her mouth was watering as she watched her portion taking shape on the newspaper.

'Salt and vinegar?' the frowzy woman serving behind the counter asked.

'Yes, please,' she said, and watched as the condiments were liberally added. 'Do you have any scraps?' she asked, meaning the bits of batter that fell into the boiling fat to become crisp, then had to be scooped out and set on one side. In Gosport, the fish shops added them free to orders, if asked.

The woman glared at Trixie. 'No!' she said, in an aggrieved voice. 'That'll be sixpence.' The wrapped portion of fish and chips now sat on the counter and the woman's hand was palm up waiting for the payment.

Trixie gulped. The chip shop at the bottom of Alma Street only charged twopence for fish and a penny for chips. The woman saw her hesitation. 'It's plaice, ducky. Plaice is dearer. This is the London Plaice!'

Trixie handed over the money, picked up her parcel and waited while Hen and Vi were served. Carrying their wrapped fish and chips, they walked in silence down the road until Waterloo Bridge came into sight.

Vi said, 'I hope this tastes as good as it smelt in the shop.'

'It should do – it cost enough,' said Trixie. 'Sixpence! And that woman would have probably charged another tanner for scraps!'

'There are some steps near the bridge, let's sit there and eat,' said Hen. She claimed a step, and sat down, immediately opening the newspaper, putting her fingers in and pulling out a golden chip. 'Yum-yum,' she declared.

Trixie, after wiping the grease from her lips, said, 'Yes, London prices but worth every penny!'

People were walking past, stepping around them, but Trixie couldn't have cared less. As she ate, she watched the tugs and barges, and workers going about their business on the banks of the great river.

'A cup of tea would be nice,' said Vi. She sat back against the stonework of the bridge and looked down at the river Thames. 'I think we'd better wait until we get back to the station, though. It'll probably be cheaper there.'

Trixie watched as Hen rolled her newspaper up tightly and looked for somewhere to put it. There was litter on the steps and the pavement but she knew Hen was too tidy-minded to add to it.

Trixie said, 'Give it here.' She jammed the wrappings inside her gas mask case. 'There's rubbish bins on the station. I'll get rid of it all then.'

'Ted was telling me that Waterloo Bridge has only just reopened to traffic,' Hen said. She smoothed back her hair: a golden strand had come loose from a pinned plait and blown across her face.

Trixie looked across to where building work was still being carried out. 'It's a big bridge,' she said. 'Still, it's got to be to span the Thames.'

'Over four hundred yards long and about twenty-six wide,' said Hen.

'How d'you know that?' piped up Vi.

'Ted told me.'

'Who's Ted?' Vi asked.

'The sailor from the train,' said Trixie.

Vi pulled a face. 'I can't keep up with all her men. And how come you, Hen, remember all those figures?'

'It's my job as a measurer not to forget numbers, silly!' Hen said. 'Ted also told me that because of the war, with our men away fighting, three-quarters of the building work was and still is being done by women, so they've nicknamed it the Ladies' Bridge.'

Trixie watched as Hen stood up and looked across the murky waters to the grey buildings on the other side. 'I'd like to live in London,' she said wistfully.

'I couldn't stand the noise,' Vi said. 'And it's dirty.'

Of course, it was dirty, thought Trixie. Ol' Hitler was forever trying to bomb the guts out of the place. And it was noisy not just because of the traffic sounds and the people but the river was busy with boats loading and unloading goods, the grey-green water burbling and smacking against the landing stages. And it smelt of fish, she thought. But this was London, lovely London, where the King, the Queen and the pretty little princesses lived.

Vi threw down her fish-and-chip newspaper and it nestled among the rest of the debris. Trixie sighed, picked it up and stuffed it into her gas-mask case with the rest of the wrappings. Just because Hitler was bombing England so that it was beginning to look like a rubbish dump there was no need for them to add to it. 'Let's get back to the station for a cuppa,' she said.

Chapter Thirty

The train whistled and smoke was still billowing across the station as Hen and Vi stepped down onto the platform at Portsmouth Harbour closely followed by Trixie, lugging her suitcase.

'You can tell we're home again. Listen to the rain!' Trixie remarked. It was hammering on the roof of the station, and as she looked through the windows to where Nelson's flagship was moored at the Dockyard, she saw needles of rain sheeting across the sea and blowing against the rigging of HMS *Victory*. It swept across the slope that ran down to the jetty where a green and white ferry waited to cross the harbour to Gosport. 'We'll have to run for it,' she said.

At the ticket office Trixie paid threepence for three tickets and, with squeals of laughter they braved the elements, running, with their suitcases, handbags and gas masks, beneath the tin-roofed canopy while the oilskin-and-sou'wester-clad crew member clipped their tickets and allowed them on board.

It was barely light in the downstairs cabin, packed tightly with people escaping the rain. The air was chokingly full of cigarette smoke that seeped into the damp. She heard the engine start and then the steady throb that said they were well and truly on their way home.

Trixie remembered the last time she'd sat waiting for the ferry to begin its short journey across the stretch of water between Portsmouth and Gosport. Cy, Hobo and the pea-jacketed American sailors from USS *Ready*, moored in the Dockyard, had entertained her, playing a harmonica and encouraging her to sing along to the popular songs. It was the first time she'd met the young man she'd fallen in love with.

Was it really such a short time ago?

She wanted to tell Hen and Vi about him and that early-morning boat trip. How his brown eyes had held flecks of gold. How his lips had felt when he'd gently kissed her goodbye . . .

But she didn't. Instead, she looked at Hen, who was giggling. Somehow the hairgrips holding her long plaits in place over her head had come adrift and one plait was hanging damply across her cheek.

They were wet through, all three of them. Trixie

remembered them deciding it wouldn't be as cold in Gosport as it was in Scotland. They hadn't considered it might rain.

Hen's tight silk costume looked moulded to her body. Vi's calf-length dress clung and slapped against her legs. And Trixie's pink fluffy jumper that she thought complemented her grey slacks was so wet it resembled a drowned animal wrapped about her.

'Come here, you,' Trixie said, pulling Hen towards her, removing pins and re-setting the coils around her head.

'She even looks pretty,' laughed Vi, 'when she's caught in a deluge!' She smoothed her own straight bedraggled hair down at the sides of her head and pulled a comical face. It caused more giggles.

When the short journey had ended, the girls allowed the crush of people with their dripping umbrellas to make their way up the metal stairs before they moved from where they'd been standing. Eventually, out in the open air again, and walking up the gangway in the gusting rain, Trixie could see the green double-deckers waiting at the bus station.

She pulled Hen to one side before her friend stepped onto the platform of the bus that would take her to Alverstoke.

'You've got my mum's address, haven't you?' she asked, shoving Hen's case into the luggage compartment below the stairs. They'd agreed it would be sensible to exchange addresses, despite making arrangements to visit each other, before the journey back to Scotland. With Hitler's bombers doing their best to obliterate the south coast, anything could happen.

'I have,' Hen said. The concerned frown creasing her forehead deepened. Her words came out in a rush. 'I'm not really looking forward to seeing my parents and going home,' she said.

Trixie was taken aback. It was a peculiar thing for Hen to say, she thought. She moved to allow more passengers to enter the bus. 'What d'you mean?' she asked. Vi was standing guard over the two remaining suitcases, sheltering against the brick wall of the public toilets. People were huddled against doorways, beneath trees, in corners, anywhere in a bid to escape the downpour. The bus Trixie and Vi needed hadn't arrived at the terminal yet, and there was very little shelter from the rain.

Hen sighed. 'This isn't the time or place to talk. You'll see what I mean when you get to Western Way. You might have to ignore . . .'

Trixie could see through the fogged windows that the conductress and her driver were hurrying from the Dive café, through the rain towards Hen's bus. She wanted to ask Hen what she meant but there was no time.

'They mean well,' added Hen, 'but they don't think the way I do.'

The driver climbed into the cab at the front of the bus and the conductress jumped onto the platform, shedding a shower of raindrops.

'Move along the bus,' she grumbled at Trixie.

'I'm not coming,' she managed, while stepping off into the rain.

'Make yer mind up, luv!' the conductress retorted She rang the bell and the driver started the engine.

Trixie raised her hand in a half-hearted wave at Hen, who was now sitting just inside, and the Provincial bus moved away from the terminal. Hen looked close to tears.

'Cheer up. We'll see her in a couple of days,' said Vi.

Trixie leant close to the wall to shelter from the worst of the rain. 'She said something funny.'

'Like what?' Vi used a hand to wipe the wet drops from her face and stared at Trixie.

'Like we might have to ignore what we'll find going on at her parents' house.' Trixie watched Vi carefully as her words were assimilated.

'Perhaps she was trying to tell you her dad makes his money by robbing banks.'

Trixie dug Vi in the ribs.

'Ouch! That hurt!'

'It was meant to,' Trixie said. 'Be serious.'

'Look! Hen's people have money. Hen has nice clothes. She went to a posh school.' Trixie could see Vi was trying very hard to keep her feelings under control. 'What on earth has she got to apologize for? The other side of the coin is me. I've asked you to come home with me because I'm terrified of going there on my own! But I do need to make sure my mum's all right!'

For a moment Vi was silent. Then she let out a deep sigh. 'I'm sorry, Trixie. This sounds like I'm aiming to persuade you into letting me win the "Who Comes from the Worst Home" competition. When we met, I was covered with bruises and I promised you one day, because I want no secrets between us, I'd explain how I got them. But I'm not getting into any rivalry about home-life with Hen. We're two very different people, with different problems, leading up to different reasons why we wanted to leave our homes and become lumberjills, which even you must admit has to be one of the toughest jobs, ever and takes guts to do.'

Trixie let her friend's words sink in.

During the time the four girls had lived alongside each other, three of them working together, it was as if their Gosport lives had ceased to be. Coming home had stirred up memories, feelings, not all of them happy.

'In Scotland we've been living in a fool's paradise,' said Vi.

'I shut out what had happened down here. I've lived a dream at Shandford Lodge. My life and where I live down here is what nightmares are made of . . .' She began to cry, tears mingling with the raindrops falling on her face, sliding down her cheeks and showing her vulnerability to life and its changes. To Trixie this was another Vi, one she hadn't witnessed before. Trixie pulled her close, pressing her to the fluffy jumper that was now a sodden rag and hoping the heat from her body would give Vi some comfort.

'It's all right,' Trixie whispered into Vi's lank, soaking hair. 'We don't have to go to your home.'

Vi sniffed back tears. 'That's just it, Trixie. I do have to. I can't move on if I don't.' Her body gave a shudder. She disentangled herself from Trixie's grasp. 'I'm sorry,' she said. 'I'm sorry for thinking that because Hen's family has money her problems pale into insignificance beside mine. Can you ever forgive me?'

Trixie smiled at her. 'Nothing to forgive,' she said.

Just then the Provincial bus that would travel down Forton Road, pausing at various places until it reached the Criterion picture house, Trixie's nearest stop to Alma Street, drove into the terminal and pulled up so the passengers could disembark.

'Thank Christ for that,' said Trixie, as the last person had left the bus. 'Now we can get inside, out of the rain.'

Chapter Thirty-one

Trixie didn't utter a word as she waited for the conductor and driver to return from their tea break in the Dive café, one of the most popular working men's cafés in Gosport. She was in the dry, steaming gently in the warmth, away from the rain that was still pelting down outside and thinking of Vi's outburst and what could have caused it.

Vi and Hen were two different people. Actually, all four of them were as different as chalk and cheese, herself and Jo included. Never had they talked about their lives and what had happened to them before they'd signed on to become lumberjills. It was as if living in Scotland had become a new beginning for all of them.

A flicker of guilt ran through her as she remembered how she had chattered on and on about Cy. So happy about her love that she hadn't thought how it might affect others.

She'd also played the piano, showing another side to her character. She sincerely hoped the girls hadn't taken it as a sign of 'showing off' because it went deeper than that. Allowing the music to flow through her fingers helped her to gather her thoughts and be herself.

What did she really know about Hen? That her parents had money and she had gone to a posh school. She also drew men to her.

Jo, too, was an unknown quantity. Mercurial moods yet one of the kindest people Trixie had ever known. But why hadn't she wanted to come home and see her family? Trixie glanced at Vi, who smiled back warmly. Vi was courageous, down to earth and Trixie was glad to have her as a friend.

'Are you sure your mum doesn't mind me staying the night?' Vi's voice cut into her thoughts.

'She'll be happy to meet you,' answered Trixie, catching sight of the conductor and the woman driver making a dash through the rain towards their vehicle. Buses had arrived and left the terminal, and now it was their turn. Soon Trixie would be with her mum again and she couldn't wait.

Trixie looked at the bus ticket in her hand. It wasn't a long ride to the Criterion, which was their designated stop, and if it hadn't been for the rain, they'd have walked. Watching through the windows, she'd become aware of the damage that had been done to Gosport in the time she'd been away. She was so busy looking at the awful destruction, which her mother had written to her about, opposite the picture house, when the bus stopped, and Vi had to chivvy her up to grab their suitcases from the luggage space beneath the stairs or the bus would have carried on to the next stop.

This Gun for Hire, starring Veronica Lake was the film advertised by the stills in the glass-fronted display cases outside the picture house.

'That reminds me,' said Trixie, looking at the sultry star's peekaboo hairstyle as she gazed adoringly up into Alan Ladd's eyes. 'I have to bleach my hair when I get in. I can't possibly let anyone see me like this. I never expected my natural colour to come through so quickly while we were in Scotland.'

'Couldn't you have done it at Shandford Lodge?' Vi asked.

'I would have if I could have bought the stuff to do it with,' Trixie said. 'It won't take long.' She grinned at Vi and pointed to their reflections in the glass case. 'Anyway, look at the pair of us, like drowned rats. The sooner we get dried off, the better.'

As they passed Watt's the greengrocer's, Trixie saw the closed notice on the door. That's a shame, she thought. She would have loved to pop in to say a quick hello. 'That's where

I worked before I signed on the dotted line to become a lumberjill,' she said. She was struck by how small the shop appeared. Time and distance did strange things to minds and memories, she thought.

'Anyone can serve in a shop,' said Vi. 'But it takes guts and strength to wield an axe and do what you've been doing for England. You should feel proud of yourself, Trixie.'

Trixie stopped walking and looked at Vi. 'Proud? I don't know about that. I only hope when we get back to Shandford we can continue working in the forests somewhere else.'

And then they were walking up Alma Street and standing outside her mother's front door. The street, full of little terraced houses, suddenly made her realize how small and insignificant she was.

Trixie slipped her hand through the letterbox and pulled out the key on the string. A delicious smell wafted out from inside the house, and as she turned the key in the lock the door swung open and her mother gathered her into her arms. 'I've been waiting, my darling girl,' Rose said.

Trixie was being held so tightly she could almost feel her mother's heart beating. With her breath squashed from her body, she just managed to say, 'Mum, I've missed you! And this is Vi.'

Her mother released her and stepped back inside the

passageway. 'Come inside, the pair of you, and out of the rain. And welcome to my home, Vi.'

Vi grinned. 'Hello,' she said.

Trixie took a deep breath of the familiar smell of home. Wood burning in the kitchen range, food, polish . . .

'Try not to make too much noise, Trix. Des is asleep. He's on nights, remember?'

Trixie did remember. Des, the widower who loved her mother and worked at the War Memorial Hospital. Des, whose hair was flame red and whose tall thin body reminded Trixie of a Swan Vesta match. Des was one of the reasons Trixie had decided to join the Women's Timber Corps. She was aware of her mother's love for him but she knew for that love to grow Rose and Des needed to spend valuable time together, without her hindering love's progress.

Des had moved into Rose's home but to stop neighbours' tongues wagging, he was Rose's 'lodger'.

'You look so well,' Trixie said to her mother. And she did, she thought. Trixie stood in the kitchen alongside Vi and watched as Rose bustled about, going into the scullery, lighting the gas stove and filling the kettle.

'Of course, we won't wake him, Mum,' said Trixie. 'Do you mind if I sort out my roots before I do anything else?

I left some stuff to bleach my hair in the cabinet in the scullery. Is it still there?'

Rose passed towels to the girls. 'If you left stuff in the scullery, Trix, then that's where it'll be. Now rub yourselves as dry as you can. We'll have a cup of tea and a chat.'

Trixie couldn't contain herself any longer, 'You've made my favourite, haven't you, Mum?' She didn't wait for an answer. 'I can smell corned-beef fritters!'

Rose, back in the kitchen now, nodded towards the black-leaded range. 'Of course,' she said. 'They're keeping warm. I've also made blackberry and apple tart. I know how much you love blackberries and I picked them fresh yesterday,' she said. She turned to Vi, who was energetically towelling her hair. 'I hope you like the meal I've prepared, love.'

Trixie saw Vi pause, her hair all tousled. 'Oh, I will. And you're very kind,' she said. She looked away and went on towelling her hair but not before Trixie had caught the brightness of tears in her eyes. Vi wasn't very good at accepting kindnesses from people, she thought, however small they were.

Rose finished making the tea, then went into the hall to bring in the girls' suitcases. Wiping the damp off them with a striped tea-towel she said, 'There's time, before Des has to get up for work, for you both to have a wash in the scullery and change your clothes.' She paused. 'Trix, I don't know if you feel up to it, especially as you've both been travelling for such a long time, but Ellie and Merv at the Alma asked me if I thought you'd both mind popping down there and having a drink.'

'You mean they'd like me to play the piano, Mum?' Trixie's smile went from ear to ear. There was nothing she'd like more. And Ellie, famous for cobbling together snacks from next to nothing, would put on a good spread, which she knew Vi would appreciate.

'Only if you feel up to it, love?' Rose said.

Trixie looked at Vi. 'What d'you think?'

'It's you they want, not me,' Vi said.

Trixie guessed sudden shyness was holding Vi back from saying what she really felt. Trixie wanted her to know she was proud to have her as a friend because she was the best friend anyone could have, and hadn't she already proved herself to be someone to depend on?

'We'd like you to meet our neighbours and friends.'

Vi blushed. 'Of course,' she said. 'But didn't you say you couldn't go anywhere until you'd sorted out your hair?'

'That won't take long.' Trixie grinned. 'I've only got to mix together the peroxide and ammonia, then use an old tooth-brush to put it on my roots.' She disappeared into the scullery.

Rose said, 'If you want, Vi, you can lay this table for you, me and Trixie. The knives and forks are in that drawer.'

Trixie came back into the kitchen, just as Vi was opening the drawer.

'Got you working, has she?' She grinned at Vi. Then she said, 'If I do my hair first, you can have a wash in the scullery before me. I can wash after you.' Before Vi had a chance to say anything, Trixie was gone again.

'I think then we'd better eat.' Rose said. 'Des'll want feeding before he goes off to work. And I hope you don't mind but the pair of you will have to share the bed in the back bedroom.'

The back bedroom had always been Trixie's room.

A blush crept over Rose's face. 'I can't put you in the front room, Vi. As soon as Des moved in, I made up the bed to look like he sleeps in there.' She smiled at Vi. 'His clothes are strewn all over the place and every so often I leave the door open so nosy neighbours can see he's the lodger!' Her blush deepened. 'Well, they don't need to know he shares my bed, do they?' She paused. 'Anyway, all this deceit won't be for much longer.'

Trixie's head, covered with a pasty wash of bleach, came into view in the kitchen doorway. 'What d'you mean by that, Mum?' she asked.

Rose was about to drop a log into the top of the range. 'You're the first to know that we've decided to tie the knot at Christmas time. Not just to stop tongues wagging but because we care about each other. We chose Christmas because, my darling girl, we thought you'd be able to take time off from wherever you'll be working and come home for the wedding.' Rose looked at Vi. 'And you, Vi, of course!'

Trixie flew towards her mum and threw her arms about her. 'Oh! I'm so glad! So very, very glad!'

Rose had to hold on to the arm of the chair beneath the window to stop herself falling over in the embrace. 'Trix, I'm glad you approve but could you show your pleasure after you've washed that stuff off your head? It stinks to high Heaven! One of these days you'll wake up to find you've gone bald putting all that rubbish on your hair!'

Trixie grinned at Rose. She'd heard her say the same thing a hundred times before. She didn't like her naturally mousy hair and preferred to be blonde. She looked at Vi. 'Five minutes and you can have the scullery to yourself,' she said.

Vi, who was now drinking her tea, put her cup down and said shyly, 'I never expected to be going out and meeting people.'

Trixie hadn't forgotten that Vi's clothes weren't up to much – hadn't she lent her frocks to wear to the Yellow Duck?

Sometimes Vi wore her lumberjill clothes. Now she knew that Vi was worried about what to wear because she didn't want to let her friend down. 'You can borrow anything of mine, of course you can.' She reached the scullery door and turned back. 'When Des wakes up and we take our stuff up to my room, why don't you and I go through the clothes that I never took to Scotland? A lot of them I don't want.'

'I couldn't allow you to give me—'

Trixie put her finger to her lips, 'Ssh! Let's not wake Des. If there's anything you'd like you're more than welcome.'

Trixie disappeared into the scullery. Again, she'd seen the glitter of tears in Vi's eyes. She guessed that Vi hadn't been shown much kindness in her life. She quickly rinsed her hair and stared at it in the mirror hanging over the stone sink. No dark roots showed through. She towelled it almost dry, then took from the cupboard the paper bag containing cut-up pieces of material. Within minutes she'd wrapped and twisted her damp hair in rags, ready to be taken out and brushed into her Veronica Lake style when it had dried. Wiping out the sink so everything would be spotless for Vi, Trixie thought, Hen doesn't know how lucky she is to be a natural blonde.

Chapter Thirty-two

Trixie sat back on the kitchen chair and patted her full stomach. 'That was one of the best meals I've eaten in ages,' she said.

Vi nodded. 'It was delicious,' she said.

'I thought you said the food at Shandford Lodge was good,' Rose said, gathering up empty dishes. Trixie and Vi had been careful not to leave any mess in the scullery for Rose to clear up.

'Nothing beats your cooking, Mum!'

Rose smiled at her lovingly. 'Well,' she said, 'now I've shared Des and my news with you, isn't it about time you told me what's going on with you and Cy?'

Trixie left the table and foraged in her case. Her mum had just come back in from the scullery as she set on the table a brown carrier bag with string handles.

'I've no idea where we'll be going, I might even be sent home,' she said, 'but I want you to look after my letters, Mum.'

Rose wiped her hands on her wraparound pinny. 'That lot must have given him writer's cramp,' she said, taking the photograph Trixie passed to her. She studied it intently. 'Oh, Trix, no need to ask which one he is.' The photograph Trixie had shown her was of Cy with his best friend Hobo. 'He looks lovely! He's a real charmer,' she said. 'And his letters will be safe in the bottom of my wardrobe.' Like everyone else Rose refused to think they'd ever be bombed out of their home by one of Hitler's planes. 'And another thing,' she passed the photograph back to Trixie, who put it face up on the table, 'stop being so negative, thinking you won't have passed your training. From everything you've told me I think they'll be lucky to have the pair of you working for them.'

Rose had just finished speaking when Trixie heard footsteps coming down the stairs, the kitchen door opened and Des's smiling face, topped by his bright red hair, looked in. He was dressed in trousers with braces dangling, and a collarless shirt.

'Hello, you two,' he said, smiling first at Trixie then at Vi, but going straight to Rose, putting his arms around her and holding her tightly.

'Has she told you our news?'

'Of course!' said Trixie. Rose looked at him lovingly.

'I suppose I should have written and asked you if you were in agreement about me asking your mother to marry me, Trix, but you'd left home to give us time together so I didn't think you'd mind,' he said.

'Mind? I'm over the moon about it,' she answered.

He left Rose's side and put his arms around Trixie. 'Thank you,' he said. 'I haven't as yet been able to buy her an engagement ring, but I'm working on it.' He smiled fondly at Rose. 'I promise I'll look after her.'

Trixie kissed his bristly cheek. 'I know you will,' she said, stepping back as Des turned to Vi.

'You must be Vi,' he said. He moved towards her, arms outstretched, but as he did, she froze.

Trixie could see Vi's hands were clenched tightly, her face a mask of fear, as she turned away from him.

There was an awkward moment of silence.

Frowning, Trixie watched as Vi gathered herself together and said, in a stilted voice, 'I'm sorry, I'm not used to being . . . Sorry . . . I hope you'll both be very happy.' Vi sat down on her chair. She stared at Trixie as though looking for help.

Des, startled by Vi's reaction, and obviously trying to

atone for something he didn't understand, picked up Cy's photograph and said, 'So, this is Cy Davis, the young man who's stolen your heart, eh, Trixie? And you don't have to tell me which he is. I remember in a letter you said his friend plays the harmonica, so I guess Cy is the one without the musical instrument in his top pocket!'

He looked at the photo for a long time. 'Cy has an honest face. I like that in a man.' He passed the photo back to Trixie. Slowly, Trixie realized the awkwardness of the past few moments was being healed.

Vi was sitting quite still, breathing steadily. She must have felt Trixie looking at her for she suddenly smiled at her. Trixie felt relief flow through herself. Whatever had just happened, she thought, Vi would no doubt share with her later. Had Des frightened her in some way? Trixie didn't think so, but she'd never seen Vi in the company of any man, not by choice. She smiled back at Vi, remembering how quick Vi had been to hit Ben Tate with the watering can at the Yellow Duck.

Trixie watched as her mum bent down and opened the oven door of the range where she had put Des's dinner, with a plate over the top, to keep warm.

'Des, love, eat your dinner. We've had ours.'

With a teacloth wrapped around her hand, she carried the

hot plate towards the kitchen table and Trixie knew that was the signal for her to take Vi and their suitcases upstairs. Her heart lifted. Now Des was awake, they could make as much noise as they liked – she could even play her gramophone. She'd promised Vi she could look through the clothes in her wardrobe. Trixie hoped she hadn't offended her, suggesting she might like to have some of the clothes Trixie had grown tired of. She hadn't meant it as a patronizing gesture. There was every possibility Vi might have left all her prettiest clothes at her own home and taken only the most serviceable to Scotland, though somehow Trixie thought not.

Leaving her mother and Des in the kitchen, Trixie and Vi went upstairs. Her room at the back was just as she'd left it and memories flooded in as though she had been gone for years, not just a few weeks, when she stood at the window looking down at the garden below. Trixie pulled the blackout curtain across.

Vi, carrying her suitcase, stood in the doorway. 'You're lucky to have so many people care about you.'

Trixie paused while winding up the gramophone. 'I realize that,' she said. She'd already taken the twelve-inch record from its sleeve and put it on the turntable. The strains of 'Amapola' filled the room. 'It's not only Donnie who's fond of this piece of music,' she said, 'I am, too.' She sat on the bed and looked at Vi. 'Are you going to tell me why you flinched when Des got close to you?'

Vi, in the process of taking her nightdress from the case, stopped what she was doing. 'I'm sorry about that. I didn't mean to cause him any offence. I don't really know how to behave around men. I'm scared of them.'

Trixie stared at her. 'No one could be scared of Des – he's as soft as butter.'

Vi sighed. 'Look, can we just forget about it?'

'Yes,' said Trixie. 'Of course.' Then she added, 'If you look in that cupboard over there,' she nodded towards the fireplace, with the grate cleaned and a paper fan standing in it, 'you'll find all sorts. See if anything takes your fancy. There's only a few bits of clothing I didn't take to Scotland with me that I want to keep.' Trixie had said she'd forget about Vi's behaviour. Except she couldn't. And now she remembered that while they'd been working at Shandford Lodge, Vi had never shown the slightest interest in men. Unlike Hen.

In the Yellow Duck, Vi had sat near the piano most nights, never moving.

The man she'd had most contact with was Alf, which was necessary because of work. And Vi had been especially suspicious of Ben Tate. But that was with good reason, wasn't it?

The record finished and Trixie took it off the turntable and replaced it with 'Chattanooga Choo Choo'.

Vi laughed. 'You have a lovely bedroom,' she said.

Trixie's eyes roved round her room, taking in the iron double bedstead with the curly bits that were painted gold. The bed had a patchwork quilt that her mother had made from pieces of their old clothing. There was a bamboo table with the gramophone on top, and space for her records below, a chest of drawers with a three-way mirror, and another chair with a padded seat, on which she used to pile freshly washed clothes before she put them away. The wallpaper was patterned with sprigs of flowers and she liked it better than the paper in her mum's room that featured evil-looking peacocks. Her curtains, beneath the blackout material, were also made of patchwork. A pile of books, mostly prizes she had been presented with at school, included *Black Beauty* and *Heidi*.

Trixie laughed back at Vi, 'I like my bedroom, too,' she said.

Vi held out some clothes. 'Can I try these on?'

'Of course,' said Trixie. She put up her hand and felt her knotted curls, pleased that in the warmth of the little house, her hair was almost dry.

Downstairs, she could hear her mum laughing. It made her feel happy inside.

*

'That was one of the best nights I've ever had. Thank you.'

Trixie heard Vi's words in the darkness and smiled. Her bed felt just as comfortable as she remembered it. Trixie yawned. It had been a lovely evening down at the Alma, like old times, with her sitting at the battered upright piano while the customers joined in with the songs they loved to hear. So many had come up and asked her about her life and work in Scotland that she'd begun to feel quite special.

Rose had sat in the alcove with some of the neighbours, smiling proudly whenever Trixie looked over at her. It was a pity that Des couldn't be there but work came first. Rose had been lucky to be granted a couple of days off from her cleaning job at the War Memorial Hospital. She enjoyed the camaraderie of the other women she worked with. It was where she and Des had first met. Though she was often teased about how they'd managed to meet, with her working days and him on nights!

Ellie, the manageress of the Alma, had produced hot sausage rolls that she had made earlier in the day and warmed up. Trixie swore there was more bread than sausage inside them, but there was a war on and all the plates went back empty to the bar.

Mr Watt, from the greengrocer's, had stood beside the piano and said, 'I miss you in the shop, Trixie. It's not the same without you, and the customers are always asking after you.' He'd asked her to play 'Thanks For The Memory', telling her it was his favourite, and he'd sung along in his scratchy voice while she played. 'There'll always be a job for you at my shop,' he'd added.

Trixie could hardly keep her eyes open. Not only had they travelled back from Scotland, leaving Shandford Lodge at some unearthly hour, but the excitement of seeing her mum and Des, then being in the Alma and meeting old friends had practically wiped her out. She was so glad now to be in her own bed. She took a deep breath of the familiar smell of her room.

Briefly she wondered how Hen was faring. She'd find out the day after tomorrow, when she and Vi visited her in Alverstoke to collect her for the trip back to Scotland. A weekend wasn't really long enough when there was so much to do, she decided.

She heard Vi sigh.

'Can't you sleep?' Trixie asked.

'There's so much on my mind. I understand why you became a lumberjill. It was partly to give your mum and Des time and space to show their true feelings to each other. Now they've decided to marry, you could come home.'

'I don't want to,' Trixie said. 'I'm enjoying my new life.

Discovering different stuff. And I like being with you, Hen and Jo—'

'I'm worrying about when you come to meet my mum,' Vi broke in. 'How you'll feel about her.'

'Don't,' answered Trixie. 'I'm *your* friend, not your mum's.'

'I know,' answered Vi. 'I just hope you'll go on being my friend.'

The words were hardly out of her mouth when Moaning Minnie's shrieks rent the air. The bedroom door opened and Rose stood there in her candlewick dressing-gown, a hairnet over her curls.

'You girls, come on down, now. We must get into the shelter.'

Vi rolled off the bed.

Trixie said, 'Take my dressing-gown. I've got a coat I can slip on.'

'I need a hand to make a few sandwiches and a flask,' called Rose, already downstairs. 'There's no telling how long it'll be until the all-clear sounds.'

'I'm coming,' called Vi.

Trixie sat up in bed. 'Bugger!' All the time she'd been in Scotland they'd never used a shelter because there'd been no raids. Now she was so tired she could have slept on a clothes line, and on her first night back in Gosport, ol' Adolf was sending over his planes.

The darkness engulfed her as she knelt on the end of the bed, pulled back the blackout curtain and peered into the sky. She could see them! Usually, she obeyed her mother and made straight for the garden shelter, but in Scotland Donnie had encouraged her to join him outside in the open air to watch enemy planes, Dorniers, fly to the aerodrome at RAF Leuchars and it had fascinated her.

Silver shapes in the sky, a swarm of planes, heading towards Portsmouth. Too many to count, and the nearer they came the louder their engines hummed. And then she could make out smaller versions, fighter planes, threaded about the swarm.

Trixie, mesmerized, watched as black dots dropped from the bombers, falling to earth.

Next came the *whump!* of explosions as the bombs found their marks or missed their targets. The planes were over-head now, the noise an unbearable cacophony of sound. Through the racket she could hear her mother screaming, 'Trixie!'

And still she watched, safe in the knowledge that, with no light behind her, she could not be seen. She couldn't tear herself away. Even though, instead of watching, any moment she might become a participant in the scenario unfolding before her.

Smoke was billowing on the skyline. Coming from the Dockyard, she thought.

Red and orange mingling with the grey of the blasts. And now the searchlights were waving backwards, forwards, trying to pin down the perpetrators so the anti-aircraft guns could eliminate them from the sky.

Trixie became aware of her mother's voice behind her. 'Drop that curtain and come down to the shelter with us immediately.'

Trixie did as she was told. She scrambled from the bed and practically fell into her mother's arms. 'Mum, it's horrible,' she cried. 'I never really took it all in before, but it's so horrible.'

'Ever felt you might have made a mistake in volunteering for this job?' grunted Hobo.

Cy stopped hurrying and carefully set down the heavy panniers hanging from the yoke about his shoulders. The palm-leaf bags were filled with gravel and he didn't want to be on his hands and knees picking it up if he spilt it. Not in this heat. He wiped the sweat streaming from his forehead with one hand, then used the other to massage his aching back.

'I did it for the extra rice, ya big jerk! Didn't mean you had to do the same.'

Food had soon deteriorated, both in portion size and content at the camp. The bowl of miso soup, now little more than flavoured water, had been reduced to a cupful. Meat was practically non-existent and the bread seemed to consist of more sawdust than flour.

'Weren't no volunteering, though, was there? Forced to do it, anyways,' said Hobo, staggering past him with his own panniers. He paused, knees shaking due to the heavy weight, then emptied one bag of gravel onto the stone surface of the road. The sound suddenly reminded Cy of waves breaking on a shoreline. Hobo guided his second pannier to the road, tipped it and emptied the bag. He removed the yoke and stood up straight, rotating his shoulders and straightening his back.

Cy looked across at Hiroshi, their guard, falling asleep beneath the shade of a palm tree. Hiroshi had told them all Japanese names had meanings. His meant 'generous' and 'a blessing'. Cy thought it suited him. He was affable and talkative, and gave the men he was guarding certain privileges. He was wise enough to understand that, as long as he sometimes looked the other way, the work would continue.

Wearily, Cy elevated the wooden yoke back across his shoulders and ferried his bags to join Hobo's. After tipping the gravel he and Hobo stood back and surveyed their achievement. Cy was aware of the honeyed smell from the flowers blooming on the shrubs about them. He, too, removed his yoke, and stretched.

Hobo dug around beneath a nearby pikake vine and produced a Japanese aluminium water bottle and pulled out the stopper. He drank sparingly then passed it across to Cy. After drinking, Cy said, 'Thoughtful of the Japs to provide these.' He passed the bottle back to Hobo who tucked it back in the shade. 'They know we'll work better if we have water, the bastards,' he added. Cy watched Hobo pick a white petal from the vine, put it into his mouth and chew it thoughtfully.

'One of these days you'll poison yourself,' said Cy. Hobo's face wound had healed but the long scar would remain. He reminded Cy of a pirate.

'Not me, my dad taught me about plants too well. They make perfume from this pikake vine and also use it to flavour tea. It's really jasmine. Now if you want poison, plumeria is quite likely to upset you.'

Cy stared at him. Sometimes he wondered how his buddy's brain could contain so much information. An outlet for his knowledge was the vegetable garden he was attempting to dig, back at the compound, on the days they weren't re-establishing the highway.

The reconstruction of the road, previously bombed by Japanese aircraft and leading towards the devastated runway of the airport, meant clearing jungle foliage, digging out palm roots, flattening a road bed, bringing in stones from the quarry, stamping down the surface, then putting on a layer of gravel also hauled from the nearby quarry.

Cy realized that the sooner the Japanese could put the airport back in commission the sooner they could use it for themselves. Especially as they now occupied the tiny Pacific Island of Pearlien, which was about five miles long and three miles wide, surrounded by coral reefs and with a lagoon in the middle. It was inhabited now only by birds, insects, small mammals and a profusion of palms and plants. The Pan Am employees were dead or departed. Japanese enemy prisoners were tucked safely into a newly built concentration camp.

Hiroshi was asleep. Cy sank down thankfully beneath the shade of a palm next to the road.

'Ever thought about escape?' Hobo asked, crouching beside him.

Cy stared at Hobo. 'What's the point? Where would we go? We'd need a boat, which we don't have, and the only way off the island is the way we arrived, via a jetty guarded by Japs. We'd be brought back and killed. Tadamichi Yamamoto promised ten men would be executed for every prisoner who escaped and was recaptured.'

'Ben Tate said—'

Cy didn't let him finish: 'Why d'you listen to that sleazeball?'

'He provided you with your shoes, didn't he?'

Cy looked down at the worn rubber-soled footwear he'd been overjoyed to accept because his bare feet had been cut to ribbons when they'd come to Pearlien.

'It doesn't mean I have to like him.' Cy didn't trust him. Ben Tate was out to make a fast buck. He could provide stuff but he wanted paying back threefold. His footwear had cost Hobo his harmonica. Cy had been unconscious, out cold at the time, or he'd never have let Hobo give up the instrument he loved. The English in the camp called Tate a 'spiv', just not to his face.

Their guard was still sleeping in the shade.

'I wonder when we'll get our postcards,' said Hobo.

'Changing the subject, are we?' Cy asked. The Red Cross had supplied the camp with postcards for the prisoners to fill in so they could be sent home to stop relatives worrying. 'We may never get 'em. The Japs don't want us writing. They may have signed the Geneva Convention but it's believed they aren't honouring it.'

Hobo sighed. 'If they hand them out, who will you write to? Your ma or Trixie?'

Cy knew Hobo's postcard would go to his mother. He had already decided his own would have to go to his ma, as his next of kin. He'd furnished her with Trixie's home address so Trixie would eventually hear any news. Trixie, having ended her probationary period for the lumberjills, could now be posted anywhere.

Cy had thought long and hard about the very real possibility of something happening to him. Dysentery, malaria and scurvy were rife in the camp. He'd lost weight, but hadn't they all? His fingers went to the tattered photograph in his pocket. God, he loved that girl. How the future panned out depended on karma, didn't it? He put his face up towards the sun, feeling its heat upon his skin. This short break from hauling stones had done him some good. A movement at the corner of his eye caught his attention. Hiroshi was waking.

'Hobo! Back to work,' he hissed.

Chapter Thirty-three

Trixie stood on the bridge, her suitcase at her feet, staring down into the murky waters of Workhouse Lake. On the other side of the creek the dour red-brick Alverstoke House of Industry loomed. Once a thriving workhouse, it was now a home for the elderly and less fortunate of Gosport. The building made Trixie shiver. The less fortunate families of Gosport were now struggling to live elsewhere in the town.

'My home is three doors away from the Robin Hood pub, and this street and the surrounding area are notorious for trouble,' Vi said.

'It's not places that make trouble, it's people,' said Trixie. She didn't add that just as Alverstoke was known for its affluent society, these streets, overshadowed by the gas works and poorhouse, were acknowledged as grim.

She watched the late sun brighten the rubbish thrown

into the water. The pavement was clean. The heavy rain of yesterday had swept away the dust and dirt. Swans were swimming around broken furniture in the lake as proudly as if they were paddling in a willow-fringed village pond.

She was tired. The all-clear hadn't sounded until the early hours of this morning. The horrific noise of aircraft and close-by bombing had kept them wide awake and terrified in the Anderson shelter. It must have been around four when Rose, Trixie and Vi trudged wearily back into the house, which was still standing, and climbed thankfully into their beds.

Nobody had woken until Des returned from work. Trixie had been worried that Vi's mum would be wondering where her daughter had got to, but Vi's reluctance to visit her mother was obvious.

Now Trixie looked away from the swans and said firmly, 'We don't have to go to your house.'

Vi slipped her arm through Trixie's and said, 'But we do. I need to know my mother is all right. And as I can't talk to you about my life, the bruising to my body, and tell you why I decided to join the lumberjills, I have to show you. You're my best friend, I can trust you and, like I said before, I don't want secrets between us.'

The house had an overgrown garden that led to a front

door with a hole where the letterbox should have been. Remnants of cardboard tacked to keep out the draught hung torn, useless.

Vi took from her handbag a key and opened the door. 'We don't leave keys on strings around here,' she said.

In the darkened hall Vi flicked up the electric light switch but nothing happened.

'Might have guessed,' she said, turning to Trixie. 'I need to put money in the electric meter.' Trixie heard the snap of Vi's handbag catch as she fumbled for her purse. Then, 'Move to one side, Trix. The meter's on the wall behind you.'

Trixie obliged. She heard the twist and click, then the chink of falling money. The house smelt of damp, and when the bulb hanging in the passageway lit, she saw that the walls were glistening with moisture. Patches of black mould were dotted here and there on the wallpaper.

'Is your mum here?' Trixie asked.

'I expect so,' Vi answered. Leading the way, Vi added, 'Leave your case.' She pushed open a door and went inside. Trixie followed.

She didn't expect to see the woman lying listlessly across the sofa. She thought at first she was asleep but she heard her say to Vi, 'You came, then. I didn't think you would after—'

'I'd have come before but—'

'I know, love.' There was a great deal of meaning in those three words. 'It's better you abide by the regulations. You start messing people about, taking time off, and they'll think you're unreliable.' The woman looked at Trixie. 'So, you're Trixie?'

Trixie nodded. She wasn't sure what was expected of her. That the woman, presumably Vi's mother, even knew her name amazed her because, to the best of her knowledge, Vi wrote regularly to no one and seldom received letters.

Vi knelt on the threadbare mat in front of her mother, who moved so she could cup Vi's chin in her hand and look into her face. 'Lovely girl,' she muttered. Then her hand went to the cushion at her head and, with great difficulty, she pulled out an envelope. 'Birthday card,' she wheezed.

The movement and the talking were too much for her and she began to cough. Vi fumbled beneath the sofa's cushion and took out a handkerchief, which her mother held to her mouth. Her wrist and arm were like bones held together with skin. The coughing began to subside but not before Trixie had noted the blood, bright red, on the cotton material.

She averted her eyes and looked around the room. The sofa was part of a three-piece suite, with two chairs at either side of the fireplace where the remains of a fire had been left to burn out. The room wasn't cold. It was stuffy and smelt of sickness. A single bed was pushed against the other wall. It was made up and covered with a well-washed candlewick bedspread. A clean chamber pot peeked out from underneath. A nightdress was draped over the bed. Across the room there was a sideboard and on top, sitting on lace doilies, framed photographs. Most were of Vi at various ages, some with her mother, and one, at the back, of a very young Vi, held in the arms of a man with fair hair.

Vi must have seen her looking at it. 'That's my dad,' she said proudly. Then she asked her mother, 'How long have you been in the dark? Have you eaten?'

'The dark doesn't worry me and I'm not hungry.'

'I didn't ask if you were hungry,' Vi said smartly, rising to her feet. 'Trix, can you stay here while I pop up to Mathews, the corner shop?'

'Of course.' Trixie didn't say she would have preferred to be the one going to the shop. Vi, as a rule, was a girl of few words. She hadn't told Trixie anything about her home life. To be left with Vi's sick mother worried her. Whatever would they talk about? What if she had another coughing fit?

'It might be a good idea if you could also take our cases upstairs to my room,' Vi said.

'Yes,' said Trixie, glad she wasn't be expected to stay and make conversation.

Vi gathered up the envelope and handed it to her. 'Can you take this up as well? My bedroom's the one at the end of the hallway.' Then she looked at her mother. 'When's he due back?'

Her mother, who had been watching Vi, looked away. She sighed. 'No idea,' she answered. 'Depends on the time of the last race, the last punter.'

'Right,' said Vi. 'I'll be back before you've noticed I've gone.'

Trixie heard the front door close behind her. 'Do you need anything? Er, can I get you something?'

'Not a thing, Trixie. My neighbour, Irene, is a good friend who comes in when she can. You can call me Alice, my love.' It was, thought Trixie, as if Alice knew she felt uneasy and was trying to help her. 'Why don't you take your things upstairs to the bedroom?'

Glad to escape, yet at the same time wondering why Vi hadn't told her that her mother was ill so that she could have prepared herself, Trixie went out into the hall and picked up the suitcases. There was a coat-rack with assorted clothing, mostly women's but a man's overcoat hung there with a Homburg hat. She wondered if a male lodger lived at the house. There had been references to a man. Could it be the man in the photograph, her father?

The stairs, leading up from the hallway were dimly lit. There were three doors leading off and Trixie, carrying both suitcases, approached the furthest. Her attention was immediately focused on the door knob, which was at a peculiar angle. As she put her hand on it, she felt it move. The lock had obviously been broken.

Inside the sparsely furnished but clean room there was a double bed, a chest of drawers with a foxed mirror leaning against the apple-green wall. There was a chair to put things on and another as a table against the bed. The room was functional but Trixie could understand why Vi had enthused so much about Trixie's comfortable bedroom. Setting down the suitcases, Trixie took the card from her pocket and put it against the mirror on the chest of drawers. She went over to the window and looked out. Gasometers hovered over the long, thin scruffy back gardens like beings from another world. Trixie shuddered.

She could see into the yard at the back of the pub. Wooden barrels were stacked against a dirty wall that had once been whitewashed. A broken-backed chair was next to a barrel that held a large glass ashtray. Even from this distance she could see the dog ends swimming in the dirty rainwater that filled it. Clearly the chair and makeshift table made up someone's idea of solitude.

Looking at the bed with its blue candlewick counterpane reminded her of how tired she was. It looked inviting. But it wouldn't do for Vi to return and find her asleep. She knew if she lay down for just one moment, she would drop off.

She heard Alice coughing again and a needle of shame pricked her. She should be downstairs seeing if she could help her.

Alice smiled at her when she entered the room. The handkerchief was gripped in her hand. 'Vi thinks a great deal of you. I need you to promise me that if ever she thinks of leaving the Timber Corps you'll do everything to persuade her to stay, and not come back here.'

It took Trixie a while to take in the words. 'I can't make her do anything and there's no guarantee we'll even be working together when we go back. The past few weeks have only been a training period.'

She shook her head, 'You two apparently make a good team,' she said. She fixed her eyes, so like Vi's, on Trixie. 'They'll keep you together. She mustn't come back!'

Trixie was taken aback at the force of her words. From so frail a person it appeared to have taken a great deal of energy from her. There had to be an enormously important reason why a mother as ill as Alice was didn't want her daughter around her. 'I'll do what I can,' she said.

Apparently, it was the right answer for Alice smiled again at her. 'Thank you,' she said. Relief seemed to ooze from her every pore.

Trixie heard the key in the front door. Vi came in with a carrier bag, which she dumped on the floor. Trixie could see tins of food, including corned beef, butter in greaseproof paper, and a fresh loaf. She stood looking at her mum. 'I'm going to make you some soup and watch while you eat it,' she said to her.

Trixie had no idea how Vi had managed to buy rationed food and doubted she would tell her if she asked. Vi surprised her: 'Money talks round here.' She moved close to her mother. 'I've paid what's owed at Mathews'. Your slate's clean. Old Mathews said he won't tell him.' Then she turned to Trixie and said, 'C'mon, we've got a meal to cook.'

At the door Vi said, 'Irene knows I'm here. She says you know where she is if she's needed and I've told her I'll see to you up until I leave tomorrow. Now, if you don't need anything, have a little doze while I cook.'

Vi picked up her shoulder bag, extracted some pennies from her purse and said, 'If there was no electric, there's bound to be no gas.'

Trixie watched her put the money into the meter.

Chapter Thirty-four

Trixie had eaten well. She was washing the last of the pots in the stone sink and paused to look around the scullery. In truth she'd seen better dishes and pans at jumble sales but everything, though old, was well used and mostly clean. She pondered bits of conversation she'd overheard but hadn't understood.

Damp patches decorated the walls and cobwebs, too high to worry about, dangled in the ceiling corners. The long garden that she could see through the yellowed net curtains was a mass of weeds and brambles, though the remains of sunflowers, their seeds already pecked by birds, still stood tall.

True to her word Vi had fed her mother as much soup as she was able to take. She'd washed her, made her comfortable, and had managed to get the wireless going again by fiddling with the back.

'Oh, I have missed the music,' Alice said.

And now Vi closed the blackout curtains before they settled to listen to Geraldo and his orchestra. Alice hummed along to some of the tunes.

'I like listening to ITMA best,' Alice said. 'My favourite character is Mrs Mopp, the charlady . . .'

'Can I do yer now, sir?' Interrupted Vi using practically the same voice that Dorothy Summers used for her programme character.

Alice laughed so much she almost choked, and afterwards Vi had to hold a cup of tea up to her mother's mouth so she could swallow properly again.

Trixie yawned.

'You two ought to get to bed,' Alice said. 'I doubt you got much sleep last night with the raid and tomorrow you'll be travelling overnight back to Scotland.'

'Actually, it's nice sitting here with you, talking and laughing,' said Trixie.

And it was, she thought. Vi might not have written much to her mother but she seemed to know a great deal about their lives at Shandford Lodge. She decided that before Alice had become ill she had been a vivacious woman. There were still traces of beauty in her face, despite the sunken cheeks and prematurely grey hair.

At last, the excitement of Vi and Trixie being there, their laughter, and their jigging about to the band music now issuing from the wireless began to tell on Alice, and Vi admitted it was time to call it a night.

'You go on up and I'll follow when I've settled Mum for sleeping.'

Upstairs, Trixie washed herself in the bowl using water from the jug on the chest of drawers, then got into bed. She looked at the envelope containing the birthday card. If it was Vi's birthday, why hadn't she said anything?

She wondered how long Alice could survive the tuberculosis that was wasting her away. As she lay waiting for Vi to come up, she could hear raucous laughter coming from the pub. There were so many questions running around in her brain that needed answering. The awful bruising that had covered most of Vi's body when they'd first met? And why wouldn't Vi tell her how it had happened? But she would show her, she'd said, only if she came home to stay with her.

Tiredness claimed her and she was almost asleep, despite the noise still issuing from the Robin Hood, when Vi climbed into bed beside her.

Sleepily, Trixie decided there was little point in talking now, when they had to visit Hen in Alverstoke tomorrow and begin the long journey back to Scotland. As she felt the mattress give way to Vi's weight, she managed to whisper, 'Goodnight.'

Bang!

The noise woke Trixie. Alarmed she sat bolt upright in bed.

The bedroom door, previously closed, had shot back against the wall with great force. Vi's hand covered hers. 'He won't do anything to you,' she said.

Trixie tried to understand Vi's words. 'Who?'

'Alec,' said Vi, now out of bed and facing the moustached and suited man who had stepped into the room. Vi stood with her hands on her hips, staring at him. Trixie could almost feel the hatred oozing from her. The man had halted upon seeing Trixie. Shock and confusion showed on his face.

Trixie scrambled from the bed covers and into her dressing-gown as a smell that reminded her of something wafted to her . . . She swallowed to stop herself gagging. Whisky. The man wasn't drunk but he'd been drinking spirits.

'Hello, sweetheart.' He was addressing Vi. His confusion at seeing she wasn't alone was now replaced by cockiness and shown in the arrogant smile that covered his face. 'I heard you'd come home.'

His dark hair was Brylcreemed to a sheen and Trixie thought

he'd have been a good-looking man if his face wasn't so chis-elled. Her heart was beating fast. Sleep had slid away from her and her senses had returned. Trixie found her voice. 'Who are you? What do you want?' She wasn't used to being woken up by strange men pushing through the bedroom door. It sud-denly occurred to her, thinking of the broken lock, that this wasn't the first time he'd entered the room like that.

'Doesn't matter who I am, lovey.' He drew himself up to his full height, which was probably well over six foot, and said, 'But you're the deterrent all right.' He nodded towards Vi. 'Trickery, eh? I didn't know you'd have a friend with you. Oh, well! I can wait.' He gave a mocking smile that showed small, very white teeth, shark-like, thought Trixie. Then, without another word, he strode away. Trixie heard another door opening, then slamming shut.

For a moment there was silence, which Trixie broke as she sat down heavily on the edge of the bed. 'That was terrifying! What did he want?' Suddenly she realized what Alec had wanted: Vi.

Vi sat beside her. 'I'm sorry,' she said. 'Please believe me when I say I knew he wouldn't harm a hair on your head. If his boss Billy Hill found out he'd broken into a bedroom where an unknown young woman was sleeping, not far from one of his establishments, he'd kill him.'

Trixie looked at her. 'Billy Hill? Isn't he some kind of gangster? You've got to tell me what's going on, Vi.'

Vi nodded. 'All right. You'd never have believed me if I'd tried to tell you. I had to show you. Alec's made my life a misery. But he's scared of his boss. Billy Hill is London's number-one gangster. And he's got ethics where his henchmen are concerned. Women and children shouldn't be harmed.'

'Alec works for him?'

She nodded. 'He's a bookie's runner, Billy Hill's runner.'

'Street gambling's illegal, isn't it?' Trixie asked.

Vi nodded. 'Billy Hill has bases in pubs and relies on runners, like Alec, to collect bets and pay off winners. Lookouts warn Alec when the police are about.'

Again, there was silence as Trixie tried to take in Vi's words.

'So,' Trixie said, 'Billy wouldn't be pleased to find out Alec had burst into my bedroom unannounced?'

'Exactly,' said Vi.

Trixie's eyes went to the knob on the bedroom door. 'That wasn't the first time he's broken in, was it?'

Vi shook her head. Trixie saw tears in her eyes. 'He's been hurting you, hasn't he?'

Vi had covered her eyes with her hands. Her voice was quiet as she answered, 'It's got worse.'

Trixie put her arms around her. 'You've got to tell me. Now.'

Vi said, 'All right, I'll start at the beginning. But please don't judge me. I've been going through hell.' Vi wiped a hand across her wet cheeks.

'Alec came to live with us a couple of years ago. He was nice. He made my mum laugh and she hadn't laughed much since my dad died of influenza. At first, we were like a family. I think Mum was glad there was a father figure about, because she said having him here had quietened me down. When I was younger, I was always getting into trouble, not stealing or anything like that. There's a lot of that goes on round here. But I could tell lies and get other kids out of trouble because people believed me. My mum and Alec, they were always kissing and cuddling. Mum knew what he did for a living but round here a job like that earns you respect. Mind you, we didn't know then who he worked for.

'Last year, when Mum got poorly, the kissing and cuddling stopped.' Here Vi started to cry again but she took a deep breath, wiped her eyes and began talking once more.

'Mum had to have stuff to help her to sleep. Alec would stop by my bedroom to chat. He'd sometimes sit on the bed. Then he began touching me. I knew it wasn't right but I didn't know what to do about it. I told him I'd tell. He said no one would believe a liar like me. I couldn't say anything to Mum because I didn't want to hurt her. Sometimes I thought even she might not believe me, because she loved him. It stopped for a while when he found himself another girlfriend, a young one. There were always women around him because he had cash, you see. He still looked after us, then, with money. But the more poorly Mum became the more he stayed away and, honestly, I was glad about that.

'When he was home, I used to push the chest of drawers in front of the door but he'd kick it in. I used to take the bread knife to bed with me. One night when he was trying to get at me, I slashed him across the arm and the blood just spurted out. He tied his belt around it and it stopped bleeding. Then he disappeared, probably up to the pub, telling them some made-up story.'

Trixie didn't say anything but it ran through her mind that that was where Vi learnt to tie a tourniquet.

'I couldn't run away and leave Mum, could I?' Trixie shook her head. 'But as I was old enough then to get a job, Eric Mathews took me on in the corner shop, delivering orders . . .'

Trixie frowned. She didn't understand. She was trying to work out how old Vi was, but Vi had begun talking again.

'Mum's friend Irene was and is a godsend. She'd come in

and look after her when I couldn't be here. She's married to a good man who's employed at the gasworks. He doesn't know the half of it. She still cooks and looks after Mum now. I send her money for Mum.' A smile touched Vi's lips. 'That's why I don't have money to spend on frivolous things for myself,' she said. 'Alec hardly ever puts his hand in his pocket for us now.'

Vi ran a hand across her forehead. 'I never wanted to come back here, Trix. That bloke frightens me to death. I think he's decided that if he can't have my body he'll just carry on beating me. But I did want to see my mum . . .' She took a deep breath. 'When you asked me about all those bruises, I thought if I told you the truth you wouldn't believe me. I was so proud you wanted to be my friend—'

Trixie interrupted her. 'But from the way your mum spoke tonight, she knows what's been happening, doesn't she?'

'Yes. The night he broke the lock on my door, Mum heard the kerfuffle and don't ask me how she did it but she left the front room and came upstairs to see what was going on. I was on the floor. I was determined he wasn't going to touch me. I'd curled myself into a ball but he kicked me. Mum told him to get out. He said he would, for that night, but he'd come back because when she died he'd have the house.'

'That's awful,' said Trixie.

'Mum said she didn't care about the house, but she was sure Billy Hill would want to know that one of his men was a kiddie-fiddler.'

Trixie must have frowned because Vi added, 'A kiddie-fiddler is an obnoxious man who touches young kids.'

Trixie almost couldn't believe what she was hearing. But she'd seen Alec and knew he could certainly be capable of such cruelty. Again, she wondered about Vi's age.

Vi carried on speaking. 'The next day Mum made me look for a job away from home. That's why I joined the lumberjills.' She sighed. 'I didn't want to leave Mum. But she and Irene persuaded me. They both said if I wasn't around, he couldn't hurt me. In the end I saw the wisdom in their words and gave in. By the time I had a medical, my bruises had almost healed. Alec didn't know I was going to leave home. When he found out, I got another hiding. It was the night before I met you on the train.'

So, at last Trixie knew how Vi had come by all those bruises. How awful for her having to hide them, and being too ashamed to tell anyone about them because she feared she wouldn't be believed. Her heart went out to the girl. And what of Alec? He was a despicable man. Trixie wasn't going to waste time thinking about him. Not when she firmly believed that what went around came around. One day, he would get his just deserts. She just knew he would.

'That's why you're frightened of men, isn't it?' Trixie's words tumbled from her lips. She remembered how Vi had turned away when Des had tried to hug her.

'Wouldn't you be?' asked Vi.

Trixie picked up her hand and held it.

'Wasn't there anyone else you could go to? The police?'

'No one goes to the police for anything in this part of Gosport. The police are the enemy. If they can't stop Alec being a runner, do you really think they'd take notice and help me? No, my mum was right. I had to leave.'

'Yes, of course,' Trixie said. Then she added, 'That's how you knew Ben Tate had put whisky in my orangeade, isn't it? I smelt whisky when Alec barged in here.'

'I learnt to loathe it,' Vi said. 'And when I saw Ben Tate had taken you out of the hut while Dolly was dancing, I knew exactly what he hoped to do. I was so angry I couldn't help myself. I belted that man with the nearest thing to hand, that watering can!'

'I was so proud of you that night,' said Trixie. 'And grateful.'

'Please tell me you're not angry with me and that you understand why I didn't want to come home unless you were with me.'

'I understand, Vi. I'm not saying I agree with you.' She took a deep breath. 'I'll be glad to leave tomorrow.'

Vi got up, went to the door and closed it. She leant the chair against the door.

'He won't come back but I think you'll feel better knowing this will make a noise if the door's touched.' Vi said. 'Perhaps it's better if we try to sleep now.'

Trixie didn't say anything but she climbed back into the bed and as she did so her eye fell on the envelope on the chest of drawers. 'When's your birthday, Vi?'

'Tuesday,' Vi said. 'I'll be sixteen.'

Trixie's mind was spinning again. She wanted to scream about the injustice of everything. But she didn't. She'd thought Vi was nearer her own age, not that that would have made any difference to what Vi had gone through. During the past four weeks of training Vi had proved how adult she was. Trixie was well aware that many girls had lied about their ages to become lumberjills, some just thirteen. The basic age requirement was seventeen. Girls were leaving school and working at fourteen: hadn't she done so herself? Vi might be the youngest of the four of them, herself, Jo, and Hen, but she'd been forced to live an awful lot of life in those few years, thought Trixie.

Chapter Thirty-five

'Come on, you two. Wakey, wakey! I've made you both tea and if you go on sleeping, you'll never get round your friend's house.'

Trixie opened her eyes to see a small woman in a flowered wraparound pinny, her hair in an untidy grey bun with wisps falling around her face, wearing a grin a mile wide. On the chair beside the bed were two mugs of steaming tea. From downstairs came wafting up from the wireless the dulcet tones of Frank Sinatra.

Vi, next to Trixie, was already struggling to a sitting position. 'Is he . . .' Vi started.

'Gone? Yes, the devil's not in his room, so we're all alone in the house and your mum's fine, love.'

'You're an angel,' she said to the woman. Then to Trixie, 'This is Irene, Trixie, and she really is an angel.'

'Hello,' said Trixie. She took the tea as Vi passed the mug to her.

'Irene, I've been thinking—'

'Stop before you go any further! If you're going to come out with any rubbish about staying in Gosport, you'll break your mother's heart.'

Trixie looked at Vi and it was quite clear from the look on her face that she had been considering this.

Vi swallowed some tea. 'Right, Then we'd better wash and dress and get out of here, hadn't we?'

Irene said, 'Good girl. I'll be making toast for you so don't let it get cold.' And then she was gone.

There was so much Trixie wanted to ask, to say, but Vi beat her to it: 'Trixie Smith, now you understand why I loved spending time with you at your mum's house and why being a lumberjill means so much to me. I suggest we do exactly as Irene says.'

Later, walking through Foster Gardens towards Alverstoke, Vi said, 'Can I ask a favour?'

Trixie said, 'Of course. Not sure I'll go along with it, though.'

Vi set down her case and said, 'I hope you do. As we won't know until we get back to Shandford Lodge whether we'll be staying together, could I ask if we could keep between us two what happened yesterday?'

Trixie said, 'I won't say anything to anybody. Your private life is simply that, private.' She smiled at Vi. Then she remembered how unhappy Vi had been at the start of their training. 'I know now why you kept yourself to yourself and didn't talk to anyone. However, you might find things easier to cope with if you do confide in people. I don't mean shout your business from the tree-tops but talking about bad things helps to put them in perspective. In the meantime I'm here if you need to share your fears and I'll help in any way I can.'

'I'm grateful to you,' said Vi. Her eyes were bright with unshed tears.

Trixie said, 'That's what friends are for.' She added, 'You know why I joined up to be a lumberjill and now I understand why you did. One day, if we're still all together, we might find out why Hen and Jo signed on the dotted line.'

Vi nodded. She looked at her watch. 'We're a bit early for visiting Hen. Think she'll mind?'

Trixie replied, 'Considering she didn't want to go home, I wouldn't think so. She might be very pleased to see us.'

'C'mon, then,' said Vi. 'Western Way, here we come. Let's go and see how the toffs live, Trix.'

The two girls stood at the bottom of the long driveway that led to the very large house. A double garage, doors open showing a dark-coloured saloon car, was built on at the side and another vehicle was parked in front. Immaculate gardens surrounded the building and Trixie could see apple trees at the rear, enclosed by a wooden fence. She remembered Hen telling them her dad owned an orchard and supplied local shops with fruit. The place looked lovely, Trixie thought, like a picture in a story book. Even the air smelt fresh and clean in Alverstoke.

'Look at that car!' Vi gasped.

Trixie eyed the sporty dark green MG TA standing on the gravel outside the porch at the front door. 'That wouldn't last five minutes down my mum's street,' she said. 'The kids would be crawling all over it.'

Vi giggled. 'A whole five minutes, eh? Where I come from it would have been dismantled or sold in two.' They laughed.

The front door swung open. 'I refuse to wait any longer,' a thin man in a suit bellowed from the doorstep. His voice was unusually high and reedy. 'Your mother promised you'd come around to her way of thinking. You haven't! I've had enough!' The front door slammed before either of the girls saw who he was shouting at.

Trixie and Vi watched as the man leapt into the open-top

car without using its door, gunned the engine and roared down the driveway towards them.

'Watch out!' shouted Vi, pulling Trixie aside before the angry man could clip her suitcase as he screeched onto the road.

'Maniac!' shouted Vi, too late now he had gone. He hadn't looked back.

Trixie was almost too shaken to speak but she managed, 'Who the hell was that? Hen's father?'

'Much too young,' said Vi.

And then Hen was running down the drive towards them, her long blonde hair streaming out behind her.

'I'm sorry! I saw what happened from the window. I'm sorry you had to witness that! Are you hurt? No? Thank God! I'm so sorry,' she repeated, throwing her arms first around Vi and then Trixie. She stepped away from them, took a deep breath and said, 'I've only got to pick up my things. There's no need for you to come inside. I won't be long.'

Without waiting for either of them to speak she had turned and was running back up the driveway towards the house, her hair reminding Trixie of a long pale scarf as it floated on the breeze.

'Well!' said Vi. 'What d'you make of that?'

'No idea,' answered Trixie, 'but I dare say we'll find out.'

Vi grinned at her. 'I'm not waiting on this driveway. Have you seen the size of that other car in the garage? We'll be pancakes if anyone drives that at us. Let's wait outside on the pavement.'

Trixie picked up her case and followed Vi out to the road. They parked themselves on a low wall.

'Wonder why she didn't ask us in?' Trixie said.

'I reckon there's a row going on in that fine house, right now. To be honest, I don't want to get involved, do you?'

Trixie shook her head. She looked along Western Way.

Large houses in huge gardens stretched as far as the eye could see. The trees were ablaze with reds, yellows and browns where the autumn was changing the tint of their leaves. Trixie thought of Alma Street. There weren't any trees, and the back gardens that might once have been filled with flowers had now been dug for victory and vegetables grew there instead. Trixie could no more imagine what it would be like to live in one of these fine houses than fly to the moon.

'I know what you're thinking,' said Vi. 'These places might be lovely to look at, but it'd be murder cleaning all the windows, wouldn't it?'

Trixie was still laughing when Hen, shamefaced, reached them.

'Glad to see someone's happy,' she said sharply.

Trixie thought she looked different, somehow. Vi picked up on it straight away. 'Why are you wearing those old-fashioned clothes?'

Hen looked down at the brown knee-length A-line skirt. She had on a darker- brown jumper that hid her curves. On her feet were heavy brown shoes almost as ugly as what was provided for the lumberjills. Thick brown lisle stockings completed her frowsy look.

Hen wearily put her hand to her forehead as if she was trying to remember or forget something. 'Let me get away from this place before I go mad and then I'll tell you.'

Trixie raised her eyebrows at Vi, whose mouth had dropped open, watching Hen, with her suitcase, marching determinedly down the road, leaving them to follow her.

Chapter Thirty-six

Cigarette smoke swirled in the air above the wooden tables of Annie's Café. Trixie had a go at picking up her overfilled mug without spilling any of the tea, but didn't manage it.

'Damn! Why do they fill cups so full,' she moaned, putting it back on the table. She helped herself to a piece of greasy bread pudding and bit into it hungrily. 'This is good,' she said. She pushed the plate containing the other two pieces towards Vi and Hen. 'Have some.'

Vi said, 'Hen, are you going to tell us why you're dressed up like a school-marm?'

Hen took a deep breath. 'When I got in the other day wearing my blue silk costume, wet through because it was raining, my father took one look at me and instead of saying, "Hello, Henrietta, lovely to see you, come and get dry," he said, "You look like a damned streetwalker. Go and take off those disgusting clothes and get rid of them."'

'That wasn't very nice,' said Vi. She was just about to take a bite of the bread pudding but stopped with it halfway to her mouth. 'You never got rid of that lovely silk outfit?'

Hen nodded. 'I have an allowance. He doesn't worry how much I pay for clothes, only that they're suitable for the occasion. Of course, he doesn't see all the clothes I buy.' She gave a small sarcastic laugh. 'A tight wet costume, apparently wasn't right to come home in!'

'I thought you looked lovely in it, Hen,' said Trixie. 'Before you got rained on!'

Trixie was unsure how to deal with Hen. She was still trying to get her head round the dark slice of life she'd witnessed at Vi's home. She'd always believed money solved problems and Hen's parents weren't short of a bob or two. But Hen really was very upset.

'What else did he say? Did you go and get changed?' Vi asked, and took a bite of bread pudding. 'You're right, this is nice,' she added. 'I'm surprised he knows how streetwalkers dress.'

Hen ignored her. 'I changed my clothes. Mum lent me these. He monitors what she wears, too.' She looked down at her suitcase, then at herself. Words streamed from her mouth like a waterfall: 'I must find somewhere to change. I'm not travelling to Scotland in this outfit. My mum and I usually obey my dad. My mum said Geoffrey was calling round. I can't stand him. They want me to marry him. Plenty of money but a simpleton.'

'You don't fancy him, then?' Vi asked.

Hen glared at her. 'No, I don't, and I never have, and if he was the last man on earth, I still wouldn't marry him. I joined the lumberjills because my parents kept me on a tight leash, never letting me go anywhere unless Geoffrey tagged along.'

'Was he the bloke in the sports car?'

'Yes, Trix, he was.'

'We heard him shout that he'd had enough. Is it all over between you two, now?'

'No, Vi, because he says that to me every time I turn him down. I honestly wish he'd take the hint and I wish my parents would allow me to choose who I go out with. It certainly wouldn't be Geoffrey Wolstenholme!'

'What do you mean you can't go out with men you like? You made a meal of every feller you came in contact with in Scotland!' Trixie couldn't help herself.

Hen pushed her hair away from her face. 'That's only because I'd never been on my own with a man before.'

Vi had taken a mouthful of her tea and spluttered it out. Trixie produced a handkerchief from her gas-mask case and handed it to her.

'Are you telling us the truth?' Trixie asked. She stared hard at Hen.

'Look, I was at a girls-only school until I was eighteen. In Winchester, that was. We fantasized about boys but that was as far as it got. I was then sent to London to Evaline Porter's finishing school. Have you heard of it?' Hen looked enquiringly at Vi, who raised her eyes heavenwards. 'Probably not,' Hen said. 'Well, I can type, my maths and English are excellent. I can make polite conversation in company. I know how to sit up straight without touching the back of my chair. I know how to fold a napkin, which should be folded towards me so I can lift the outer facing corner and dab my mouth on the inside. But I longed to know what it felt like to kiss a boy and I never found that out until I became a lumberjill. Which I joined, by the way, without my parents knowing about it. To save face they sent me off with good grace. I thought I'd escaped Geoffrey Wolstenholme, who is destined for the Cabinet, so I keep being told. I don't care. He's boring, he has a whiny voice, he's arrogant, he doesn't listen to me and his breath smells of rancid cheese!' She burst into tears.

Trixie and Vi, both unsure how to deal with Hen, allowed her to cry. After a few minutes and some looks from other customers. Hen hiccuped, then used her jumper to wipe her tears, running her dripping nose along her sleeve.

'Bet you didn't learn that at finishing school,' said Trixie.

Hen began to laugh. After a while, she said, 'I left my sodden silk costume in the kitchen. Dad picked it up to throw it out and discovered Ted's address in the pocket. He asked me about it. I didn't lie, I said it belonged to a sailor I'd met on the train. He almost had a fit. Called me a lot more names, some I'd never heard before.' She gave a huge sigh. 'I wish I'd never come home. I should have stayed in Scotland like Jo. I hope when we get back to Shandford Lodge they have work for me. I couldn't bear to have to live with my parents again.'

'Freedom is very special, isn't it?' said Vi. She was quiet for a few seconds, then added, 'You've already been chosen to be a measurer. I think you'll be fine.'

Hen said, picking up her mug of tea. 'I hope you're right and I do so hope we can all stay together.' Trixie remembered Hen coming out to say goodbye to Alf and Lulubelle and how, when she'd been tongue-tied, Hen had said all the right words to him for her. She thought of the apples Hen had provided for the horse. She hoped she and Hen wouldn't be separated.

Hen put down the empty mug. 'My father has always been very protective towards me. I'm an only child, you see. Geoffrey's family are very well connected but I can't marry him just because the two families expect it, can I?'

'I should say not,' said Vi. Trixie saw she was looking hungrily at the remaining piece of bread pudding left on the plate.

'Do you want that?' Trixie asked Hen.

'I don't even know what it is,' Hen replied, peering at it. 'It looks dreadful.'

'It's dried fruit, sugar, fat, marmalade, cinnamon and stale bread, and it tastes lovely. It's also a shame to waste it,' chimed in Vi.

Trixie said, through gritted teeth, 'Eat it then, Vi!' She was beginning to think that maybe money didn't solve problems but instead presented new ones. She understood why Hen had wanted to leave home, why Hen needed to experience life and men, especially men. Everything seemed to fall into place.

She, Hen and Vi had never worked so hard as they had in the forests, chopping down trees, loading them on transport to be taken to sawmills and used to help win the war. And it was exceedingly hard and heavy work. But its saving grace was that working away from home was giving each of them a new perspective on life and how precious it was. She was shaken out of her reverie by Vi using the grubby net curtain to wipe the condensation from the café's window, and saying, 'Do you see what that street opposite is called?'

Trixie shook her head. She knew they were in a little café near Ann's Hill and had decided afterwards to wait at the stop along the road to catch a bus to the ferry, cross the water, and wait for the London train at Portsmouth Harbour station. The overnight train from London would take them to Dundee where they would be met to drive back to Shandford Lodge. Trixie would be very glad to reach their destination. Vi was peering at the street sign tacked to the remaining wall of the derelict shop on the corner.

'It's Bedford Street,' said Vi. 'That's where Jo lives. Shall we go and say hello to her mum and let her know Jo's doing fine in Scotland?'

'No!' said Trixie. 'Jo must have had a very good reason for not wanting to come down to Gosport to visit. It's not up to us to push our noses in where they're not needed! I'm sure Jo wouldn't like it. She can be moody and I don't want any bad feelings directed at me.'

'I only made a suggestion,' said Vi. She sat back on her chair.

Hen spoke in her usual cut-glass tones, 'I'm going to ask

the woman behind the counter if I can use her lavatory to change my clothes.' As she moved past Trixie, carrying her case, Trixie smelt her familiar flowery perfume. She was wondering whether she should suggest they bought more tea, when she heard the assistant say loudly, grouchily, 'This is Annie's Café, not the bleedin' Ritz. We ain't got no lavvy for you to use. There's a public convenience about four streets up.'

Chapter Thirty-seven

'What number Bedford Street does Jo live at?' Vi asked, peering at one of the remaining houses left standing.

'Number nine, I thought she said,' Trixie also thought it was presumptuous of them to knock on a stranger's door, tell them they knew her daughter and ask if their friend could change her clothes. Not that there were many houses remaining in Bedford Street. Trixie shivered as a cold autumn breeze seemed to blow from nowhere, reminding her that summer was gone.

'This place certainly caught it in the bombing,' said Vi.

'That woman's looking at us from behind her net curtain,' said Hen.

'It's a natural pastime in Gosport,' said Vi. 'Anyway, how do you know it's a woman?'

'She's got curlers in her hair.' Hen snorted.

Trixie's eyes went back to the small terraced house shored up with wooden struts either side to stop it collapsing. It looked quite lonely standing on its own with rubble stacked each side of it where once other homes had flourished. The tiny front garden had been mostly cleared of detritus, and mauve Michaelmas daisies asserted themselves. The net curtain quivered, and Trixie looked away lest the occupier of the house thought she was staring. But within seconds the front door opened. A woman with metal curling pins in her hair and a pinny stood on the doorstep, her arms now folded. 'You girls looking for someone?'

Her bright eyes were inquisitive in her sharp-featured face. She moved her stance from one foot to the other in her tartan pom-pommed slippers. The left one had a split in the side through which a large bunion peeped.

Trixie decided it was only polite to answer. 'Our friend Jo's mum lives along here somewhere—'

She got no further for the woman nipped smartly from her front door down the short path to her gate, shaking her head.

'Oh, no, no, no, my dear. You've got it wrong. They were bombed out weeks ago!'

Hen said, 'That can't be right, we—'

'Are you telling me I don't know what goes on in my own

street with my own neighbours?' The woman looked Hen up and down.

Trixie saw her eyes harden. 'I'm sorry, we didn't know Jo that well.'

The woman's whole demeanour changed. She smiled, showing bright white dentures. 'I'm just going to put the kettle on. Would you like a cup of tea?'

Before Trixie or Vi could answer, Hen said, 'Would it be possible for me to come inside your lovely little house and change into something more suitable to travel in? I've—'

'My dear, of course you can.' The suitcases evidently hadn't escaped the woman's beady eyes. She opened the gate, then began walking back along the brick path, obviously expecting the girls to follow her, so they did.

Several brightly polished brass ornaments twinkled in the warm kitchen. Most were of cats in various poses. Along the top of the mantelpiece above the range there was a line of tightly packed china cats. The smell of cat wee pervaded the room. A table in the centre had four chairs around it. A comfortable velvet armchair near the window held a long bag with knitting needles and heather-mixture wool poking out. Curled, asleep, on the armchair was a huge orange cat. It opened one eye at the girls' entrance, closed it again and continued sleeping.

Trixie heard the pop of the gas beneath the kettle in the

scullery and hissed to Hen and Vi, 'Be careful what you say. Jo's a very private person.'

The woman put her head around the scullery door. 'I've a nice bit of seed cake we can have with our tea.'

Hen walked to the scullery doorway and asked brightly, 'Where can I get changed?'

'Take yourself into my front room, love. No one'll disturb you in there,' came her answer.

Hen disappeared with her case. Trixie and Vi pulled out two chairs and sat down at the table.

Trixie didn't want to be in the woman's house. If it hadn't been for Hen wearing her mother's clothing, she wouldn't be trapped in this nosy neighbour's kitchen waiting to be grilled about Jo, for she was sure that was what the woman intended. She was shocked that Jo's home had been razed to the ground before Jo had arrived at Shandford Lodge, and Jo had never told them. But it was Jo's business and they'd all kept secrets from each other, hadn't they?

Now she was beginning to understand why Jo hadn't wanted to come back to Gosport, and why she was sometimes moody and depressed.

The woman was talking inanely as she carried in a tray filled with cups, saucers, spoons, a milk jug and a tea pot. A china plate held cake cut into slices.

'That looks nice,' said Vi, breaking into her chatter about the war.

'Thank you, my dear,' said the woman, putting the tray on the table. 'Shall we get acquainted? My name's Molly Brown. I've lived in this street all my life.' She paused obviously waiting for information from them.

'I'm Vi, and I'm a Gosport girl,' Vi said.

'Trixie,' volunteered Trixie. She heard footsteps coming along the lino in the passage. 'And that's Henrietta,' she said, as Hen appeared in a tightly belted green woollen dress with front box pleats that Trixie had seen her wear before. It gave her figure an hour-glass effect. Nylons and black high heels completed the look.

Hen smiled. 'Did you say your name's Molly?'

The woman nodded.

'Well, Molly, I hope you don't mind but I've left the clothes I was wearing folded on the small table by the window. I have no further use for them. Could you dispose of them for me? Perhaps a rummage sale.'

'Of course,' said Molly. She had a gleam in her eye as she began pouring the tea.

Trixie felt trapped in the small house. She wanted to leave. Instead, she heard Vi ask, 'When was the heavy bombing that demolished most of the street, then?'

'It was June, when that devil Hitler sent over his planes and they practically flattened this place,' said Molly. 'Gosport took a beating that night.'

Oh, my God, thought Trixie. The intake of girls for the Timber Corps at which Trixie, Hen, Vi and Jo had first met, had travelled to Dundee just weeks later.

'Jo had gone out on her own,' Molly continued, 'to the Criterion picture house to see *Hold That Ghost*, with Bud Abbott and Lou Costello. Her mother-in-law was looking after little Harry. He was giving Jo merry hell because at three months he had a tooth coming through.'

Molly took a deep breath. She'd poured out the tea, though no one had moved to drink it. They were listening to her intently and she obviously liked being centre stage.

'Gwen was coping better than Jo about her Army husband, Barry, that's Gwen's son, being missing, presumed dead. She was convinced Barry was still alive. She said she would know if her son was dead. She preferred to believe he was in one of those prisoner-of-war camps and would come home to them, safe and sound, after the war. Moaning Minnie went off. I toddled to the public shelter at the bottom of Ann's Hill. Good company in there, sing-songs and everything.' She picked up her cup and took a sip of tea. Put it down again and carried on. 'Gwen and baby Harry went in their Anderson at the bottom of their garden. Oh! Gwen's husband Peter died in the Great War. She only ever had the one boy, Barry. So, in love Jo and Barry. They didn't want Gwen to be on her own so they came to live with her after they got married. Got along fine, they did.' Molly stared at Vi. 'Have a bit of cake, love, I made it myself.'

Vi never moved, or answered, just stared at Molly intently.

'Oh, well, perhaps in a minute, then,' said Molly. 'Now where did I get to? Ah, yes. I was in the public shelter and the bombing went on all night. Eventually we got out when the all-clear went, must have been about five o'clock in the morning. I couldn't believe my eyes when I got here and saw there was only a couple of houses left in the street. This little house was still standing but Gwen's place was just a pile of rubble. The bomb had done for the shelter. And her and the baby. Straight hit, the warden said. A lot of my neighbours died that night. Some preferred to hide under the stairs,' she said, 'especially those who were shaky on their pins. Them Andersons can get very damp, can't they? Down by the shop there was tarpaulins on the pavement with the dead underneath waiting to be identified. I saw Jo. She looked grey and dazed, having a cup of tea at the WVS van. I sent word by the warden that she could stop with me. Well, she had nowhere to go, did she? See, I tried to talk to her but she wasn't taking anything in. I took in Sid Clements and his dog. Only for the night, mind. Sid's dog and my Toby,' she waved at the orange cat, 'don't get on. I never saw Jo again.' Molly's eyes brightened. 'But you say she's all right?'

Vi said, 'She's fine, she—'

Trixie anticipated Molly's next questions: she'd want to pass on titbits of information. 'Look at the time, girls, we must be off.' She stood up, went to Vi and pulled her off her chair, hissing, 'Don't want to be late, do we?' Luckily, Vi got the message and made a grab for her suitcase. Hen, however, had tears in her eyes and had picked up her cup of cold tea for a bit of comfort, so Trixie had to take the cup out of her hand, replace it in the saucer and practically manhandle her out of the kitchen and down the passage.

Once out on the path, having manoeuvred Vi and Hen onto the pavement, she turned to Molly and put her arms around her. 'Thank you for being so kind. We do appreciate it, Molly.'

'Think nothing of it,' Molly managed to say, as the girls walked away.

Nobody spoke until they reached the bus stop.

'It's not my business,' Trixie said. 'What you two do is up to you, but I feel terrible that Jo has had to carry the burden of all that unhappiness by herself. I feel worse that I now know something she didn't want me to know about.' She took a deep breath. 'I just wish we'd never set eyes on that Molly.'

Hen was dabbing at her eyes with a clean handkerchief. Vi's lips were clenched in a thin line.

The number three bus trundled down Forton Road and pulled up at the bus stop. The girls got on, stored their luggage in the designated space beneath the stairs and still no one spoke, except to the taciturn bus conductress, until they reached the Gosport ferry.

On the boat Hen said, 'I expect you'll think about your Cy every time you come across on the boat, won't you?'

Trixie, whose mind had been so full of other things since she'd been back in Gosport, said, 'This weekend has been so eventful I haven't even thought about writing him a letter. But I do hope there's letters waiting for me when we get back to Scotland.'

Hen smiled. 'You're so lucky to have someone to love you like that.'

'I do know,' Trixie said. She now felt bad about making scenes because she'd not heard from him. It was so little in the bigger scheme of things, she now realized. She remembered the night she'd sat on the snag with Jo, drinking

Coca-Cola. What was it Jo had said to her? 'Accept your good fortune and let the future take care of itself.' Jo had tried to make her feel better yet she had been carrying around the most awful sadness. No wonder her emotions were all over the place. Trixie suddenly saw what a special person Jo was, working through all that grief but telling no one.

The London train was waiting when they arrived at the station. Seats were, as usual, at a premium but they managed to find three together and, ignoring the tobacco smoke, the chatter, the smell of sweat, rattling newspapers and rowdy children, Hen and Vi soon fell asleep. Trixie kept watch over her friends until at last she, too, slept.

At Waterloo they drank tea and ate sandwiches at a café. While Vi and Hen were still eating, Trixie slipped out and bought a paperback novel, *You Can't Keep the Change*, by Peter Cheyney. Vi had promised she could have *Mildred Pierce*, when she'd finished but she was still reading it. She also purchased a card for Vi because tomorrow would be her birthday. She could hardly believe Vi was younger than herself. There had been times when Vi had shown more sense and courage than all of them put together. But then, she thought, age was simply a number, wasn't it?

On the train to Dundee the three of them talked, laughed

and chatted to the other passengers and servicemen. But it was all dialogue without saying anything. Trixie thought that perhaps they had delved too far into each other's lives. Tiredness made it easy to sleep away the journey and when, finally, the lorry deposited them and the other girls who had travelled south for the weekend, outside Shandford Lodge, very early in the morning, all she wanted to do was go to the hut, make up her bed and sleep.

Jo was waiting in the doorway of the medieval-themed hallway, wearing dungarees over a thick shirt. It was noticeably colder than it had been in Gosport. Trixie shuddered anew at the stuffed animal heads and antlered stags. A huge smile covered Jo's face. She threw her arms around each of them in turn.

'Did you have a great time in Gosport?' she asked. Then, without waiting for an answer, she said, 'I haven't had breakfast. I thought I'd wait for you. I've really missed you lot.'

Trixie said, 'I've missed you, an' all.' Because she had. She could also smell fried food and hadn't realized how hungry she was.

Jo began walking down the polished hall towards the dining room but when she arrived at the door, she barred the way. She glanced down at the cast-iron Scottie dog keeping the door open. 'How about we have breakfast after we've looked at the notice-board outside Maud Styles's office?'

The tiredness Trixie had been feeling disappeared immediately. 'You mean the list is up?'

Jo nodded. 'I know exactly who is going where but I won't spoil it for you.'

There was a sudden scramble to be outside the office. Other girls were staring at the typed paper. A couple walked away muttering. A few were smiling.

Trixie saw the listings were compiled of estates, the names of girls who had been assigned to them and where in Scotland they were situated.

The noise around the notice-board was considerable.

Trixie allowed her eyes to find her own name. There it was. Next to, MacKay Estate, Talmine, Sutherland.

She didn't really know how she felt. She consoled herself that she had passed her training so she wasn't going home.

She quickly found Vi's name. It was next to MacKay Estate, Talmine, Sutherland. So, they'd be together. Vi pinched her arm.

'Good, eh?' Trixie grinned at her.

'I'm going to MacKay Estate, in Talmine, Sutherland,' said Hen. 'With you two.'

'So am I,' said Jo. 'We're all staying together.'

'I thought you wanted to stay here and work in Lachlan MacLeod's sawmill?' Trixie said.

'That was then, and this is now,' Jo said mysteriously. 'I value my friendship with you lot.'

'We're stayin' together, we're stayin' together, we're stayin' together,' sang Vi, tunelessly.

'There's only one thing wrong,' said Trixie. She frowned.

'What?' questioned Hen. She looked worried.

'Whatever's the matter, Trixie?' asked Jo.

Trixie took a deep breath before saying, 'Where on earth is MacKay Estate, Talmine, Sutherland?

Acknowledgements

Enduring gratitude to my agent Juliet Burton. Heartfelt appreciation to editor Celine Kelly. Thank you, as always, to Florence Hare and Jane Wood for believing in me; also to the incomparable Hazel Orme. To all at Quercus, I am, as always, indebted to you. Thank you.